Praise for

A Last Time for Everything

"Such a funny, heartwarming tale full of hijinks that perfectly captures the precise and complicated feeling of departing early adulthood. I loved following Wren and Arthur through their adventure of remembering who they were, deciding who they want to be and what they're willing to fight for."

—Natalie Sue, author of *I Hope This Finds You Well*

"A smart premise that's written with wit, *A Last Time for Everything* portrays a couple preparing to cross through one of life's biggest milestones. Evan Porter expertly reminds us that within the tiniest details of these funny, messy, vulnerable characters there are universal truths that connect us all."

—Sidney Karger, author of *Best Men* and *The Bump*

"As tender as it is funny, *A Last Time for Everything* is a big-hearted, often bittersweet ode to the special kind of growing pains a young couple faces on their way to becoming a young family. I *loved* it."

—Laura Piper Lee, author of *Hannah Tate, Beyond Repair* and *Pot Shot*

"*A Last Time for Everything* tenderly explores the uncertainties, disappointments, and joyful surprises we face as we leap from one stage of life into another. Arthur and Wren are full of love and relatable insecurities, and I loved getting to follow them on their journey to parenthood. Evan Porter's second novel is warm, funny, and, best of all, achingly human."

—Jamie Harrow, author of *One on One*

"From a jar of adventures to the jarring swerve life takes when a baby arrives, Evan Porter delivers a slightly madcap, laugh-a-page heart-warmer of a novel. Despite competing with one oversize mouse, a raven (or, more accurately, a Raven), a decrepit dog, and even a tarantula, it is the human relationships that truly land in this endearing book and make it so relatable and enjoyable."

—Andy Abramowitz, author of *Thank You, Goodnight*

Also by Evan S. Porter

Dad Camp

A LAST TIME FOR EVERYTHING

A Novel

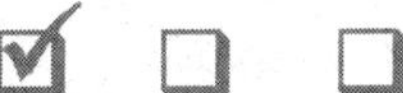

EVAN S. PORTER

DUTTON

An imprint of Penguin Random House LLC
1745 Broadway, New York, NY 10019
penguinrandomhouse.com

Book design by Kathleen Soriano-Taylor

LIBRARY OF CONGRESS CATALOGING-IN-PUBLICATION DATA

Names: Porter, Evan S. author
Title: A last time for everything : a novel / Evan S. Porter.
Description: New York, NY : Dutton, [2026]
Identifiers: LCCN 2025048874 | ISBN 9798217044078 paperback |
ISBN 9798217044085 ebook
Subjects: LCGFT: Domestic fiction | Novels
Classification: LCC PS3616.O768 L37 2026
LC record available at https://lccn.loc.gov/2025048874

Printed in the United States of America
1st Printing

The authorized representative in the EU for product safety and compliance is Penguin Random House Ireland, Morrison Chambers, 32 Nassau Street, Dublin D02 YH68, Ireland, https://eu-contact.penguin.ie.

For Sarah. Here's to never growing up. I love you.

A LAST TIME FOR EVERYTHING

PROLOGUE

December

ARTHUR PETERSON STOOD PATIENTLY IN the hallway, waiting to find out if his life was about to change.

Positioned just outside the bathroom door, he could hear everything. The cheap, builder-grade material had a way of not only not dampening sounds but somehow amplifying them. On quiet nights, when the upstairs neighbors weren't stomping around and violently dragging heavy chains across the floor or whatever it was they did up there, Arthur and Wren could hear each other wipe. Wipe! Safe to say there were no secrets in this household.

The amphitheater-like properties of the apartment's layout were working overtime tonight. Arthur could hear every rip of the box coming from inside the bathroom, every peel of the wrapper, and soon, every single drip-drop that would determine the next eighteen-plus years of his life.

He waited, leaning against the wall, but not too hard lest the plasterboard give way. (Arthur knew almost nothing about construction, home repair, or general handiness, but he knew deep in his soul that the drywall in their apartment had to be thinner than the standard. Glorified papier-mâché.)

He waited still and heard nothing.

"Babe? Did you fall in?"

"Yes," Wren called through the door. "I've fallen in and am now making my way through the Baltimore City sewage system."

"Oh, that's not good," he said flatly. Wren wasn't a strong swimmer, he knew that much.

"I did briefly drop the test in, though. Five-second rule is a thing, right? It's probably fine."

"You should get another one. God knows what kind of residue is floating around in that toilet. If that one's positive it might mean *I'm* pregnant."

"Ugh," she groaned. "Hold on." There was a shuffling, another ripping of a box, and more crinkling wrappers.

Arthur didn't love the idea of Wren in the cramped bathroom, sitting on the perma-yellow toilet (they cleaned it frequently—*he* cleaned it frequently—to no avail), going this alone. He wanted to be in there with her, to hold her hand, even though he wasn't certain it would help the situation. While it seemed romantic in a sense, practically, holding hands with someone who was peeing would have its challenges.

"We don't have to do this right now, you know," he reminded her. It hadn't exactly been the most well-planned-out operation. Wren had . . . something. Call it a feeling, a gut instinct, or a feminine intuition. Some magical, almost spiritual divination that a miracle was occurring inside her. Or "My fucking tits hurt," as she had so eloquently put it at the time. A quick trip to the Dollar Tree for a six-pack of tests and here they were.

"Yes, we do. I won't be able to enjoy the New Year's party knowing the champagne might be poisoning the baby, if there is a baby."

Their friends Charlie and Tristan were hosting a gathering for everyone to watch the ball drop. There'd be fancy dress, passed hors d'oeuvres, and many loud arguments about whether Dick Clark was still alive. It could easily be settled by a two-second Google search, but it would be more fun to shout back and forth about it instead.

"You could just not drink," Arthur said. "I mean *we* could just not drink."

"I'm not even going to acknowledge that."

Silence. The anticipation was going to kill him if this went on any longer.

"I think I forgot how to pee," Wren said after a few moments.

"Sorry?"

"You know when you become aware of every blink or breath and suddenly you don't remember how to do it automatically anymore? I think I've got the opposite of that. I can't remember how it's supposed to work. Can you distract me?"

She was probably dehydrated. The woman was incapable of drinking water, only energy drinks, coffee, and red wine. He had to trick her into drinking water by sweetening it up with those little squeeze pouches, pure extract of Red 40. It was like trying to get a kid to eat broccoli by chopping it up and hiding it in mac and cheese. At least, he'd always heard that was a good technique, until he saw a psychologist on TikTok declare that it caused kids to develop trust issues later in life.

"Um . . . Got any New Year's resolutions?" he asked. It seemed an appropriate question to pass the time. Midnight was just a few hours away, after all.

"Nothing concrete. I want to do something new with my hair, maybe."

"Already?" She'd just gotten it cut short a few weeks ago on a whim, unable to wait until summer to chop it all off. He liked it at every length. She always asked him for his opinion, as if he'd have one other than she'd look great whatever she decided to do.

"I might go shorter, or try a new color."

"Or try shaving it all off. I've always said you have a sexy head shape."

"Aw, babe, that's sweet. How about you?"

"I'm mostly just thinking about this potentially-becoming-a-father thing."

What was he supposed to do with this impending news, finally get that six-pack he'd always wanted? Run a half-marathon? Download a chess app and get obliterated by eleven-year-olds from Germany? No. Self-improvement would have to wait.

"There's gotta be something. Maybe this could finally be the year you make some progress on grad school?"

"I have been making progress. I'm just going at my own pace."

"You narrowed it from, what, ten schools down to eight? You're a machine."

"Yes. And I'll whittle it down further when I'm good and ready."

"Oh, classic Arthur," she chuckled.

She didn't get it. Couldn't get it. Wren liked to do things willy-nilly, off the cuff. For example, she never took a list when it was her turn to grab groceries, which was lunacy to him, and exactly how they ended up with so many gimmick foods in the pantry and fridge—things like Cool Ranch Oreos, Dunkaroos-flavored coffee creamer, Sour Patch Kids–infused wine. He shopped the sales and made an attempt to consider the entire spectrum of nutrients the human body needed; Wren shopped on vibes and vibes alone. She went with her heart and her gut, and he loved those things about her. But going back to school to get his master's was not a willy-nilly decision. He wanted to make the right choice, not to mention make sure he got the timing just right. His future depended on it. Their future.

But before he could think about it any further, a sigh of relief came from Wren. A moment later, she flushed the toilet and stepped out, dark hair clinging to a slightly damp forehead. Her usually pale cheeks lit up with just the faintest bit of red. Her skin freckled with goose bumps. She was frazzled but silent.

Come on, out with it, woman! he thought.

"So?" was all he could think of to say. He was suddenly warm, his skin all tingly. If there were any more words in him, they were all stuck in his throat.

"It has to bake for a few minutes." Right. Of course. He knew that. "You want a drink?"

She pushed past him and crossed the small living room, which didn't take long, and curled around the wall and into the kitchen. The entire apartment was only a handful of strides long, covered in thick, stiff carpeting that had apparently been the victim of a horrible glue spill at some point. In certain spots, it was hard enough to break skin. Arthur followed, carefully.

In the kitchen, Wren whipped the fridge open and grabbed a beer (Natty Boh, the city's official beer even though it wasn't technically made there; it was all Wren ever bought) and shoved it into Arthur's chest.

"What's this for? How long do we need to wait?"

She moved to the microwave and set a timer for three

minutes, pressing extra hard on the finicky buttons, the thin protective layer of plastic meant to protect them from splatters bubbling and peeling off in chunks, then turned back and took a deep breath.

"I have to tell you something before we look. You know, just in case."

Now he was the frazzled one. *I have to tell you something.* Right now? It had to be bad. If the adrenaline hadn't gotten to him yet, it was happening now. His heart began to thud and he felt sweat quickly pooling in all the most embarrassing places.

"OK," he said. The beer hadn't seemed appealing or necessary at first, but now he suddenly found himself taking a long pull.

She took a breath, as if gathering herself, and he prepared for the worst. Maybe there was a baby, but it wasn't his. Or maybe, and more likely, this was just the catalyst she needed to realize that she didn't love him. Wasn't in love with him, anyway. Not anymore. *I'm having your baby, and also I'm leaving you*, he imagined her saying. And why not? The noticeable hotness differential between them had always made him a little uneasy. Wren was edgy, with piercing blue eyes and an "I woke up like this" beauty that any living human, man or woman, would kill for. In photos, Arthur often felt like the bafflingly average-looking boyfriend draped on the arm of an A-list celebrity, the one who people figured had to be a rich producer or something. Nerdy but not in the sexy way, thin, a beard that didn't look quite right at any length.

And, though they had been together for about eight years, give or take, they weren't married.

He began to strategize: What would he do if this was the day he'd always feared might come? What would he say if—

"Arthur?"

"Hey," he said, snapping back to the moment, embarrassed at how quickly he had spiraled just now. It was just the nerves chattering inside him, that was all. He had to suppress the urge to draw finger guns in order to show her how cool and casual he was.

"Yeah, hi. I said I need to tell you something. And since the test will be fully baked in about"—Wren looked at the microwave clock—"two and a half more minutes, you'll have a limited amount of time to be mad at me, so here goes."

He gulped, braced himself as if about to be hit with hurricane winds.

"I kind of . . . quit my job."

"Oh," he said, instantly feeling ridiculous but not fully processing the words at all, only feeling relief that his imagination had been lying to him.

"Oh?"

"Oh. Oh? . . . OH!" Now he was beginning to understand. "Wait, you what?!"

"Can I just explain?"

"Please, yes." Arthur was having another vision now, of raising the baby together, but in a cardboard box. He wondered if soup kitchens had baby formula, then immediately felt bad about being so flippant. His parents couldn't get through a single conversation without begging Arthur and Wren to come stay in their finished basement for a weekend, in their large home tucked away in the mountains of the Pacific Northwest. They were never there anyway, always off on adventures in their camper, so if he and Wren ever wanted the place to themselves, it was all theirs. Somehow, by the grace of God, he and Wren would be OK. But that didn't keep him from beginning to spiral again.

"My boss, you know my boss, right?" Wren said, as nonchalantly as if she were discussing the traffic on her morning commute. She grabbed various bags of chips from the cupboard and ripped them open, dumped them into cheap plastic bowls.

"Yeah, the asshole." Arthur rubbed his temples and took another swig.

"Yeah, you know him. Anyway, he's always had a weird habit of hiring pretty young girls right out of college. Like, only pretty young girls."

"OK?"

"Which I always thought was gross, but I'd never seen him be inappropriate, you know? I've seen him be a shithead, but he's always been an equal opportunity shithead."

Arthur looked at Wren, looked at the microwave clock. He had no idea where this story was going and gave her the universal "wrap it up" hand signal.

"Long story short, I found one of the résumés he marked up after an interview. Apparently, he and one of the other managers have actually been scoring girls on their looks; it was right there on the paper. I couldn't believe it."

Arthur softened a bit. "Well, that's icky."

"Right?"

"So what did you do?"

Wren hesitated, then popped a chip in her mouth and casually walked away, speaking over her shoulder through a mouthful of crumbs. "Nothing much, really, just sent a photo of it to everyone at the company. And my resignation letter."

"Wait, why the resignation letter?!" Arthur chased after her, around the tight corner of the other kitchen entrance, which led right back to the living room. Wren sat the bowls on the ottoman slash coffee table.

"Because I obviously can't work there anymore."

"Couldn't you just report him? He should get fired, not you."

"Oh, I'm pretty sure he's getting fired. But you know how it is. If it's rotten, there's no fixing it. Time to move on. Head for greener pastures." She painted the invisible horizon with a brush of her hand, as if she could see said pastures. All Arthur saw was their kitchen window, which was actually below ground and covered with several inches of dirt and grime. Quite the view.

There was no use arguing it with her. She had already quit. The damage was done. Now they—he—was going to have to find a way to deal with the fallout. He flopped on the couch, took another sip of his beer, while Wren scuttled into the kitchen and returned with a handful of prepackaged dips.

"This city has to be running out of CEOs you haven't verbally or physically flipped off," he said, almost thinking out loud, estimating how much a crib might cost, one of those special baby trash cans, a few pallets' worth of diapers—and how he would pay for it all on his public school teacher's salary. Would Target accept "making a difference in a young person's life" as payment for a stroller?

"What's that supposed to mean?"

"Well, you have to admit you've been through a lot of jobs. I know you'll say you can get another one, but at some point . . . I'm just saying that you're really flirting with the limits of the acceptable résumé length-to-age ratio."

Arthur had a sudden feeling of déjà vu. They had had this conversation many times over the past couple of years. Wren would find good work, be happy for a while, and then either quit over some minor grievance or find a way to get herself fired, often resigning in disgrace with some big, showy gesture before she could be called into a surprise meeting with

HR. It was always something. And this time, the timing was far from ideal.

"And who is all this food for?" he added.

She grabbed his face and peered into his soul like she was delivering a message of grave importance: "If this test says what I think it's going to say, I am going to eat. My fucking. Face. Off."

He couldn't help but chuckle, and as he did, he felt the stress and worry slide right off him. Wren had a way of doing that. She might put them out of house and home with her impulsiveness, but at least they'd be laughing.

"We're a good team, aren't we?" he asked, running a thumb along the edge of her foot as she settled onto the couch beside him.

"We are. As long as you keep doing that."

"We'll figure it out. Whatever it says." Then: "Shouldn't that timer have gone off?"

Arthur and Wren both shot off the couch and into the kitchen, where they found the microwave blinking ERR, ERR, ERR over and over.

"Piece of shit," Wren cried, spinning around and sprinting toward the bathroom, Arthur in tow. She squeezed through the narrow doorframe a half second before him, her body blocking his view of the pregnancy test she'd left sitting on the bathroom sink. She stared at it for several seconds as Arthur tried to peer around her, unable to read her reaction from only the back of her neck.

"Come on, don't torture me. What does it say?"

When she turned around, he knew the answer. Her face said it all. Her eyes were wet and afraid, her mouth turned up in a beaming smile; the goose bumps and flushed skin were all there. She was experiencing the full spectrum of human emotion all at once, and now it was washing over him. He felt warm and light-headed, like he might float away or pass out. He wrapped his arms around Wren and squeezed her tight, as if she were the only thing that might keep him on the ground.

"This is really happening," she said, and he couldn't tell if she was making a statement or asking a question.

"Oh my God. It really is. How are you feeling?" He still hadn't let go. Finally, she pulled away, looked back down at the test as if to confirm she hadn't hallucinated the whole thing. Then she took a deep breath, opened her mouth as if preparing to spill all of her hopes, dreams, and fears in this sacred moment.

"Pregnant out of wedlock," she said. "What a hussy."

"Wren . . ." But he couldn't help laughing.

"What?"

"Do you mind? This is supposed to be a moment."

If only there had been more time to plan. There could have been candles, gentle music, maybe even balloons or flowers. He'd have certainly worn something better than the droopy T-shirt and pajama pants that were just barely concealing the tremors vibrating through his body.

"OK, but I have one more," Wren said.

"Go ahead." He sighed. She was going to keep making jokes whether he approved or not, so he might as well give her the green light.

"What would my parents say?" she said, then before Arthur could respond: "Good thing they're dead!"

Arthur winced. This was always Wren's response when met with any amount of sentimentality. The gooier and more earnest the moment, the darker her jokes. She had to be really overwhelmed to bring up her parents.

"Are you done?"

"I think so, for now." She sank back into him, resting her head on his shoulder and nuzzling deep.

"I'm so happy," he said, meaning it. This was exactly what he'd been waiting for, planning for, and hoping for since the day he met Wren. There had never been a doubt in his mind.

"Me too," she said.

"Really?"

"I'm excited. It wasn't what I was expecting, I'll admit. Or when I was expecting it. But that's what makes it . . . kind of thrilling?"

They held each other for a moment before Arthur could feel her vibrating.

"You want to call Charlie, don't you? Even though you're not supposed to."

Charlie was Wren's best friend, on a level that Arthur could barely comprehend. If Wren had an unusual bowel movement, Charlie would know about it before he did, and she would have a photo. There's no way Wren would be able to keep this to herself. Plus, somehow, Arthur doubted they'd be making it to Charlie's party later that evening. They might never make it to a party that started after 9:00 p.m. ever again.

"See, you get me," she said, kissing him on the cheek.

She pulled away, walked into the living room to grab her phone. Arthur watched her go, already looking at her differently. She was carrying precious cargo, and was she even already glowing? No, that was just the cheap lamp in the corner spilling a dim yellow light over the whole room. But still, it looked good on her.

"Hey," he said as she excitedly dialed. "We can do this. We are ready for this."

"I know," she said back with a smile.

1

WREN MORRIS WAS READY, ALL right.

Ready for everyone to get the hell away from her.

It had been Wren's idea to have the all-gender baby shower outside, but she never said it was a *good* idea. Charlie had put the whole thing on, and admirably so considering how busy she was with her own wedding coming up in just a few short weeks. She had handled everything from the decorations (Baltimore Ravens tablecloths draped over plastic folding tables) to the food (wings, dips, and brownies that looked like little footballs) to the games (trivia: How many kids did famous NFL players have and by how many different mothers?).

But Charlie and her fiancé, Tristan, were just getting settled into a new place and couldn't host. And money was tight because of certain unnamed, rash career decisions Wren had made. Hosting at their own minuscule apartment was a nonstarter for myriad reasons, including space, bugs, and nonfunctioning appliances.

So Wren suggested just doing the thing in the grass outside their building.

As the party wrapped up, she was deeply regretting the

choice. The suffocating late July heat had left Wren—who in addition to her height and weight had, at thirty-five weeks now, developed a new measurement: circumference—sopping wet and riddled with mosquito bites.

"Thank you, thanks so much for coming, thank you," she said, smiling at exiting guests. She realized no one was listening to her, only touching or talking to her belly, murmuring absurd goo-goo-ga-ga nonsense to it. "Namaste. Happy birthday. Congratulations. Cowabunga," she began saying to the line of well-wishers. No one noticed.

A few not overly close friends she'd picked up at her last couple of jobs, a small gaggle of Arthur's ripe-smelling teacher colleagues, and that was it.

The party was finally over.

Wren hurried over to Charlie, who was neatly boxing up the leftover food, her flowy sundress moving gently with the breeze. Wren looked down at her own outfit, which she had put very little effort into—an old Ravens jersey and maternity pants—and thought her friend looked more like the mom-to-be than she did.

"Thank God that's over," Wren said.

"Gee, thanks."

"You know what I mean. I'm just hot and my feet hurt and I talked to way too many people about my vagina."

"OK, but isn't that normal for you?"

"My feet don't usually hurt."

Charlie rolled her eyes but couldn't fully suppress her laugh.

"Come inside and veg with me," Wren said. "I've been hankering for a relisten of the entire Ford the River discography, and 2000s pop punk always slaps harder when I listen with you."

"Who's gonna clean all this up?"

"Arthur's got it."

Arthur, who was in danger of being crushed under the massive pile of presents he was carrying, even had one balanced on his chin as he wiggled through the door to their building. She loved him, but he was not a well-built fellow. He looked like the Slender Man had picked up a part-time job with a moving company.

"See? Now, come on."

"I—" Charlie stopped, hesitated.

"What?"

BEEP. A car horn blasted from the parking lot some twenty yards away. Wren turned and saw a shiny sports car with Tristan hanging a tan arm out the window.

"Sorry, Wren. I gotta go. Tristan's taking me to dinner and he hates to be late."

"What's the restaurant? Maybe we could tag along."

"It's not a restaurant, per se, it's more of a culinary experience. One of those dining-in-the-dark places, where the servers are blind and you can't see the food before you taste it."

"*A culinary experience.* Woman, just call it a restaurant." Wren realized she was snapping at the person who had dropped everything to throw her a baby shower. "But, hey, of course I get it if you guys need some time together."

"We've just been so busy with everything going on."

Wren fought not to roll her eyes. She appreciated her friend, she really did. But she and Tristan had just gotten back from the Maldives, and Banff a few weeks before that. A fancy dinner—sorry, *culinary experience*—tonight. Having a sought-after wedding planner taking care of everything, and seemingly no budget limits to speak of, sure sounded like a lot of work.

"I totally understand. Thank you for all this, really. It means a lot."

Charlie leaned in for a quick hug, then hurried off to the car.

"Hi, Tristan," Wren called as Charlie got in on the passenger side of the all-white, all-electric sports car. It managed to be both environmentally conscious and incredibly obnoxious at the same time, which was an impressive feat. For people who wanted to save the planet but *also* let everyone know they were insecure about their penis.

"Hey, Wren."

"Whadya got for me today?"

He ran a hand through his jet-black hair and took a deep, calming breath before speaking. "Don't deny the world your gifts. Step into your greatness."

"Hell yeah. Will do."

Tristan was the douchiest sales bro in the entire city, Wren was sure of it. She didn't know if he actually worked in sales, but the title seemed fitting. He did business, that's all she knew. And apparently did it quite well. More interesting to her, he was a grab bag of personal trainer catchphrases. A self-development podcast come to life. A walking acai-berry smoothie. She was endlessly tickled by him, and though she hated to admit it, he pulled the ridiculous car off pretty well through sheer earnestness or at least a profound and enduring commitment to the bit.

"You sure you don't need help cleaning up?" he offered. "I don't mind."

"You guys go; I've got Arthur."

Somewhere inside the building, a tumbling sound rang

out, like an aluminum cake stand falling down a long flight of stairs.

Wren watched them drive off, and soon enough Arthur was back by her side, panting, sweating, greatly disheveled from a half dozen trips carrying things inside and up the stairs.

"Charlie can't stay?" he asked. She shook her head. "Well, maybe they're just in a hurry," he offered.

"Tristan didn't seem to be. He offered to help clean up."

"He offered to *what*?"

"Nothing."

Arthur was still out of breath and looked briefly annoyed before softening.

"I'm sorry," he said, throwing an arm around her. "I'm sure you guys will figure it out."

There wasn't much to figure out. Wren hadn't planned on getting pregnant, hadn't planned on the due date being so close to Charlie and Tristan's wedding (September 3 and September 12, respectively). She'd give anything to be there, but there was a 99 percent chance it just wouldn't be possible. In another world, she would have been the maid of honor, and if not that, then definitely the drunkest at the bachelorette party. Instead, she wasn't even in the wedding party. Eventually, Charlie would realize that it wasn't Wren's fault. Eventually, she'd come around.

"I know what'll cheer you up," Arthur said. "Opening presents."

❑ ❑ ❑

"I feel worse."

Wren had initially been optimistic, and excited even. There was a Target gift card, which was always fun, and a high-end bottle of wine for her to drink literally as soon as medically permissible.

But things went downhill from there. A four-pack of Aquaphor jumbo tubs. A rectal thermometer that looked like an elephant.

But it was the jar of nipple cream that really did her in.

"Where is all the cool shit?!" Wren whined, tossing wrapping paper into the air and out of the way as if sifting through a mound of feces for something, anything better.

"Admittedly, it's a little dry," Arthur said, holding a package that contained a long blue tube with what looked like a mouthpiece at the end. "But this is all important stuff we're going to need. You could have helped me with the registry, you know."

"I'm the mom. I don't need some list on a random blog to tell me what my baby needs. I have millions of years of evolutionary wisdom stored in my DNA."

"OK," he said. "Then what's this?" He held up the blue tubey thing.

"A straw," Wren said confidently. "For breast milk." She mimed popping one end of it onto her nipple. "That way, your arms don't get tired from holding the baby. It can just lie down and chill while it eats."

"So close," Arthur said. "It's for sucking boogers." Wren retched dramatically.

In reality, she knew they needed all this junk. She'd read the stupid lists. But, come on, it *was* boring. And worse, the whole pregnancy had been dreadfully boring. Nausea and aches and pains and being really tired all the time was hardly the adventure of a lifetime she was hoping for the day she found out she was pregnant. Today, at least, she would have loved more of an ironic baby shower, like one of those "Over the Hill" birthday parties where you gave people piles of gag gifts. She wanted a comically large bra with a beer tap on each nipple, a pair of mom jeans that came up to her ribs. A wine-glass the size of a globe, preferably one that said something stupid on the side, like *When the kids whine, mom wines.*

Worst of all, she was not gifted a single piece of "Live Laugh Love" paraphernalia.

"This one, though," Arthur said, ignoring her and scooting over a gigantic box wrapped in adorable stork wrapping paper. "This one looks like fun. Help me open it."

She sighed and stuck out a hand, and Arthur hoisted her up from her comfortable spot on the sofa. They both grabbed a loose corner of the wrapping paper.

"One . . . two . . . two and a half . . ." Arthur counted down, trying to get her to join in.

"Oops," Wren said, ripping the paper on her side clean off.

"Wow. No showmanship at all, but OK." Then Arthur got a sliver of a look at what was inside, and his face lit up. He excitedly ripped the rest of the package open.

"You promised me something exciting," Wren said.

"This is the Graco Lock-tite 4000 XL," Arthur said. "Only the most cutting-edge car seat on the market. It's ridiculously safe. Someone on the internet said if you get in an accident, it's more likely to kill the person that hit you than leave a single scratch on your baby. Indestructible. We're talking airplane black box material. What could be more exciting than that?"

"Oh, you poor sheltered boy."

"Scoff all you want, I'm stoked. We could never have afforded this on our own."

"Who's it from?" Wren tried to bend down to find the tag and found she couldn't. Couldn't bend down, that is.

"It didn't say," Arthur said, still marveling. Then he took out his keys and sliced open the top of the box. "Just want to get a look at it."

"So this marvelous piece of safety technology, you're gonna install it?"

"Yeah, who else?"

Wren cackled.

"Why's that funny?" Arthur said, picking out the instruction manual from the box, or rather hoisting it out. Holding the thick, three-hundred-page tome caused a noticeable tension in his forearm muscles.

Wren shot him a look, which he instantly understood. "Yeah, I better see if we can find someone to do it."

She stepped over the carcasses of opened presents and kissed him on the cheek. "Smart boy." Again, loved the guy, but she couldn't help but think back to when they first moved in and were assembling furniture. She said they needed a screwdriver and Arthur replied that they were out of orange juice. Of course, they were practically babies back then, but he hadn't changed much.

Then, a knock at the door.

"Sit down, take a load off," Arthur said. "I'll get it."

"If that's a pizza that you secretly ordered, I'm gonna sex you so hard."

She'd not really hit the mythical horny phase of pregnancy everyone talked about, but a thick-crust extra cheese might just do it. Wren flopped on the sofa—getting hungry now—just in time to hear Arthur open the door and two voices she recognized yell out:

"SURPRISE!!"

So. No pizza, then.

❑ ❑ ❑

Arthur's parents, Neal and Laura Peterson, were standing in the living room for the first time in years. They were immaculately dressed in polos and shorts, looking like a silver-haired couple plucked right out of an erectile dysfunction commercial.

"How about a tour?" Neal boomed, clapping his hands together loudly as required by Dad Law.

"It's the same place it's always been," Arthur said.

"I know that, knucklehead. We want to see what you've done with the place."

Wren could see Arthur's cheeks grow just the faintest bit rosy. What they'd done with the place in the five or six years since his parents visited was exactly nothing. Hung a Goodwill painting of a vase of flowers. Bought new pillowcases once or twice. But it was an apartment—what were they going to do, add on a deck?

"*Wait!*" his mother cried out. "Before we start . . . just one more hug? It's been too long."

Arthur smiled sheepishly and reluctantly stretched his arms out, but Wren cut him off.

"Pretty sure she was talking to me there, buddy boy. Go get your own hug."

And, indeed, she was. Laura wrapped Wren in the warmest, gooiest hug she'd felt in forever. It was like being smothered in half-baked cookie dough. A weighted blanket of pure maternal energy and comfort washed over her, and she felt so safe there in that woman's over-perfumed bosom that she briefly considered staying forever.

"I'm just still in shock," Arthur said. "I can't believe you guys are here."

"It's long overdue," Arthur's dad said. "Sorry we missed the party, by the way. Traffic in the city was a nightmare; that didn't help. Now, come on, let's not waste any more time, show us around like it's all new to us."

Wren briefly wondered if Neal Peterson was being nice and showing an interest, or if he had genuinely forgotten what his son's apartment looked like.

"Well, you're basically looking at it," Wren said, scanning the living room, which, to be fair, made up about 74 percent of the apartment. "Is it big? No. Is it cozy? Also no. But we don't mind it for now."

"Square footage?" Neal asked.

"Dad," Arthur groaned. "I can't remember exactly, not off the top of my head."

"Was never very good with numbers, this one," Neal said, jabbing a teasing thumb in Arthur's direction for Wren's benefit. "He had every Shel Silverstein poem memorized as a kid, but I'd send him off to get one measurement and he'd forget by the time he came back to tell me. Every time." He reached out and playfully rubbed Arthur's shoulder.

Wren laughed.

"Well, it worked out OK. I'm an English teacher, after all, and a pretty good one at that."

Wren's laugh quickly died out. Her eyes flitted back and forth between the two men, who were both smiling stiffly, as if in competition to see who had the thicker skin. It was always like this with Arthur and his dad. Friendly at first, then a bit prickly, nobody daring to break the tension and actually say what they were really thinking. Personally, Wren didn't really get it. Neal was a little old-fashioned, a little rough around the edges at times. But he was here, warts and all, and Arthur didn't seem to realize how lucky that made him.

"Can we see the nursery?" Arthur's mom asked, slicing the tension.

"Well, funny thing," Wren said, guiding everyone single file down the very brief hallway from the living room to the bedroom, looking back over her shoulder once or twice as if they might get lost on the long journey. "It's a one-bedroom. So this is it."

Wren didn't love Arthur's parents standing there, staring at their bedroom, scanning and judging. It didn't look anything like a nursery, save for a small white high chair assembled and stuffed into the corner, and a messy pile of blankets and extremely plain infant clothes on the floor waiting to be put away properly. Arthur had picked most of it out, and it showed.

No one said anything for a beat. A long beat. A significant amount of time passed. The longer this went on, the worse Wren began to feel. Their bedroom, which she ordinarily found quite comfortable, began to look like a prison. Sparse. It was far from homey, with very little on the walls and not much furniture beyond the bed and nightstands. It looked . . . temporary. Functional, at best. Spartan, at worst.

Truthfully, that had been the idea. Intentional. She wasn't going to be like every other mom with their murals of forest animals and soothing pastel colors. She wasn't going to fundamentally change the way she lived, or who she was, and she *liked* that their apartment looked like they could just pick up and disappear at a moment's notice.

Only, having it all on display for Arthur's parents was suddenly making her feel painfully self-conscious about the whole thing. What the hell was wrong with her that she was feeling so casual and detached? Why couldn't she just be like everybody else?

Then Neal spoke.

"What's that noise? Sounds like dripping." He mimicked it by popping his lips three times. "Anyone else hear that?" And then he ducked out to investigate. Arthur shrugged at Wren and followed.

"Well, I think it's smart that you don't want to commit to any design choices you might regret later," Arthur's mom said finally, having fully taken in the space. "You know, especially once you find out the sex."

Arthur and Wren had decided to keep it a surprise until the big day. Even they didn't know. Arthur had been adamant that they find out as soon as possible, but it was an argument Wren won easily. Being the one actually growing the damn kid was pretty much the ultimate trump card. And where was the fun in knowing everything?

"Yeah," Wren said, trying to sound optimistic. "I mean I read that the baby really only needs a little bassinet for a while, like a few months at least. And I think they're blind for the first couple of weeks, right? Or is that kittens? Anyway, we have some time to zhuzh it up."

"I'm sorry." Laura laughed. "I don't mean to sound judgy. I try so hard not to that sometimes I end up putting my foot in my mouth."

"No, not at all," Wren said, even though this was definitely true.

"Tell me about the shower. It must have been fun celebrating with all your friends."

The ones she couldn't get to leave fast enough? And Charlie, whom she wanted to stay, but wouldn't? Yeah, totally.

"It was."

"Were either of your brothers able to make it? I know it was mixed gender so I was hoping. So modern, by the way. Love that."

Wren suddenly realized that Laura was affectionately playing with her hair, running her fingers through, giving just the tiniest bit of scalp massage. It was heaven. It was all Wren could do not to start purring like a cat.

"No, sadly. They couldn't come."

Could be because Wren had chickened out of inviting them at the last minute, along with barely speaking to them for the last decade-plus of her life. She loved them, obviously, but there were a lot of bad memories there, and now was not the time to dredge them all up.

"Too bad. Because it is true what they say, about it taking a village. You need a strong community around you, one way or another. I hope you two have that here."

Wren could only force a smile.

"Now." Arthur's mom peeked her head out the door, then led Wren farther into the room, sitting them both down on the bed. "I don't know where the boys have gone off to, so I don't know how much time we have."

"For what?"

❑ ❑ ❑

Later, they all stood outside in the parking lot, admiring the Petersons' shiny Airstream trailer. It was sleek and silver, modern but classic, futuristic but from an era when everyone thought for sure we'd have flying cars and robot butlers by now. It was hooked to a beefy pickup truck, the tires sprayed with mud.

"You sure you guys can't stay?" Arthur asked without much fight in his voice.

"No can do," Neal said. "We're on a tight schedule, continuing on to Acadia National Park so we can wrap up in time."

Wren had heard all about their tour of national parks. They'd seen dozens of them. There'd even been an agonizing slideshow presentation earlier, endless photos of mountain views that all looked the same. The only thing worse than the photos was the apparently Herculean task of Arthur and his dad trying to stream the slideshow onto their horribly outdated TV. But to be fair, that was at least entertaining to watch, Wren and Laura sharing private snickers as the men fuddled and failed.

It was beautiful, Arthur's parents doing this together in their twilight years, but there was also something about it that bummed Wren out deeply. Laura could whip up ten different kinds of chocolate chip cookies without once looking at a recipe book but had never seen the Grand Canyon until earlier on this voyage. It added a frantic "Everything must go!" quality to their trip. It felt like, now that they were in their late sixties, there was no guarantee how much time either of them had left, the grim reaper hot on their tail, riding a sick Harley, so best to keep moving and soak up as much as possible. Still, for all the stories and the many, many photos of bison, they hadn't mentioned their journey coming to a close anytime soon.

"Wrap up in time for what?" Wren asked.

"In time to meet our first grandchild, of course." Laura smiled.

"Just a few more weeks," Neal said. "We'll be ready; just give us a call if you need anything at all."

The eyes of all four of them, that is to say, eight individual eyeballs, were growing wet. Neal feigned a cough and wiped at his tears before they could form proper drops; Laura couldn't hold hers back. Even Wren, despite her best efforts, was getting a little misty.

"We do have something for you, before we go. Neal?" Laura elbowed him gently, and he stuck his head inside the truck, rummaging around before returning with a cardboard box. He handed it over to Arthur, who accepted it with a mix of pride and wonder, as if it were some great family heirloom finally being passed down.

"Been meaning to get this to you for a while," Neal said.

"What is it?" Arthur asked. Maybe his father's old toolbox, or some old children's books Arthur used to love as a kid, Wren thought. Perhaps a sentimental something that Neal wore as a baby in the sixties; a onesie made of pure asbestos.

"It's the last of the junk out of your room. Some stuff from college, I think. Figured it was time."

"Can't have you still tied to us when you're getting ready to start a family of your own." Laura sniffled.

"Aaaaand, we could use the space," Neal clarified. "We're turning the room into a gallery. Your mom's been experimenting with photography and actually has quite the knack for it."

Wren watched the air leave Arthur's body and his shoulders sag as he muttered a weak, "Oh, thanks."

A last round of hugs and then the Petersons said their prolonged goodbyes. Arthur and Wren soon watched the Airstream drive away, navigating the tight, mazelike parking lot. They watched for a while without saying anything, either of them, until finally:

"You OK?" Wren asked. "You look a little shell-shocked."

"I'm OK," Arthur said. "You? How did it go with my mom?"

"Fine. What happened with your dad earlier?"

Arthur sighed. "Recap?"

"Recap."

They held hands and trudged across the parking lot back toward their building, Arthur awkwardly carrying the sagging box of junk under one arm.

"Can we be eating?" Wren asked.

"Of course."

2

THEY ATE DINNER AT THEIR favorite neighborhood sub shop. It was called Sub Shop. The place was right in the middle of a nondescript shopping center near the apartment, one of many, sandwiched between a defunct laundromat and an unnaturally well-lit Mattress Firm.

They sat at a wobbly plastic patio table stuffed into a corner of the tiny shop. Wren tore into a gooey meatball sub the size of her entire torso, while Arthur nibbled on a cheesesteak. Arthur found he didn't have much of an appetite. Too busy replaying the visit over and over in his mind. Thinking about his great gift, the box of crap, and whether his parents realized or cared that they lived in a one-bedroom apartment with no storage.

"This is the best sub I've ever had," Wren said between bites.

"That's what you said last time. And the time before that."

They had eaten here, or had the food delivered, frequently during the pregnancy. It had hit the sweet spot of satisfying Wren's cravings in the early days, and somehow the sandwiches—despite being soggy with grease and mayonnaise—were among the few things that didn't make her nauseous.

"And I mean it every time." She chewed some more, savoring every bite.

"So, you called this meeting," Arthur said. "What's on your mind?"

Wren held up a finger, swallowed a colossal lump, and then spoke. "We're not ready."

"Not ready for . . ."

"When your mom and I were talking, I realized we have absolutely no clue what we're getting into."

"What do you mean? We have a car seat, we have a booger sucker, we have diapers. I've got my time off all set up with the school. We have enough money saved up. Well, enough for now. Speaking of . . ." He trailed off.

"What is it?" A piece of shredded lettuce shot out of Wren's mouth and landed on the table in front of him.

"My dad tried to cut me a check. Slip it into my palm like some sort of mobster. Can you believe that?"

"That's amazing. How much?" She lit up.

"No, Wren, it was not amazing." It was patronizing, insulting, and infantilizing. Like Arthur couldn't take care of his own life, his own family. Like he hadn't been scrimping and saving for years to prepare himself for this phase of life. He'd worn holes in almost every pair of socks he owned just to make sure the baby would have enough bibs—which, come to think of it, he had forgotten to buy—and the absolute gall of his father to think he didn't have things under control.

He didn't, to be clear, but still—the *gall*!

The offer had also come with a lecture on cutting back on "luxuries," like Netflix, his cell phone, and the odd dinner out. Like any of that was going to make a difference.

"It doesn't matter, I wouldn't take it."

"You're kidding. Why not?" She shook her head disapprovingly. "If I know anything, it's that when people feel like being generous, you should let them."

"It's not generous, it's . . . Can you just be on my side here?" She always did this, especially with his parents. Saw them with rose-colored glasses. Why couldn't she see that this was a passive-aggressive power move? Her insistence on seeing and believing the best in people could really be obnoxious.

"OK, I'm on your side," she said, hands up in surrender, then miming zipping her lips shut, locking them together, and throwing away the key.

"Thank you for lying. I just wanted to tell you, in the interest of not keeping secrets. But to your earlier point, we are absolutely ready. We took those classes, practiced our diapering and swaddling. Met pediatricians. What else is there?"

Wren spoke but refused to open her lips. All that came out were stifled mumbles, as if her mouth was duct-taped shut.

"Still locked, right," Arthur said, reaching over with his own imaginary key and opening her lips back up, zipping them free.

"Ah, thank God. It was getting hard to breathe." She took a few dramatic, labored breaths. Arthur rolled his eyes. "I was trying to say, we haven't talked about names. Not once."

"My mom was grilling you about baby names? We decided not to find out the sex, so . . ."

"Yeah, but shouldn't we have a short list or something?"

"OK, so let's make a short list."

Wren paused. "But I don't wanna."

"OK . . . I'm confused."

"She was asking about my birth plan, Arthur. What the

fuck is a birth plan?! My plan is to push the baby out and not die. That was like the best-case scenario a hundred years ago; I didn't know I needed more than that."

"Did you say that to her?"

"No, because then she started asking me about gentle parenting versus authoritative, and burping techniques for stubborn gas, which just . . . ew. And was I going to breastfeed exclusively or not at all or a mix? And I had no idea what to say about anything."

"Well, she's overly inquisitive and involved; we know that about her."

"Or maybe she could just tell that we needed help. That I needed help. She was being nice, I think. Wasn't she?"

Arthur sighed. "She loves you, Wren. You're like the daughter she never had."

"Really?"

"Believe me, she never stops talking about it." His mom had never explicitly verbalized her disappointment at never having a girl, but when Arthur was growing up, it was impossible not to notice. He was always uncomfortable with the forlorn sort of way she'd look at his short hair. Always trying to coax him into watching rom-coms with her or attending Shania Twain concerts. "And as her de facto daughter you're going to have to master the art of not trying to interpret her motives and just tuning her out when she gets pushy."

Wren balled up her sandwich wrapper, picked completely clean, and chucked it in the nearby trash can.

"Whatever, either way, she's right! Our bedroom, for example. Like, that's what we're bringing our baby home to? Why haven't I been *nesting*? I keep waiting for this magic maternal instinct to kick in and make me give a shit about burping and blowouts and nursery aesthetics and it just . . . I feel nothing."

As much as Arthur wanted to reassure and soothe Wren, he could relate to what she was feeling. The surprise visit from his parents had rocked him, too, left him feeling horribly inadequate.

"So you know how me and my dad disappeared for a while?"

"Yeah, thanks for that, by the way."

"Well, he found out that our bathroom sink was dripping, and I told him I'd call the leasing office. And he said, 'Why wait for those bums?' And he dragged me out to the hardware store and we bought this little rubber thing called a gasket—I thought he said we were going to get a *casket* at first; you should have been inside my head for that one—and we came back and he asked me where my toolbox was."

"You don't have a toolbox."

"Exactly. So that was humiliating. But lucky me, he had his in the Airstream, because of course, and so he popped our faucet open and fixed the leak in like five minutes."

"Wow."

He'd imagined himself growing gracefully into the role of "man of the house"—whatever that really meant. Someone in the family had to have the know-how to occasionally wield a set of pliers, and if there was anyone more hopeless than Arthur, it was Wren. She was competent enough, it wasn't that, but he knew she could have lived with the dripping faucet until the Earth simply ran out of water. Stuff like that just didn't bother her. So that left it up to Arthur. During the brief visit, though, it was deflating to see just how far he really had to go. Not just when it came to fixing things: His dad had always made good money, provided, knew the right way to handle every situation. Arthur was just . . . Arthur.

"You know, it's not too late to become a plumber," Wren added. "You've got the butt crack for it."

"Thanks."

Wren reached across the table and grabbed his hand with hers. It was so warm. She'd been running hot lately, which had really emphasized the inadequacy of their air-conditioning unit this summer. But right now it felt nice against his own nervously clammy skin.

"You're being too hard on yourself, like always. Maybe you're not your dad. But I like you." She had read his mind. Always could.

Arthur sighed. "I guess it's not a fair comparison. When my dad was my age, he had already served in the navy, seen the whole world, and started his own contracting business. Plus you could buy a big house in the suburbs back then for, like, forty nickels. The money went farther. The world was so different."

"I'm telling you, if women could vote, I would so go back." Wren sighed.

"OK, my parents aren't *that* old."

"You about ready to go?" She laughed.

He nodded, and go they did. They stood up, exited Sub Shop, made a sharp right, and moments later opened the door to the Mad Cow Creamery two doors down. Its frigid, vanilla-scented air was welcome relief from the hot, oniony atmosphere of the previous stop.

"I'll grab the table and spoons," Arthur said as Wren approached the counter.

"You want anything tonight?"

"I'm so full I could explode. I literally don't know how you do this."

It had become their ritual. Some nights they even had queso at the Salsa Casita, hitting the three spots in succession like the Big Bad Wolf laying waste to the piggies' homes. Admittedly, eating out like this was more expensive than cooking at home, and Arthur hated spending the money. (*In this economy?!* he joked whenever Wren wanted to go out. But he wasn't really joking. He usually ruled the budget with an iron fist, but there was also a much more serious cost to consider of not keeping the pregnant lady happy.) On the plus side, due to some kind of mailing list error, they received multiple copies of the local coupon mailer every week and always had one freebie or another coming their way. They made it work.

Soon, Wren sat down with a tremendous caramel-drizzled sundae piled up to her chin and dug in.

"I'm serious," Arthur said. "I know you're eating for two, but it's still impressive. Maybe you should go for a spot on the wall."

Wren's jaw dropped. "I've been telling you that for years! Look at all these losers," she said, gesturing to the wall: a row of yellowing portraits featuring customers who'd been able to finish the famous three-pound sundae named the Heifer. The cheery, optimistic before pictures and the bloated but triumphant afters. "I could have outeaten any of them, and that's before I got pregnant. Now? Not a single person on this wall could hold my jock. But you never let me do it."

"Whoa, *let* you? It costs thirty dollars to even try, and what do you get? Your photo on the wall and diarrhea?"

Wren's eyes flew open, and she put her spoon down. She

wasn't done eating, so the move caught Arthur by surprise. Pregnant Wren was not known for taking breaks mid-meal.

"What are you doing?"

"Shut up, I need total silence. I have a nugget of an idea and I'm trying to sift it out of the brain fog. I think it's a good one."

"What is—"

"Arthur, if I lose this idea, I'm gonna make you do maternity photos with me in a pumpkin patch."

Arthur zipped his lips and watched nervously as Wren paced and chewed at her fingernails for some time, periodically mumbling to herself. Suddenly, she spun around to face him.

"I've got it," she said. "I know what we have to do."

3

"ARE YOU SURE WE WROTE them down?" Arthur asked.

Wren sat cross-legged on the floor of their bedroom closet. Around her, the walls seemed to stretch toward the sky and close in. Hanging clothes pressed so tightly together they threatened to snuff the oxygen right out of the room. Damn, this apartment was small, but hey, at least it also had roaches.

A junk box sat in front of her, overflowing with crap, picture frames and obsolete electronics cords peeking out from underneath the lid.

"I'm absolutely certain that we did," she said in defeat. What she was looking for was not in the junk box. She grabbed another from behind the loose, flowy ends of some hanging dresses and dragged it out. She popped the lid off the container. It had CHRISTMAS LIGHTS scrawled on it in faded Sharpie and crossed out, then BOOKS crossed out, then, finally, ETC. The top layer of this one, too, was all cords and cables for long-deceased cell phones and digital cameras. She grabbed a spaghetti-like mess of them and chucked them into the trash bag next to her.

"OK," Arthur said, sitting back on his heels next to her.

Out of the corner of her eye she could see Arthur pulling the cables out of the trash and giving them an extra look. She was certain he'd end up saving them just in case there was an emergency need to charge an iPod Shuffle from 2005. And he thought he wasn't ready to be a dad. "Are you sure that this actually happened and you're not fabricating the entire thing?"

"Yes, asshole. If I could rotate my spine I'd give you the worst death stare right now. I can't believe you don't remember."

"Where were we?" he asked.

"I don't know."

"When? What year was it?"

"I don't know."

"Well, I have to say you make a compelling argument."

"OK," Wren said, resigned. "Some of the details are a little foggy. But I distinctly recall staying up late one night and writing down all the things we wanted to do before we turned thirty. Our bucket lists. We wrote it down, and we saved them . . . somewhere. I'm sure of it. We bared our souls to each other and you can't even be bothered to remember."

"We were high, weren't we?"

"Or tipsy. Maybe both. I can't remember."

"You mentioned that."

"Will you just help me look?"

Wren scraped her way down into the next layer of the box like a geologist studying rock formations and reached the frames. Old pictures of her and Arthur that had been replaced on the walls with newer options. There was the first photo of the two of them ever taken, both glassy-eyed and slightly blurry in the college dorm, canoodling uneasily like brand-new lovers. A photo of one of their first dates, mini golf. Wren holding the score sheet with a victorious smile on her face, Arthur sagging dramatically, as if in anguish, hamming it up.

Noticeably absent were any photos from the past few years. Sure, on the walls they had hung exactly one set of professional portraits taken in an orchard, but Wren had found it buggy and sweaty and too difficult to walk and laugh and gaze lovingly into each other's eyes at the same time without looking like a total psycho. She'd vowed to never do portraits again. And inside the box, there were a few snapshots, mostly taken in the low light of this very apartment. But Wren felt like there should have been more. Maybe the obligatory photo of the two of them holding up the Leaning Tower. Instead, here was a bland selfie, sitting on the couch eating macaroni.

"I'll help you find it. But can you explain the idea one more time? I think all the food hit you in the car and you started nodding off while you were explaining it. You weren't making a lot of sense. At one point there was mention of pirates."

Wren groaned, growing mildly frustrated. She was feeling unnecessarily antsy. Like time was already a-wasting. And there wasn't much left of it to begin with. In just a few weeks, the baby would be here and this would all be moot.

"I had a major epiphany when I was devouring my sundae," she said. "I've always wanted to take down the Heifer. Talked about it, put it off, said, 'Ah, tonight's not the night,' a hundred times. But what am I waiting for? If not now, when? Right? Soon I'll be too busy spooning rapidly melting bites into a toddler's mouth to give two shits about getting my face on the wall."

"If it's that important to you," Arthur said, "you should have just said so."

"It's not just about the Heifer." She sighed. How could she articulate this to him? His life was about to change forever, but not in nearly the same way as hers. For some reason she thought of a Nat Geo documentary. She'd be the haggard lioness feeding a brood of cubs and wasting away in the heat, and he'd be the proud male lion off loafing in the sun, getting fat, and banging whoever the hell he wanted. Arthur would never do that to her in the real, human world, outside the Wild West of the Serengeti, of course. But there was something more permanent and binding about her role in all this that she couldn't quite put her finger on; that much was for sure. "It's my maternal instinct, or lack thereof. I think the reason it hasn't kicked in yet is because I feel like I have unfinished business. The ice cream is just a representative example. A metaphor, if you will."

"Unfinished business. That's something a ghost would say. Are you planning on haunting someone?"

She ignored him and continued.

"I've never left Baltimore, not once in my life. We've been holed up in our apartment, trying to save money, just trying to get by." And nobody had ever told them that just getting by would be so goddamn hard. That it would require working all day just to come home and eat dinner so you could go to bed so you could get up the next day and work some more, and all that fifty-some weeks a year just so you could live in a shitty apartment and watch your life get more and more expensive without ever actually getting the chance to live any of it. "And I haven't minded being patient, I always knew that our time would come, but there's just so much left to do. So I think my body is physically rejecting the idea of settling down permanently."

"Like a bad hair graft."

"Exactly."

"I think I'm getting it," he said. "Just like I feel like I'm missing the wisdom and experience that I'm going to need to be a great dad. And the way we fix that is . . ."

"The bucket list. If we can just find the damn thing."

Arthur stroked his beard, professor-like. Except Wren could tell he was momentarily distracted by a patchy spot, and he was considering what it might look like to chop the whole thing off. "We can always remake it," he said, refocusing. "Come up with new ideas."

"No, that completely defeats the purpose. I want to go back and remember who I wanted to be before being an adult fucked it all up." She wanted to remember what her hopes and dreams were when they were pure and untainted. Would nineteen-year-old Wren be proud of who she turned out to be? Twenty-nine, living here, hopping from job to job, getting pregnant her greatest accomplishment to date? Adult Wren was pretty sure she knew the answer, and she didn't like it. What did she think and hope her life was going to be like, and with less than a year before she turned thirty, where had she gone wrong? She needed that list to know for sure.

"I get it. Except we've been at this for an hour and we're running out of boxes to check. The only one you haven't opened is that one with a stack of laptops in it that I've been too lazy to recycle."

Wren realized he was right. They weren't going to find it. It had to be, what, ten years old? She flopped backward, realizing about halfway down that she should have checked for a soft landing spot, but luckily her head landed in a pile of Arthur's sweaters. He had so many sweaters. "So we're doomed," she said. She exhaled. "It's OK. We can just wait, delay our adventures until our kid's all grown up. Might as well pop out a few more while we're at it. What's another couple of decades anyway? Your parents are proof that it's never too late." Damn it, she was starting to well up despite her best efforts. It felt ridiculous, all this over a couple scoops of ice cream. But suddenly it was like she could see the next several decades of her life flying by and losing herself to them completely. This was not how she was supposed to be feeling right now.

"Hey," Arthur said, reaching over and wiping away her first tear the instant it formed. "I just remembered something."

"What is it?"

"There's one more box."

❑ ❑ ❑

In the corner of the living room, the box of "college junk" Arthur's parents had so kindly brought them had been unceremoniously shoved into a corner, a blanket folded on top of it as some sort of half-hearted camouflage.

"You think there's any chance it's in here?" Arthur asked as she slid it out into the middle of the carpet.

"I think there's a good chance," she said. "You're just sentimental enough to keep something like that. And we've looked everywhere else. Is it OK if I open it?"

"Knock yourself out," he said.

"You're sure? You don't want to preview it first in case there's some steamy letter from an ex-girlfriend sitting on top or something?"

He rolled his eyes. "I only had one girlfriend before you, and I'd hardly call the relationship steamy."

"Oh, I remember her. She had a funny name . . . Chipper, Chimmy. Something like that."

"Chipmunk." Arthur sighed. "It was her camp name."

Wren cackled as she unstuck the edges of the packing tape holding the box top on. She remembered Chipmunk now.

When Arthur had first told her, she'd teasingly asked him if he liked her because she knew her way around nuts.

"Shut up, it was a formative experience," he said. "But no, I don't think you'll find any memorabilia from the relationship in there. Other than maybe the rock she painted for me."

With the tape removed, Wren pulled off the lid, singing a heavenly little *aah* as if golden beams of light might shoot out of the box at any moment.

Arthur sat down next to her and peered inside.

They sorted through stacks of papers, his Intro to Creative Writing journal with Lumineers lyrics scribbled on the front (he was one of those guys), embarrassing posters that once hung on Arthur's dorm room walls, and even his diploma still rolled up in its original casing. And there, just when they thought they were going to come up empty-handed, half-stuck to the very bottom of the box was the dried-up, slightly crispy piece of paper Wren was looking for.

4

WREN HAD BEEN DYING TO get going on their lists first thing the next morning, but Arthur reminded her that he had one final obligation to take care of. Though he'd miss the first few weeks of the school year on paternity leave, he still wanted to be at the meet and greet slash pizza party slash info session for incoming sixth graders. In fact, he had to be there. It was his last chance to grab face time with the principal and earn a little goodwill. If he wanted to get his master's (which he did, eventually) and move up the ranks (which he prayed at some point would lead to a salary that he couldn't easily beat by working at Costco), the schmoozing was important. As much as he hated it.

Wren understood, but that's not to say that she took the news easily. No, she clung to his arm like an old barnacle on his way out the door earlier that day, insisting over and over that they just find a "quick, easy one" to check off.

"I'm almost certain I wrote down 'have a threesome.' We can get that done in five minutes!"

"With who? No one in this building, I hope."

"There's a hot guy on the third floor that drives for UPS.

Well, he *would* be hot if he had all his teeth. But if he wears the uniform I think I can make it work."

"OK, goodbye," he had said, shutting the door slowly so as not to slam her pouting nose in it. "I love you!" he shouted through the door once it latched.

From there it was a fifteen-minute drive to the school, right on the outskirts of the city. It looked like a prison, all stained concrete and windows reinforced with iron bars. The school drew an interesting and explosive mix of city and suburban kids. It was simultaneously known as the best school in the city and the worst school in the county. When kids were accepted, they either got a "Congratulations!" or an "I'm sorry," depending on which neighborhood they lived in. It was where Arthur had started his teaching career, many years after being a student there himself. Initially, he was excited to carry on the school's proud tradition and help a new generation of students fall in love with his alma mater, the way he had. Now it felt more like the place was being held together by duct tape. It was far less *Dead Poets Society* than he'd imagined it. His first few years he had been exhaustingly energetic, always pushing the curriculum to its very limits, trying to really make the lessons come alive. At one point he'd even experimented with making a TikTok account of his own where he gave out lessons and homework reminders via choppy, torso-only dances. But eventually he realized the kids were laughing *at* him, not with him, and he quickly shut it down.

Lately, even he had to admit, his heart hadn't been in it in quite the same way.

He pulled into the parking lot, the sedan chugging and lurching along. Arthur prayed the car would make it a little longer or, ideally, a lot longer. It had been his in college, survived more than a handful of dry years with far too few oil changes, and was now completely paid off. It would be just his luck that it would die now.

The teachers' lot, for inexplicable reasons, was farthest from the main entrance. He drove slowly past the visitors' lot, where lines of parents exited much nicer vehicles than his and crossed the pavement toward the main entrance. They wore slacks and ties, dresses, and polo shirts. Some pushed strollers or pulled along toddlers who were too young to be left at home with a babysitter. Then he drove a little farther, past the spaces reserved for administrators, the principal, senior faculty, teachers with seniority. Basically anyone who was more important than him, which included nearly everyone. Soon he reached his own designated parking space, deep in the bowels of the overflow lot. A sappy tree branch hung so low over the space it nearly scraped the hood as he pulled in. The pavement at his feet as he stepped out was covered in bird shit, and mosquitos from the nearby woods swarmed him immediately, as if they'd been eagerly awaiting his arrival. Arthur smacked one against his neck but missed, merely smacking himself. The sun was going down now, this area of the lot poorly lit and ripe for a good mugging. Not the warmest welcome, certainly not a corner office in a city high-rise somewhere, but it was nothing he wasn't used to. If he just stayed the course, he'd have a nice parking spot one day, one that wasn't knee-deep in the brush. And maybe he'd have a car worthy of parking in it, too.

Arthur was just catching up with the herd of parents and children entering the building when he saw a breathless mom come streaking toward him out of the corner of his eye. "Do you work here?" she asked, eyeing the faculty badge hanging around his neck. He smiled and nodded and felt his heart flutter just the tiniest bit. Here was the nervous mother of an incoming sixth grader, frazzled and lost. She was probably looking for a steady hand to tell her where to go, what to do, or maybe just someone to reassure her that everything was going to be all right. It could definitely be overwhelming for parents when their kids started at a new school, and Arthur would be honored to be the friendly face she needed.

"Arthur Peterson, sixth-grade English. What can I help you with?" It sounded so official and prestigious rolling off his tongue, and he noticed his voice had even dropped an octave. Admittedly, he'd not been looking forward to tonight. Awkward handshakes and crappy pizza and a million questions about ChatGPT, that's what it would be, for the most part. But the look of relief on the woman's face, relief that she had found *him* of all people, well, it was almost enough to make him feel like a first-year teacher again.

"Can I give you this?" the curly-haired woman asked, producing what looked like a balled-up cloth or T-shirt from seemingly nowhere. "I don't see any trash cans and I don't want to leave it in the car."

"Oh, sure," he said before fully understanding the package he was accepting. In an instant, it was in his hands, the ball unnervingly warm. Worse, it felt fresh. The smell assaulted him. It was no T-shirt. And that was when he noticed the tall husband waiting by the stroller for his wife a few yards away, tiny little newborn feet poking out of the carriage. The baby's toes wiggled in the air with the sort of carefree pep that can only come from someone who's recently dropped a huge load. Arthur nearly barfed.

"You're a lifesaver," the woman said, and she hurried off to meet her family.

He stood there for what felt like a long time, holding the rancid diaper and pondering his life choices. When he was a kid and he'd go out with his dad, he remembered strangers saluting him and thanking him for his service. Neal Peterson would wear a simple US Navy sweatshirt and, as if by magic, people would let them cut in line, waiters would bring free appetizers, and occasionally a few very forward women had asked him with barely concealed hope in their voice whether he was a widower. Arthur, on the other hand, might as well have been the school janitor. Actually, that was an insult to the custodian, Miss Lily, who was beloved and revered by everyone at the school.

"AP?" A voice made Arthur snap out of it and spin around. A lot of kids had taken to calling him AP, short for Arthur Peterson. He liked to think of it as a term of endearment and not a subtle show of disrespect—he'd really prefer Mr. Peterson—but it was too late now. It had stuck.

He recognized the boy standing there as Martin Lamb, a gangly, quiet kid he'd taught the previous year. Good student, not a lot of friends—probably due to his discovering deodorant just a *smidge* later than his peers. Arthur offered a friendly wave. "Why are you holding a diaper?" Martin asked as a flicker of excitement flashed across the boy's face. "Did you have the baby?!"

"No, no, we did not." Arthur sighed and left it at that. "What are you doing here? Tonight's just for the sixth graders."

"I know. I'm trying to talk to Mr. Hernandez." The music teacher and band director. Also, a bit of an asshole. But Arthur wasn't about to bring that up now.

"I'm sure he's here somewhere, but I don't remember you being in band."

"I'm not. It's just—" Martin looked down, shuffled his feet. "Don't worry about it. I'll find him and sort it out."

"Is there something I can help you with?" He'd struck out hard with the curly-haired mom, but maybe he could still be useful to someone tonight. "Come on, it's me. AP. We're cool, right? You can tell me what's going on. I'm rizz. I've got aura."

"If I tell you," Martin began, "will you please stop?"

Arthur nodded. "Whadya need?"

The boy took a deep breath and came out with it. "You can't help me. Unless you've got three hundred dollars for a trumpet."

Arthur wished he had a drink so he could spit it out. "Three hundred dollars?!"

"Right? That's what I'm saying! I really want to do band this year, but I can't afford that. All the rental shops are sold out, too. I need to talk to Mr. H and see if there's something we can work out."

Knowing Mr. H, he of the passive-aggressive break-room notes that frequently targeted the smell of Arthur's tuna sandwiches (it was cheap protein, OK?), Arthur doubted it. And then he said something that he couldn't quite explain. It just came over him.

"I'll give it to you if you want, the money." Martin cocked an eye at him. Arthur doubled down. "I'm serious."

The quick math in his head calculating the three hundred dollars against what they had in savings was definitely painful, but it would feel good to make a difference, if he could. It damn sure wasn't happening inside the classroom, or by accepting soiled diapers from strangers.

"No. Thanks, but no," Martin said. "I'll figure it out. It's no big deal, anyway."

"OK. If you're sure. Offer stands if you change your mind."

"Six-seven," Martin said.

Arthur blinked. "I gotta tell you, I still don't know what that means."

"Honestly, neither do I." They both laughed. "But for real, though, are you gonna tell me why you're holding a diaper?"

5

ARTHUR OPENED THE DOOR TO the apartment just in time to see Wren standing immediately in front of him with a pair of long, sharp kitchen scissors. She could see the terror in his eyes. He thought she'd snapped. She knew it. Hatched a plan to kill him off and flee with the life insurance money. Perform a home vasectomy so he could never put her through all this again.

She played into it on purpose, widening her eyes like a haunted doll and keeping the scissors raised high, à la Michael Myers. "Welcome home, Arthur."

"What, uh . . . whatcha doing?" he said uncertainly.

"Arts and crafts. Come here, I'll show you." She lowered the blades and grabbed him by the hand, dragging him the rest of the way into the apartment. "Oh, and how'd it go at the school? Did you get a chance to talk to Principal Norman?"

"No, I couldn't quite pin her down."

"So I made all those talking points for nothing?" Arthur had told her that Norman was really into comics, the Marvel movies in particular. Wren took the liberty of making him a few flashcards, mostly featuring Tom Holland (Spider-Man) trivia and details of the short period of time when Tom Hiddleston (Loki) was dating Taylor Swift. More than enough to get a rousing discussion going.

"I'll get to it, I promise. I just couldn't find the right opportunity."

"Arthur, I say this with love, but have you considered the fact that you might have to make your *own* opportunities? To get what you want out of this job."

She could tell by the way his jaw set that perhaps she'd overstepped a tad. But sometimes, she knew, if she didn't challenge him, he didn't act. But before the flush in his cheeks could grow any darker, she presented him with the results of her project. "Ta-da."

On the kitchen table were the remains of a massacre. Strips and bits of paper lay everywhere, strewn about as if after a bout of snowflake cutting gone horribly wrong. Wren was not graceful with scissors, no. She had artistic talent and always had, but no one had ever accused her of being neat and orderly, of taking the smoothest route to her final destination. As a kid she was scolded constantly for it. Not content to just grab one color at a time, she'd dump the entire bin of paints out on the table. The same with markers, which would then roll off the table and become a slipping hazard for others in the household. She was practically a hoarder when it came to her coloring and drawings, carrying around great stacks of them with her and hiding them all over her uncle's house. Drove him absolutely insane. But for whatever reason, she refused to change her ways. One small act of rebellion and chaos that she clung to, she guessed.

"What are these?" Arthur said, finally dropping his bag

and examining her creation. Two mason jars sat on the table, one labeled with a construction paper *W* in glittery purple, the other with a green *A*.

"I took the liberty of separating our lists. I cut out each line item and put them into our respective jars. To retain a bit of mystery, I tried to look as little as possible. Hence the mess."

Arthur picked up one of his old neckties, which lay crumpled on the table.

"Did you blindfold yourself?"

"Like I said, I tried really hard not to peek."

She realized that the mental image of her sitting in the apartment blindfolded, running around with a giant pair of kitchen scissors, must have been unsettling to Arthur. And yes, she could have used the morning to knock out some freelance work. Should have. Arthur must have been thinking it. Her unemployment had put a drain on their savings, savings they were going to need when they got the bill from the hospital in a few weeks—sure, most of it would technically be covered by Arthur's insurance, but there would surely be fun, surprise line items along the way. She'd even heard it costs extra sometimes to actually hold your baby because, hey, America! But as crazy as it all was, that's how much this really meant to her.

"So what do we do now?" Arthur picked up his *A* jar and twirled it around in his hands, examining it like a crystal ball.

"We draw slips. And we try to get as much done as we can before I pop this baby out."

She scooped hers up, held it close to her chest.

"Can I go first?"

"Should we maybe clean up first or . . . No, never mind. Go for it."

Wren's heart began pounding. This was so exciting! Like taking the risky path in a choose-your-own-adventure book that would almost certainly lead to your character's demise but could ultimately unlock the happy ending with a bit of luck. A goose-bumpy thrill shot through her body. She dipped her fingers into the jar, felt the rough edges of the papers inside, slid past the top layer, and pressed in deeper. The pad of her middle finger touched one, and she couldn't explain it, but it just felt right. Like this strip of paper was calling to her. Its face was smooth, its temperature a bit cooler than the others somehow. Yes, this was it. This was the thing that when she did it, she would feel like herself again. It would right the course of her entire life, and the rest of her bucket list would fall into place like dominoes. She would finally become the person she had always wanted to be. At the end, she would feel completely ready to tackle the greatest challenge of her life: motherhood. But first, this. She pulled it out, flipped the paper round so she could read it, and paused before she spoke.

"Come on, don't tease me," Arthur said. "What does it say?"

She frowned. "You gotta be kidding me."

"What is it?"

She held it up so he could see. "Climb to the Top of Mount Everest."

Arthur stifled a laugh. "Shall I check Google Flights for last-minute departures to Nepal?"

"Very funny. God, I was such a basic." She was disappointed but not ready to give up so easily. She'd had this stroke of inspiration as a naive kid, back when climbing Everest wasn't such a commodity. She'd since seen the lines of people—lines!—waiting to get a glimpse of the summit. No, thank you. "No problem. Mount Everest is played out anyway. I heard they're thinking of putting in a gondola. We can do better."

She reached back into the jar. No magical intuition this time; she just pinched the first strip of paper she could feel and pulled it out. Whatever it was, it was bound to be at least slightly more practical than summiting the tallest mountain in the world.

"Bungee Jump into an Active Volcano," she read plainly.

Arthur winced. Wren sank at first, but maybe there was a way . . .

"Technically . . ." she began.

"No," he said.

"If you think about it . . ."

"Don't. Don't even think about it."

"Well then, I give up! I never would have gotten pregnant if I knew you weren't allowed to volcano bungee!"

She huffed out of the room. Just needed a minute. Just needed to sit and collect her thoughts. In short, they were that this completely sucked. Why didn't she think of this a year ago, two years ago? They had wasted so much time, and now it was too late. But maybe it didn't matter. She hadn't had the money for these things growing up, not in college, not as a young professional just trying to carve out a career and get by, and certainly not now. She would always wonder what could have been, what she'd missed out on. What kind of way was that to start their family? Would she always be bitter and resentful? She stared down at her belly and gave it a little rub. Would the baby know someday, be able to tell that her heart was never really in it, that she had settled down before she was really ready? More plainly, would it screw them up?

Thirty years from now, would they be talking about their emotionally distant mother in expensive therapy sessions?

She felt the couch sink next to her. Arthur. He placed a warm arm around her and squeezed gently, calming her immediately. In his other hand, he offered her the jar.

"One more try? There's got to be something in here we can do."

"I'm not in the mood. This was all a terrible idea. Too little, too late." She didn't want to look at a jar ever again. Peanut butter? Out. Jelly? Good goddamn riddance. She vowed right then and there to not even leave a door ajar for as long as she lived, just out of spite.

Arthur wouldn't give up so easily, though. He shook the jar playfully in front of her, rattling the pieces of paper inside.

"One more try and we'll go to bed."

She rolled her eyes, feigning resistance. In truth, she appreciated him. Her rock in moments like this. She reached back into the jar one more time and felt for a good one, whatever that meant, then pulled it out, unfolded it, and read it.

"Huh," was all she could say.

6

WREN: *Get on the Jumbotron at a Ravens Game*

A FEW DAYS LATER, THEY sat in the bland waiting room with opposing levels of patience. All the calming wall colors and Brookstone trickling desk fountains in the world couldn't stop Wren's leg from bouncing anxiously.

Arthur wore shorts, sensible sneakers, and a subtle purple shirt. Wren, to his left, wore a full Baltimore Ravens jersey with purple and gold beaded necklaces, full eye black, and tassels in her hair. A concerned-looking couple slunk through the waiting room and toward the exit, having just come from their own visit. Wren nodded solemnly to them, looking absolutely absurd in the process.

"You're sure we can't skip just this one?" Wren whispered to Arthur. "We've been waiting forever and we're missing the tailgate." She checked an imaginary watch on her wrist.

"Don't you have to know someone and be *invited* to a tailgate? You don't just show up to a magical free buffet of wings and dips . . . do you?"

"Uh, that's exactly what used to happen when I'd go with Charlie. People would offer us food, beers, shots. It was epic."

"Oh, right. Of course they did." Charlie and Wren used to

go together a few times a season. They never had tickets, but they'd also never needed them to hang out in the parking lots and be showered with free food and drink. Apparently when you look like Wren you can just walk around and be a welcome addition to anyone's party. It was not a phenomenon that Arthur had ever personally experienced. Come to think of it, though, Arthur couldn't remember the girls tailgating at all last season. Their schedules seemed to get harder and harder to line up. "Well, anyway, sorry in advance if I slow you down. I give you permission to abandon me if someone's smoking a pig."

"It doesn't matter. I just want to get down there to soak in the atmosphere," she said, leg bouncing impatiently again.

"It's just an August preseason game. Even I know that the game is meaningless. And it doesn't start for six hours; we're fine."

The fact that the game was an exhibition, would have no impact on the standings, and would feature all the teams' biggest stars hanging out in sweatpants on the sideline was the only reason last-minute tickets had been available and somewhat affordable.

"Ugh, preseason. Don't remind me. But fine—we'll stay for the appointment."

Another minute ticked by. Truth be told, Arthur was anxious, too. He always was leading up to these increasingly regular appointments. Though the pregnancy had been uneventful so far, there was always the chance that things could change. A "bad scan" could happen at any time, really. In fact, some of the worst things were the ones that showed up late in the game like this. He knew that much from late-night doomscrolling when he couldn't sleep, reading about all the worst-case scenarios. Of particular interest when he felt like torturing himself was imagining things going wrong and all of it being his fault. Yes, that was definitely on his brain's greatest-hits playlist. He'd watched more Instagram reels than he cared to admit about groundbreaking research into "low-quality" sperm and how it could negatively affect the baby or even raise the chances of a miscarriage, and he couldn't help but wonder. He'd had his fair share of booze and weed in college and exercised about as often as Halley's Comet came around. And then there were times when his diet leaned far too heavily on cheap ramen out of a styrofoam cup—it was delicious and helped keep the grocery budget in check but packed enough sodium and preservatives that Arthur sometimes worried he was being mummified from the inside out. Surely the habit wasn't good for his swimmers. He'd managed to get this far, but would these things eventually all come back to haunt him?

"Wren Morris?" a nurse called.

❑ ❑ ❑

"I'll go out on a limb and say you're going to the game tonight?"

Wren's OB, a gray-haired woman who was close to retirement and had seen absolutely everything in the entire known medical world, sat on a stool and took notes on a clipboard as they wrapped up the visit.

"Hell yeah. Ravens–Commanders. Battle of the Beltway. Primetime football, baby."

The woman said nothing. "It's my first game," Wren added. "Sort of a bucket-list thing. We're excited."

"I bet they'll score a lot of goals for you," Dr. Abadi said. Arthur imagined the woman knew absolutely nothing about American football and was quite content to keep it that way. "I hope you have fun."

"Thank you."

"But not too much fun."

Something about her tone of voice threw a pit into Arthur's stomach. Before he knew it, Wren, usually so jokey and playful during these visits, reached out and grabbed his hand, squeezing it like she was trying to wring water out of it. Wren shifted on the table, crinkling the thin medical paper underneath her. The doctor sensed their unease immediately.

"Everything's fine," she cautioned. "The baby's growing beautifully. But your blood pressure is a little higher than I'd like. Nothing to be alarmed about, just . . . take it easy."

"Are you putting me on bed rest?" Wren asked, exhaling just a bit. Arthur could see the slightest bit of moisture welling up behind her eyes, though. Being told she had to restrict all activity would be absolutely gutting. The poor woman was still coming to terms with the fact that pregnant people couldn't go high-altitude climbing.

"No, nothing like that. I'd just like you to try to relax. Avoid stressful situations if you can. Have you been walking like I told you?"

"Sure have. To the fridge, right?" Wren wheezed and held out a hand for a low five. Dr. Abadi stared at it, then reluctantly caved, giving it a polite slap. "But yes. Walking as much as I'm able." Arthur said nothing, but he couldn't stop thinking about the bucket list. What kinds of death-defying, high-adrenaline adventures were waiting for them inside that jar? If his pathetic sperm didn't ruin everything, maybe the pursuit of this bucket list would.

"Good. Keep it up. Thirty-six weeks means you're almost there, OK? I'll see you next week, and remember"—she put her hands out, fingers and thumbs looped into a circle like a meditating yogi—"*calm*."

❑ ❑ ❑

"YOU WIMPS ARE GOING DOWN!" Wren screamed. They were riding the rickety light rail down toward the stadium and she'd caught the eye of a few Commanders fans from across the train car. "YOU'RE IN RAVENS COUNTRY NOW. WE RUN THIS TOWN! WE RUN THIS WHOLE . . . GENERAL METRO AREA!"

One of the men, an older gentleman with glasses, just trying to enjoy a nice evening out on the town, take in a ball game with his young son, looked at her confused. *Please, it's just a preseason game*, his eyes seemed to plead. Arthur pulled Wren closer to him as if to physically restrain her.

"Can we take it easy? People are staring at us."

"It's football, Arthur. Trash talk is part of the game. If this is going to be our first and last time going to a game—because, let's face it, I'm not bringing a child into the Thunderdome—I want the full experience."

"And what's that?"

"Eating too many hot dogs and deep-fried desserts, for one. And I've always had this fantasy of talking a *little* too much shit to a rival fan. And since he can't beat me up, he takes out his anger on my boyfriend and the video goes viral."

"That's hot that you fantasize about me."

A random memory surfaced in his brain. His parents had taken him to a football game—one of the very first Ravens' seasons in Baltimore—and a drunk fan in the row behind them had been shouting obscene language the entire time. Some bad words that Arthur didn't really remember, but also some gross jeering at the cheerleaders, which Arthur did. His dad turned around and asked the guy politely to tone it down, words were exchanged, and the guy threw a punch. Arthur vividly remembered dropping the soda he had begged his parents for and smearing ketchup all over his shirt trying not to drop his hot dog. There was a brief fracas and before he knew it the rowdy fan was tumbling down the stadium stairs like a rolled-up carpet while his father calmly ushered Arthur and his mom away.

Arthur still related more to the scared little boy than to his father in the story.

"And of course," Wren added, "getting on RavensVision."

"Sorry, what?"

"That's what they call the jumbotron at the stadium. Come on, keep up."

Arthur was deeply regretting this whole thing. At this point, he might honestly prefer that they go bungee jumping. A football game just had too many unknowns, too much prolonged excitement and intensity. The doctor had just told them hours ago to ease up and chill out, and here they were about to walk into the lion's den. Worse, while he knew Wren was kidding, he doubted his ability to protect her from drunk, rowdy idiots who might be looking to pick a fight.

"God, I love the light rail," Wren said out of nowhere, snapping him out of his worries just as the lights on the train flickered like something out of a horror film.

"You're the only one," Arthur said. All the swaying was making him ill.

"It feels like childhood to me, if that makes any sense." She was staring wistfully out the window now, watching the city go by in a shaky blur. "The few good parts of it. My uncle was always working, so he'd buy me a pass and I would just go exploring. I always liked going to the neighborhoods you're 'not supposed to go to,'" she said, adding air quotes.

"Why?"

"I don't know. I hated how everyone wanted to pretend like they didn't exist instead of helping to make things better."

Arthur wondered if Wren ever felt like that as a kid. People, even her own family, knowing she was broken, not knowing how to help, and finding it easier to just look away.

The train lurched to a stop, squeaking horrifically the whole way, and the doors slid open.

"This is our stop," Wren said. The mass of people exited with cheers and tipsy *Let's gooooo*s, but Arthur grabbed Wren's hand.

"Maybe we shouldn't do this. We could go home, order in, watch on TV."

"Watching on TV isn't on the bucket list."

"I just . . . don't want anything to happen." *It's my job to take care of you and the baby*, he thought. And he was really doing a bang-up job so far.

"I'm not really going to get you beat up. But . . . I am getting on that jumbotron. One way or another." She pulled him toward the doors. "You coming?"

It didn't really feel like he had a choice.

❑ ❑ ❑

Their seats were so high up, by the time they'd finished climbing the never-ending stadium ramps, Arthur was sure they had reached a new climate. Not unlike Everest. There was altitude here, along with a slight haze in the air. Were they actually inside a cloud? Only a few rows from the very tippy top of the stadium, the wind whipped around and the August evening felt twenty degrees cooler. They could see the whole field, but the massive human beings inhabiting it looked tiny from where they sat.

"I leave you in charge of buying the seats and this is what happens," Wren said as she awkwardly squeezed her belly past the other people seated in their row.

"I thought 'corner end zone' sounded good." The price tag also sounded quite good. They'd worked incredibly hard to build up their savings, forgoing this exact kind of activity: expensive nights out without coupons. Not that he hadn't looked for discount codes for the ticketing app. He wasn't about to blow all their hard work now. Sadly, he found none and had to pay full freight.

The climb had left Wren famished, and so once they were settled in, he departed again in search of food. She needed good nutrients for the baby, for her overtaxed body and the growing life inside her. "Get me anything covered in nacho cheese," she had said.

Shortly before kickoff, he returned with an array of rations.

"What's this?" Wren looked at him as if he were holding a dirty diaper out for her to examine.

"Only the best snacks M&T Bank Stadium has to offer. Here's a parfait with fresh fruit and Greek yogurt. A lean turkey hot dog on a whole wheat bun." He handed the items over and she accepted them reluctantly.

"Anything to drink?"

"Yes. I got one of the bartenders to brew me a mug of decaf Earl Grey." He handed that over, too. "You're welcome."

"What a perfectly balanced meal."

"Right? They have everything here! Has the match started yet?"

"The *game*. Don't be so British." She sighed and placed the drink down. "They're lining up now." She peeled back the foil encasing the hot dog and took a look inside, winced, then covered it back up. A moment later she shrieked, "Oh my God, it's Poe!"

"Who?"

She turned Arthur's head toward the scoreboard. On the video screen, a giant black raven mascot wearing a purple jersey was running up and down the sidelines, pumping up the crowd.

"Oh, Poe, Raven. I get it. Jeez, they really leaned into this whole motif, didn't they?"

"I've always wanted to meet him. Shake his wing," Wren said wistfully, almost starstruck. There was not so much as a hint of irony or sarcasm in her voice.

"So why don't we?"

She laughed like it was an idiotic question. "You don't just 'meet Poe.' He's very hard to get to."

Of course. Some people were just untouchable. Taylor Swift, the Rock, and Poe.

"Let's freaking go, boys!" Wren yelled out as the kickoff team took their place on the forty-yard line and the kicker positioned the ball on the tee, ready to start the game.

"Why's the kicker so far away from everyone else?" Arthur asked. He'd rarely watched closely and, seeing it all in person now, was incredibly confused.

"It's the new rule."

"But why?"

"So there are fewer injuries or something."

The crowd roared as the kicker launched the ball off the tee and into the air. A Commanders player caught it and charged forward, the Ravens players now sprinting full speed looking to take him down.

"Huh. So they're trying to make the game safer?"

"Yeah, isn't that great— YES, GET HIM! KILL HIM! TAKE HIS HEAD OFF!"

Arthur couldn't help but notice a few heads turn in their direction, a few furrowed brows.

"First and ten, Washington," the PA announcer mumbled. Arthur sat down as the Commanders offense jogged onto the field.

"What are you doing?" Wren said.

"Sitting? My legs are tired."

She looked at him, silently reminding him of the golden rule. Thou shalt not complain to the pregnant woman about aches and pains, and if you do, you'd better be dying.

"You don't sit." She hoisted him back up. "Especially not when the other team is on offense. Your job is to scream and make their job as difficult as possible. Like you're the twelfth man on defense."

He groaned. "And you have to do this the entire game?"

"Yes."

"So when do we sit in the seats that we paid for?"

"Ideally, we don't."

"OK, makes sense." The Commanders quarterback fired a short pass that fell incomplete.

"TAKE THAT WEAK SHIT BACK TO DC!" Wren yelled. Another incomplete pass on second down. "YEAH, YOU SUCK! THIS IS WHY YOU DON'T HAVE CONGRESSIONAL REPRESENTATION! Oh, look, they're panning to the crowd."

She pointed to the massive video board that stretched the

entire length of the opposite end zone. On it, close-ups of fans around the stadium: a shirtless kid with his body painted Ravens colors. Pan to: a guy who looked straight out of Mad Max with spiky purple armor. The crowd went wild for them.

"What exactly is your plan?" Arthur asked.

"What do you mean? I'm passionate, pregnant, and adorable. I'm a shoo-in."

"So you don't have a plan."

"Excuse me, what do you call this?"

To Arthur's dismay, Wren began doing what looked like the Macarena if performed by a robot. It was a jerky, elbowy dance routine that deeply upset him to his core. Somehow even the knees were getting involved. He was always so proud to have Wren on his arm, but now he found himself blushing and hiding his face, not wanting anyone to associate him with this atrocity, this desecration of the art of dance. Next time they had sex, instead of thinking about baseball he was sure he would be thinking about this.

Somehow, the innovative routine failed to capture the attention of the camera operators, and the screen cut to a bored-looking grandpa fiddling with his phone, unaware he was even on the screen.

"Come on, him?!" Wren cried, winded. "Up here, damn it." She waved her arms back and forth, screamed and shouted various *whoo*s and *yeah*s, but it was no use.

"I don't think they're ever going to pan up here," Arthur said. "I honestly don't know if the cameras can go that high."

It was just meant to be an offhand comment. A harmless observation.

"Arthur." She turned to him, deadly serious, hands on his shoulders. "You're a genius."

Only bad things happened when she said that to him.

❑ ❑ ❑

Minutes later they were casually walking through the tunnel leading to Section 126. "This isn't what I was suggesting," he said.

"Just act like you belong." Wren nudged him as they walked. Arthur inadvertently made eye contact at that moment with an ornery-looking usher.

"Hello . . . again," Arthur said to the lady, adding a little wave for good measure, as if they were old friends. The *again* had just come to him in the heat of the moment. He was quite proud of it.

"Smooth," Wren said, audibly rolling her eyes.

Whatever, it worked. A few more strides and they were stepping into the glow of the stadium lights. So close they were practically on the field. Front and center, fifty-yard line. Best seats in the entire stadium.

Wren paused to soak it all in. She actually inhaled the air deeply, as if tasting the popcorn and cotton candy and stale beer. She ran her hand along the railing as they descended the stairs, feeling every bump and scratch on the metal. Arthur watched her. She was actually having a spiritual experience.

"How come you've never brought me here before?" she said, more curious than accusatory.

"I've thought about it, plenty of times." That much was true. He looked at tickets at some point every season, but before now, he'd never wanted to settle for the cheap seats. He knew how much she loved this stuff; he wanted to be able to buy her Section 126, fifty-yard-line tickets. The best money could buy. When the stars finally aligned, it was going to be perfect. He dreamed of driving Wren and Charlie downtown and surprising them last minute with the tickets he'd scored.

Being the hero. But he could never seem to get as good a deal as he wanted, and the car needed new brakes one season, and another he needed a crown at the dentist. Somehow his plans always ended up getting derailed by one thing or another, usually because something expensive broke. "But we're here now, aren't we?"

"Sure are," she said.

"This really means a lot to you," he said as they walked down the steps, getting closer and closer to the sideline.

"It does. I've never missed a game, on TV anyways, and I never will."

He truly didn't get it. Didn't get what she saw in this violent, boring game. One thing he'd never considered, until now, was how they would spend their Sundays as a family. Would they have to give up trips to the park, say no to birthday parties, forgo visits to the museum, and basically structure their whole life around not missing the football game? Arthur didn't mind throwing it on when it was just the two of them, but he wasn't sure he liked the idea of it being such an integral part of their life for the rest of time.

"But why the jumbotron? Can you explain?" All this just to be on the big screen for, what, maybe five seconds? In front of a bunch of drunk middle-aged men wearing the quarterback's jersey?

"I've never had a single person show up and cheer for me, let alone seventy thousand. Of course, I never gave anyone anything to cheer about," she joked. "But I always imagined that maybe one day I would know what it felt like."

Arthur could only put a comforting hand on the small of her back, as if he might be able to reach out and grab her if she were to begin tumbling.

"Look," Wren said, pointing a finger toward a man in one

of the rows. Spiky purple armor guy. And a few more rows down was the shirtless kid. They were really in the sweet spot now.

"There are plenty of empty seats," Arthur said. "Let's grab some."

"No." Wren shrugged him off. "We can get closer."

He followed her farther down the stairs, down, down, down, until they were standing at the barrier that separated the fans from the Ravens sideline. Beefy security personnel in bright yellow jackets stared up at them. Beyond that, actual NFL athletes. This close, they were gargantuan. Even Arthur was amazed. He imagined what it must feel like getting tackled by one of these human rhinoceroses. It would surely be the end of him.

"Here," Wren said, shimmying down the front row of seats, squeezing past annoyed fans. Arthur followed until they reached a pair of empty chairs and sat. "How sweet are these?" He had to admit, pretty damn sweet. Almost exactly on the fifty-yard line and so close to the action, they could hear the players pads popping, helmets smacking together. He watched the next play. From above, it was one of those nothingburger runs right into the line for no gain. At field level, it was all-out war. It reminded him of the great historic battles he loved reading about, of gladiators in the arena, of Roman legion formations. The game, for now, had earned his begrudging respect.

"OK." He sighed. "This is kind of cool." Cool enough to dominate every single one of their weekends each fall? To be determined.

"See? I've been trying to tell you. Now . . . heads up. It's the end of the first quarter, so they'll have to fill some time on the jumbotron while the players stand around and spit out Gatorade. How do I look?"

She tousled her hair, adjusted her jersey, and faced him. Honestly, she looked perfect. She was pure enthusiasm and joy; it radiated out of her. Her earnestness and, he had to admit, probably naivety, that she was ever going to get on this jumbotron—she, out of seventy thousand people—was childlike and incredible. It was intoxicating. He wished he could bottle it and drink it himself.

"You're looking at me like you love me," she said.

"Busted."

She blushed, just briefly, before: "Should I show more cleavage? I'm not above it, might as well put these things to good use."

"You—"

"Screw it, no time!" She gawked up at the scoreboard. They were showing more screaming fans. Wren stood up and threw her arms in the air, waved them back and forth, yelled so loud that to Arthur the veins in her face looked like they might explode.

"Arthur, this is it! They're making their way around the stadium, see. The camera's panning this way. Get up and scream!"

Arthur stood reluctantly, watched the faces pan by on the video screen, and clapped his hands together gently in rhythm with the crowd and the thumping music. He had all the zest and enthusiasm of someone half applauding a singer-songwriter in a sleepy café.

"It's not golf, Arthur! Make some noise, for God's sake!" Wren had grabbed him by the arm and was shaking him back and forth.

He tried again.

"Ahhhhhhhh!" he yelled. Better, but only slightly—this time he mustered all the conviction of someone who'd just been stabbed in a middle school production of *Hamlet*.

"LOUDER!"

He turned red. Yes, there were thousands of people around, many of them standing and screaming, but he hated anything that might draw attention to himself. What if he looked stupid? He could imagine everyone stopping in unison to stare at him for doing it wrong. For not fitting in. What if, God forbid, the camera operator decided to put *him* on the jumbotron? In front of all these people?! He'd simply combust, that's all. Vanish into a pink mist and cease to exist.

Wren was out of patience. She grabbed his face and pulled it to hers. "IF YOU LOVE ME YOU WILL FUCKING SCREAM!! AHHHHHHHH!!"

He couldn't help but join her; whether it was out of terror or love, he wasn't sure. But he did scream. Some guttural, scratchy sound formed somewhere between his chest and his belly and clawed its way out of his throat and into the nighttime air. And with it, so much of the tension he'd been holding. His shoulders dropped several inches and his chest relaxed instantly. How come no one ever told him how good it felt to scream?

Then someone tapped him on the shoulder. Arthur turned to look at the fan seated next to him, a silver-haired man who looked an awful lot like his dad. The man gestured back toward the aisle, where a stern usher was pointing directly at him.

"Babe," he said.

But Wren wasn't listening. She was beating her chest like a gorilla and howling like a wolf at the same time.

The usher was now gesturing for Arthur and Wren to make their exit. They were caught. They didn't belong and now the stadium staff knew it. Arthur's face ran hot. This is what he got for making a spectacle! For screaming like one of his feral middle schoolers! And now there would be consequences. He did not enjoy breaking the rules, getting in trouble. He was a teacher, a respected member of the community. Not respected by his students or their parents or any of the people he worked with, but respected in theory, as an educator. He was not the kind to get thrown out of a sporting event, or worse, locked away in the seedy little jail they kept in the basement for the ultra-drunk and disorderly.

"Wren, we have to go," he said. But she didn't hear him. She was still screaming and watching the screen. And now the usher was shimmying her way down the aisle, scooting along and stepping over beers. Closing in on them. Were ushers authorized to use force? Was he about to be beaten with a hidden baton? "Wren!"

"Screw it," she said, grabbing the railing in front of her and climbing the barrier's rungs like a ladder.

"Stop, what are you doing?" She was standing six rungs high, waving her arms still like a maniac, towering a good two to three feet over all the other standing fans. Arthur reached for her but simultaneously felt a strong hand squeeze his shoulder, and he looked up and made eye contact with Wren, whose face was pure elation as she pointed up at the RavensVision jumbotron. He followed her eyes and saw her there, pixelated and shouting for joy, and he also saw himself, and the usher grabbing him and leering. Arthur heard the cheers, a raucous wave of approval. He peeled his eyes away from the board and looked at Wren. She'd lifted up her shirt and was pointing to her exposed belly where she'd written *Future Ravens Fan*. But this wasn't safe, he had to get her down, except he couldn't because the usher was pulling him in the other direction.

And then she fell.

She fell four whole feet onto the field, into a pair of soft arms waiting to catch her. Well, not arms, exactly, but wings.

7

"I CAN'T BELIEVE I MET Poe!" Wren exclaimed from the passenger seat. With the seat slid all the way back, she just barely fit in the front of Charlie's near microscopic car. Which was somehow packed with far more garbage than it had any business holding on to, like a tiny ant carrying an entire potato chip. Though well-manicured on the outside, her friend had always been a slob, and that much hadn't changed.

Charlie, driving, was incredulous. "You didn't meet him, you *fell* on him, Wren. He tore his ACL. They say he'll miss the season."

"Wait, where did you read that?"

"*Barstool.*"

"Haven't I told you to stick to *The Athletic* and the local beat reporters? Those skeezeballs will write anything for clicks. Besides, he was laughing, and I definitely got the feeling that if I hadn't been super, super pregnant, he might have asked me out for a drink after. So . . ."

"Well, still. It wasn't a very flattering article."

"But there *was* an article about me. I'm basically famous."

"Relax, they didn't even use your name. The writer only referred to you as 'the belligerent woman.'"

Wren considered this. On the one hand, she felt bad about what could have happened to the mascot, you know, it being completely her fault and everything. But to be fair, he knew the risks of his chosen profession. Dancing around on the sideline of a football field? Come on. He could get creamed by a three-hundred-pound nose tackle at any moment. He should be so lucky that a civilian woman fell on him instead, and that he escaped the encounter without injury.

Wren, herself, was fine, by the way. And so was the baby. Arthur, of course, had insisted on a quick checkup with Dr. Abadi the next morning. Other than an extremely stern look and another firm reminder to be more careful, she'd gotten off scot-free, which was the universe's way of telling her to continue on just the way she was. Which she would gladly do.

And besides, it had been worth it. Those few glorious moments of seeing her joyous, pixelated face on the RavensVision screen; the entire stadium screaming for her; Arthur being accosted by a surprisingly strong female usher. It had been the thrill of a lifetime, given her a jolt of life and energy. She hadn't planned on such a kerfuffle, becoming the main character of the entire TV broadcast. It wasn't necessarily the goal to have people in the surrounding rows craning their necks to get a good look at her. But at least she felt like she mattered for once. Like someone noticed her, besides Arthur. Like her presence was having an impact on the world at large and not just the well-worn part of the carpet at home where she tended to walk frequently between the living room and kitchen.

"So . . . to Target, then?" Charlie asked. "I must really love you because you know this is so not up my alley. I don't know the first thing about babies except that they're born blind."

"Kittens," Wren said. "That's kittens. Common mistake."

After the embarrassment of showing off the "nursery" to Arthur's mom, Wren still wasn't feeling any strong nesting instincts. But she figured the least she could do was get the kid a bassinet to sleep in. Ideally one that was on sale. She'd dragged Charlie along because, well, she missed her, and with the two of them together, this would all feel like a hilarious adventure, an outing, and not a boring domestic errand. Charlie had reluctantly agreed. So far, it had been a smashing success—they'd grabbed lunch in Fells Point and then walked down a few alleys trying to see who could find the fattest rat.

Wren was determined to find a way to relieve this strange tension that had been brewing between them, and so far this outing had been the ticket.

"Think of it this way," Wren added. "You can watch me flail and fail my way through this whole debacle up close, and that way, you won't have to make the same mistakes when you and Tristan are ready."

"Wren, I . . ." Charlie trailed off, suddenly serious. "It's just that Tristan and I . . ." She took a deep breath, steeling herself.

"What is it?"

"We decided we don't want kids."

"Oh," Wren said. Charlie had said it so plainly, so matter-of-factly. So certain. Not *We don't want kids right now* or *We're not sure if we're going to have kids*. Charlie was just . . . out.

"Yeah."

"Like, ever?"

"Pretty much."

"OK." Wren took a breath, exhaled it slowly. This was fine. It was Charlie's choice, surely one she'd thought about a great deal, and her happiness and comfort with it was all that really mattered. Sure, it upended everything Wren thought her own future was going to be. Charlie was going to be her best mom friend, her confidante, her playdate go-to, chugging wine and watching cheap reality shows while the kids wreaked havoc around them. They were going to force their children into an arranged marriage regardless of what sex and orientation they turned out. They had specifically talked about it over the years, even looked at what wedding venues might be available in the year 2050.

In other words, she was going to be lonely in this. The sense of loss was immediate, and deep.

But this wasn't about her. So she sucked it up. "OK then," she said, not knowing what else to say. She knew asking too many questions was supposed to be bad, even though she had many of them.

"No, see. You're all awkward now. You feel weird."

"I always feel weird, it's nothing to do with you." This probably explained the distance between them lately. If you'd recently grappled with the decision to spend your life child-free, would you want the responsibility of a baby shower thrust upon you? Want to be asked to go bassinet shopping? The weight of the decision was probably still raw, and Wren wasn't helping.

"Do you have, like, questions or anything?" Charlie fumbled out. She was obviously feeling a little exposed. Wren knew that prying and digging would only make it worse, so she decided to take a different tack.

Her Emo Skate Punk Sad Loner Kid playlist was just getting to the good part, and she cranked the volume way up just as Yellowcard's signature violins began to whine. This music always got them in sync and screaming along together, smashing their hands around like drummers. But Charlie gently reached out and turned it back down.

"So, how are *you* feeling about everything?" Charlie asked.

"About what? Like, the state of the world? Not great, I guess, but luckily I'm an expert at disassociating." She'd given up reading the news and had gently sculpted her social media feeds to be almost exclusively cute dog videos. Though, somehow, the machines knew enough to keep squeezing the occasional momfluencer in there.

Charlie soldiered on. "You're so close now, it's got to be dredging up some . . . memories."

Wren was taken aback. What was this, an interrogation? An emotional sneak attack?

"I don't know, Charlie. I'm just taking it one day at a time and trying not to pee myself ten times a day. Can we turn up the music now?"

"It was really hard to tell my parents, you know, about me and Tristan. They didn't understand at first. By the way, you have no idea how hard the 'We're not mad, just disappointed' hits when you're thirty. Yeesh." Charlie was wiping away a hint of moisture from her eyes. "I just always wanted to make them proud, you know? I really wish your mom could see you now."

First of all, Wren doubted it. But second, no, she was not going to allow this. She didn't need some kind of catharsis right now, to be sobbing in the car as a lifetime of trauma leaked out of her. She needed to buy a bassinet, she needed to finish the bucket list, and, now that she'd put the thought out there, she actually kind of needed to pee. She didn't know the genesis of this line of questioning, but for as stubborn as she knew Charlie was, there was nobody who was capable of tearing down her emotional walls when she committed to building them up full strength. Nobody.

"If only Mom had worn a seat belt . . ." Wren said, trailing off and shaking her head for effect.

"Wren . . . Jesus. I can't with you."

"I'm just saying."

"Forget it," Charlie huffed, seeming genuinely annoyed. Even hurt. But come on. Charlie knew how Wren operated. The dark humor and sarcasm shouldn't have come as some big surprise.

They pulled into the Target parking lot. Wren was beyond eager to escape the confines of the car and this emotionally loaded pseudo intervention. She was eager to walk the store and goof around with her best friend. Like the old days, when they'd play all the demos on the Nintendo Switch in the electronics section or move a bunch of the cat and dog toys into the kids' area.

"You ready?" Wren asked as Charlie threw the car in park.

"Yeah, actually." Charlie cleared her throat. "It's later than I thought and I really should get back to Tristan. He's cooking sea bass for dinner and he's, like, obnoxiously excited about it."

"Oh."

"Do you mind calling Arthur for a ride? Or I can drop you off."

A lump formed in Wren's throat. They weren't far from the apartment, and Arthur was definitely home. (Where else would he be, parasailing?) That wasn't the issue. "So you're not coming in?"

"Well . . ." Charlie was reconsidering. "I should get Tristan his Perrier real quick. It's on sale and he'll want it with dinner. Oh, and his nighttime moisturizer. But I'll stay out of your hair."

She didn't want Charlie out of her hair. She wanted her all

up in it, hopelessly tangled like a knot from swimming in the ocean.

"Besides," Charlie said, as they both stepped stiffly out into the parking lot, "picking out a bassinet is really a you and Arthur thing. But I'll see ya around."

Wren began walking toward one of the entrances, where she knew behind those automatic doors lay a rack of candles, the customer service desk, and the baby stuff. But Charlie beelined for the other one all the way on the other side of the building—groceries, pharmacy, toiletries. There was a very brief moment where they walked toward the store together, and for a second things didn't feel so weird. But it quickly became clear they were moving at different cadences, their bodies slowly drifting in different directions. Quickly, Charlie peeled away with one more stammering "Bye!" and before Wren knew it, her friend was just another blond-haired, yoga-pant-wearing body disappearing into those hungry, looming doors.

8

WREN: *Go Skydiving*

AFTER NEARLY AN HOUR'S DRIVE south toward the airport, they were almost there, the cramped lanes of I-295 giving way to smaller roads; not quite rural, not quite industrial. Airporty. That was the only way to describe it.

"This is pointless. I know what they're going to say," Arthur said, pressing his foot to the gas pedal so begrudgingly it was a miracle they were moving at all.

"If you don't quit complaining, we're going to need to start talking about consequences."

"Consequences?"

Wren was getting annoyed at Arthur's incessant pessimism. She knew what Google would say, but there was no harm in asking, just in case they got a lenient instructor who might be willing to let a few things slide. She'd even sign a special waiver promising not to sue, if she had to. Come to think of it, she wasn't so sure a lenient skydiving instructor who wasn't super concerned with doing things by the book would be a good idea. But this is why nothing good ever came of thinking before doing.

She needed something to shut him up.

"I propose that if we refuse to do something we pull from the bucket list—or if one of us is overly naggy about it—that we give up our naming rights."

"For the baby?!"

"No, for your penis. Of course the baby."

"Absolutely not, that's crazy. Besides, we've never talked names. How do you know we won't just agree?"

She smirked. "You won't agree with mine."

"Oh God. What are you thinking?"

"Not telling."

"Wren, you're scaring me. This is an innocent child you're talking about."

"You'll never guess in a million years."

She'd gone full Rumpelstiltskin on him.

"What if I don't agree to your terms?" he asked skeptically.

"I'm the mom. I can tell them whatever I want on the birth certificate and they'll just write it. No one will even ask you."

She had him there, and he knew it. His only choice was to placate her.

"Look, fine. I agree. I'm just saying, not nagging, just *saying*. There are better uses of our time when a quick Google search will tell you that pregnant women cannot go skydiving."

"What exactly is the problem? If my chute fails to open and I go splat . . ."

Arthur winced. "Please . . ."

". . . what difference does it make? If I were some childless cat lady, it would be totally fine for me to risk my life. But because I'm some holy vessel now, I suddenly lose all agency?"

She was being snarky on purpose, but there was something

about it that annoyed her. Every day women got beaten, groped, and insulted in every corner of the country, the world even, and no one gave a shit. No one particularly cared about her when she nearly flunked out of school years after her parents died, for example, and when she had a brief phase of lashing out, getting into fights, smoking, drinking Smirnoff Ice out of paper bags like the world's frilliest little drunkard. The only intervention ever suggested was to send her to one of those Scared Straight camps for troubled teens where you sleep in a barn and they throw things at you and spray you with a hose until you agree to shape up. So the way everyone was suddenly fawning over her protectively *now*, it made her more than a little ill.

"I'm not making a moral judgment, OK? It's just the facts," Arthur said. "The act of free-falling out of a plane apparently puts a lot of stress on your body, and so Big Skydiving, their lawyers, the insurance companies, I don't know, *whoever*, has decided that it's not a risk they're willing to accept. I don't make the rules, but they do exist for a reason."

Wren stroked her chin for effect. "I've been thinking a lot about redneck names lately. I think they get a bad rap. Like Skyleigh, now, there's a good name. Or how about Kennedy with a bunch of random *h*'s thrown in there? Bri'anne with an apostrophe?"

"Look, we're here, OK?" He held one hand up as if to say, *Don't shoot*, and then returned it to the wheel to make the final turn. "We can ask them and see what they say, if that's really what you want."

She unclicked her seat belt with a satisfied *hmph* as they parked in front of a ramshackle building called Velocity Skydiving.

"But I still don't understand why we couldn't do this over

the phone," Arthur added. He just had to get that little comment in there.

"My particular brand of charm and charisma doesn't translate as well over the phone. Plus, I can't do this." She flashed him her best puppy-dog, Disney, Bambi-just-watched-his-mother-die doe eyes.

They parked and walked inside, the door chiming behind them. A preposterously handsome instructor fellow manning the check-in counter flashed them a quick smile, his triceps actively testing the tensile strength of his Velocity Skydiving polo.

"'Ello." And he had an Australian accent to boot, like he was literally made in a lab to be a poster child for adventure sports. "Can I help you?"

Wren stepped forward and gave Arthur a "follow my lead" nudge.

"You can, actually. I just had a question, about the—"

He cut her off. "No."

"Sorry?"

"The answer is no, pregnant women can't jump. No, there's no special waiver you can sign, and no, I can't make any exceptions." He smiled again. "You'd be surprised how often this comes up. But, sincerely, congratulations."

Wren's face ran hot with embarrassment. It was over, already, before it even began. She started to look over at Arthur, as if for backup, but stopped herself. He'd surely be giving her that little look, the half smile with his lips tucked in, *I told you so*. She wasn't going to give up that easily, nor was she going to give Arthur the satisfaction. She was just inquiring, after all, so who was this guy to shut her down? Wasn't she allowed to ask questions? She didn't know how they did things Down Under, but this was America the last time she checked.

"You have some nerve, sir. I am fat, and I'll have you know that I'm not ashamed of it. It's 2026 and I will not adhere to your toxic nineties beauty standards."

If he looked close enough, even through her shirt, he could probably see the distinct impression of a foot pressing against the inside of her belly. She folded her arms over her stomach just in case it might help.

"Good for you, but, lady, I don't know what to tell you. It's policy."

He wasn't going to budge, she could tell. The man was confident. And sturdy. But she had just the thing for that.

She tilted her chin down, eyes up, and gave him her best *helpless damsel in distress*. It was a good one, too, she could feel it, the muscles around her eyes having been warmed up a few minutes prior. He didn't notice, however, not in the slightest, and even walked away to disinfect a pair of goggles. That left Wren batting her eyelashes at the clock on the wall.

Arthur made his move to pull her away, save her from any further embarrassment, but she dodged his attempt to grab her arm. Wren followed the instructor man down to the other end of the counter.

"Look, let me level with you," she said. "We could argue back and forth all day about who's pregnant and who's not. But the truth is that it's my constitutional right to jump out of an airplane if I choose to."

"It's not."

"How do you know? You're not even from here. I'm not trying to be xenophobic, but it's the truth."

He smirked, not taking this encounter seriously whatsoever, maybe even enjoying it. "You know two-thirds of Americans can't even pass the citizenship test? I'll put my civics knowledge against yours anytime."

And he was on the move again, shuffling to the other end of the counter to grab a stack of what looked like release forms. Now she was staring at an empty patch of drywall.

Christ, this was humiliating. She knew damn well she couldn't go skydiving. Or zip-lining. Or scuba diving or go-karting. She had even looked up hot-air ballooning, on a whim, but apparently even gently floating around in a large basket was too dangerous. Couldn't jump off a diving board, couldn't drink coffee, couldn't take a hot bath. Absolutely anything to protect the baby. People wouldn't even look her in the eyes anymore, would they? The first and only thing they saw was the belly, including Walmart Chris Hemsworth, currently smiling at her. He didn't register her as attractive, or as young, or even as a woman, really. She was just a vessel, and she didn't matter. It would only get worse after she gave birth, she knew that much. How was she supposed to be the best version of herself for this kid if she barely even qualified as an autonomous person anymore?

Wren was out of fight. Right then, she wished Charlie was here. Charlie was never out of fight. She would demand to know where the man kept the parachutes, might even force her way into the back to see them for herself. She would not take no for an answer.

Instead, Wren had Arthur, who was staring at a photo wall of Velocity customers smiling after successful dives and inching ever closer to the door. Wren felt an overwhelming sense of melancholy. She mourned the loss of an idea, of being free to fly like a bird and stare death in the face, to be weightless and unhindered by anything at all. It was a dream she'd had since she was a kid and it had slipped away. Yeah, she could come back in a few months, when her achy postpartum body was still attempting to realign itself. Or maybe in a few years when all the babysitting and school schedule stars aligned and she found herself with a free Saturday and a hankering to roll the dice with her life. Or maybe when she was ninety and it no longer mattered all that much if her chute failed to open. It all felt so hopeless.

And she was looking at Arthur, one toe on the threshold of the exit now, when she came up with an idea.

"Well, what about him?" Wren announced, pointing to Arthur.

"Me?"

"See, *that's* no problem. You're not pregnant, are you, mate?" The instructor winked.

Arthur went ghost white. He looked like he'd stumbled across a Tyrannosaurus rex and was trying to stay completely still to avoid its motion-activated vision. Wren approached him gently and grabbed his hand.

"What do you think?" she said.

"I don't understand. It was *your* dream to do this," he croaked, fighting through dry mouth. "Not mine."

"Right. And I don't know if I'll ever get the chance. If I do, I don't want to do it alone. So what do you say?"

It wasn't really about the skydiving, not right here and right now. She just got to wondering. Would it always feel like this? Like she was the gas and he was the brakes? Would it always be her responsibility to bring the fun to their life together, to be the sole source of spontaneity? There would be times when she couldn't. She wondered if he would ever be capable of surprising her.

There was something in his eyes as he thought it over. Terror, there was plenty of that. But also a slight flicker of light, a barely visible raise of the eyebrows, that had her thinking that he might actually say yes. He might conquer his fears, right here and right now, because she needed him to.

"I think," he said quietly, finally, "we should talk about it at home."

Wren sank. What surprised her was that, for a second, she really allowed herself to believe that Arthur might do something wildly out of character, simply because he loved her that much. It wasn't a fair thought, she knew that, but it was there nonetheless.

9

ARTHUR: *Buy My First House*

ARTHUR STARED AT THE SLIP of paper in disbelief. It was his own handwriting, that much was for sure. What shocked him was that there was ever a time he was naive enough to believe it would be possible. Own a home outright. As an English major. In a time when making scrambled eggs in his own kitchen was considered a luxury.

Of course, poor young Arthur wouldn't have known anything about 2020 and what would happen after. How the chart of average sales prices for single-family homes would look like the initial lift hill on a towering roller coaster from that point forward, the big exciting drop never coming. Just up and up and up until everyone passed out and crapped themselves.

"As great as this would be, I don't think it's realistic." He sighed, handing the bucket-list slip to Wren, as if officially resigning it. She pushed it back toward him, refusing to accept it.

"Why not?"

"Because we only have a few weeks left, max? It's not the kind of decision you rush. And besides, I doubt we can afford anything half-decent." He pushed the paper back to her.

"We have savings." She returned the volley.

"Some."

"What about that special account you labeled DO NOT TOUCH, EVER, and then in parentheses, YES, YOU, WREN."

"It's not enough."

"How do you know that?"

"Because I just know. I watch the news."

"So, what, you're just going to let Jake Tapper or whoever decide the rest of our life? We should at least go see what's out there."

Arthur sighed again. "I don't know."

Frankly, he didn't need the heartbreak. He'd heard enough stories from the other teachers at school of dream homes getting snatched out from under them for 150 percent of the list price with a full cash offer. He didn't need to go looking at places they couldn't afford, or worse, at places they could. He didn't need another reminder of what a failure he was.

"Are you declaring Rumpelstiltskin already? Because you're being a total chicken right now. I may not be able to free-fall into a volcano, but there's absolutely no reason we can't give this a fair shot."

"A chicken? Really?"

"At the very least, you're being a silly goose. You're definitely some kind of cowardly bird."

"All for being fiscally responsible, for wanting a secure financial future for our family, for not wanting to make rash, impulsive, poorly thought-out decisions that could jeopardize our entire life together."

"Yes, exactly."

Arthur rolled his eyes. He hated that he'd agreed to play along with her twisted little game. While he and Wren had never openly talked about names together, he had a major preference for traditional names. Strong names for a boy, something like Jack or Ben. He'd always lamented that Arthur was an old-man name he'd spend his whole life growing into. It sounded frail, like a name that came pre-bundled with suspenders and a walking cane. He never had a chance. For girls he liked simple, like Emma, or something short and boyish, like Alex.

God knows what Wren was thinking. Moonflower or Ziggy or Natasha, probably. He couldn't afford not to have a vote when the day came.

But more than that, he'd hated the look in Wren's eyes the other day at the skydiving joint. The searing, palpable disappointment was too much for him. He couldn't bring himself to let her down again.

"OK," Arthur finally said. "OK, OK, OK. We'll go see some houses. But I need your help," he added. "I don't even know where to start."

"Oh, I've got a few ideas."

❑ ❑ ❑

Arthur craned his neck to take in the entire structure. All three levels. The sun, peeking over the ornate, castle-like crest of the home, was blinding. A crystal chandelier hanging inside, and the impossibly sparkling windows, only reflected even more light. It physically hurt to try to take it all in at once, the feeling not unlike trying to comprehend the limits of the universe and the implications of your own insignificance in the grand scheme: pain.

"It's a bit much, isn't it?" he said.

Wren said something, but it was hard to hear her over the

burbling cherub fountain, which was placed delicately in the center of a beautiful circular driveway. A hot yellow Porsche would be right at home here, or a fleet of black SUVs with tinted windows. Their gray beater sedan, parked awkwardly near a palm tree, looked horribly out of place and temporary. Like the pizza guy was going to drive it out of eyeline posthaste.

"I said, 'I think it suits us,'" she repeated as she ambled closer.

He decided to play along. It wasn't exactly what he had in mind, of course. Wrong part of town, a little stuffy. Oh, and the seven-figure price tag. But it was just like Wren to bring him someplace like this, try to get a laugh out of him. He couldn't deny her that after she'd gone to all this trouble. "I don't know." He tsked. "It *is* a little dated. Look at the columns. A little second century AD for my taste."

"That's fair."

"Plus, I'm afraid we'll outgrow it. I don't want the children being forced to share a wing."

"No, of course. They'll be teased mercilessly at school. Won't make any friends. Unless . . ."

He snapped his fingers, as if struck with a genius idea. "We buy them friends."

"I'll make the call, then."

He laughed.

"Right." Shifting back to business. "Well, this has been a great use of time. Now we know in no uncertain terms what we *can't* afford. So we're basically looking for something between this and a rotten shack in the woods."

He appreciated the gesture of Wren cheering him up. She knew it would be hard for him to look at the homes that were just out of their reach, or worse, to get his heart set on one of them. So she brought him here: the former home of Pitbull, probably. He turned to leave, but she grabbed his arm.

"Where are you off to?" she said, looking up from her phone. "Sorry, I got a text from Charlie."

"Everything OK?"

She read it aloud: "*I could really use your help at the cake tasting next week. Need your legendary sweet tooth. What do you say?*" Then: "And then there's a GIF of that guy from *Cake Island* yelling 'I love cake!' and falling over backward in his chair. See?" She showed Arthur.

"Why do you look . . . perturbed?" Arthur asked. He knew how much it had been weighing on Wren, the strain between her and Charlie. It was written all over her face.

"Eh, we had a weird thing the other night. This is the olive branch."

"A fight?"

"Just girl stuff. Nothing a pillow fight in our underwear couldn't solve."

"Wren . . ."

"I'm kidding! Jeez," Wren said. "Since when did comedy become illegal?" She deepened her voice here, doing her best sarcastic impression of a conservative pundit.

"Are you gonna go?"

"Please, you think I'd even consider missing free cake? In my condition?" She tapped out an emphatic reply, then put her phone away. Arthur wasn't convinced the issue was dead and buried, and he hated that he couldn't fix it for her—he, the master of keeping the peace, an expert at placating all parties involved. But he couldn't help, and even if he could, she would be too stubborn to let him.

"You ready to go, then?" Arthur asked.

"Go where?"

"The next stop," he said. She stared, blank-faced. "Reality," he clarified.

"But we haven't even had the tour yet."

"You arranged a tour?"

Wren hung her head sheepishly. "All I did was fill out the little form saying I might be interested, and then all of a sudden my phone was ringing."

"Oh no, what did you do?"

"I don't know!" Wren was suddenly flustered. "The lady was just so nice, she insisted on dropping everything to show us around."

Arthur went beet red. What had she gotten them into?

"*She* probably thinks we can actually afford this place. That we're mega-loaded. Did you correct her?"

"I was going to get around to it."

"Wren . . ."

The sweet hum of an electric golf cart floated into their ears, and a shiny black one rolled to a stop near the fountain. Out stepped a pantsuited woman, the Realtor, clutching the necks of two sweating bottles of sparkling water between her fingers.

"I'm sorry I'm late! Had a showing all the way on the other side of the community." The gated community, situated on the outskirts of a shared golf course, Arthur reminded himself. "Anyone thirsty?"

This was the part where Wren would come clean and they would apologize for the misunderstanding slash colossal waste of this professional's time, and they would run off with their tails between their legs. Instead, the mother of his child said,

"Absolutely," grabbed one of the Perriers, and brought it to her lips with a near sexual lip smack. "God, that's good."

"Mr. Peterson," the agent said, extending a hand to shake his.

"Doctor," Wren incorrectly corrected. "He likes people to call him doctor."

"Of course." The poor woman looked genuinely embarrassed to have made such an error. "Dr. Peterson. A pleasure. Let me just grab the key and we'll head inside."

The Realtor walked up the gargantuan steps to the similarly gargantuan front door and began fiddling with the lockbox. Arthur pulled Wren aside for a word.

"What are you doing? I don't like the side of you that lies so easily."

"I didn't say you *were* a doctor, I said you like it when people *call you* doctor. And, to be fair, you've never once told me that you don't."

"Wren—"

"OK, look," she whispered. "I didn't mean to get us into a whole situation. But you should have heard the way she talked to me on the phone. So deferential and respectful and just . . . kind. She rearranged her whole day to help us because she thinks we're important."

"What she thinks is she can make a juicy commission off of us. Don't you think she's gonna be pissed when she finds out?" Not only could they not remotely afford this house; Arthur realized he probably wouldn't even be qualified to work for the kind of person who could, even as their lowly assistant. How sad was that?

"I just, argh," Wren grunted, some pent-up frustration leaking out of her. "Arthur, I'm sick of being coupon people."

"What do you mean?"

"Like the way waiters roll their eyes at us and do that impatient little sigh when we pull out our coupons. I hate that."

"So? I don't get it."

"People are always looking at us and assuming. Assuming we don't know anything about wine or culture or travel."

"We don't know about any of those things."

"That's the worst part! That they're actually right. We don't know anything, because we haven't lived. Not really."

"Well, we don't come from old money," he said, feeling defensive. His parents had been somewhat well-off, but never anything close to this, and they'd earned it all themselves. Which is what he wanted to do, too, even though they'd offered on many occasions to make things easier on him. "So we're young and broke, earning our way up."

He wasn't sure he even really believed that. Wren certainly didn't. "We're not that young."

Arthur knew what she meant. He wasn't ever embarrassed about being thrifty, but sometimes he was embarrassed that they'd had to be. It was particularly bad going out with Tristan and Charlie, who seemed to have more money than they even knew what to do with. Tristan had once invited Arthur golfing with him and his buddies, as a gesture to score points with Charlie. But Arthur didn't have the right clothes, the right shoes, the right kind of sunglasses and hat. People kept assuming he worked there and handing him dirty balls to exchange for new ones, asking him to fetch them a fresh drink. It was miserable. On the plus side, he made a lot of good tips that day.

He and Wren had bickered about it before. Because he was always the one saying no. No to Ubering when he was happy to DD, no to a celebratory dinner when he was more than happy to cook, no to expensive new bedding when the

Amazon's Choice brand had good reviews and was basically the same thing. It was exhausting, the back-and-forth, all the little decisions. And he hated always being the stick-in-the-mud, the bad guy, but he was doing it specifically for this very moment in their lives. Because he knew what they'd be up against when they struck out on their own as a proper family, and he wanted to be as prepared as possible.

"So can we just pretend, for now? And get through this without humiliating ourselves?" she asked. "It feels goddamn amazing when people think you're rich."

"But owning a home is on my bucket list. You said we had to try, and I can pretend to be Dr. Peterson, but I can't pretend to pull three million dollars out of my ass."

"OK," Wren said, wheels turning in her head. "We'll find a way to let her down easy. Take a quick look, then tell her we think it's too big for us after all, and could she maybe show us something a little more modest. Yeah?"

Why couldn't they just come clean, tell this woman the truth? But as he thought about it, played the scenario out in his mind, he realized Wren was right. It would be absolutely humiliating. Like forgetting your wallet at a restaurant and having to wash dishes in the back as penance, while the sneering manager looked on, and all the other happy couples on anniversary dates watched as you were walked to the back like a scolded child. If such a thing ever actually happened in real life. It would be the look on the woman's face as she processed the information. How he would be able to *see* her opinion of them fall instantly, their value plummeting. Arthur hated lying, but he was pretty sure that would feel worse.

"Coming?" the agent called out, swinging open the ten-foot-tall door.

All right. He could take a vacation from being the no guy just this once. He could be Dr. Peterson for one afternoon.

❑ ❑ ❑

The tour began in the grand foyer, which featured ceilings that touched the sky, the aforementioned chandelier, and an ornate curved stairway leading to the upper levels. But Arthur couldn't stop staring at the marble-tiled floor. Not a scuff to be found on it. It was brilliantly shiny, maybe more so than their bathroom mirror at home, which always seemed vaguely foggy no matter how many times he cleaned it.

"So when are you due, if you don't mind me asking?" the Realtor chirped. Linda Kellerman was her name (and according to the pin on her blazer, GETTING YOU A GREAT DEAL was her game).

"September third," Wren said.

"So soon! You two must be eager to find the right fit, then."

He noticed that Linda was removing her shoes. It was one of those homes, apparently. He and Wren did the same.

"Absolutely," Wren said. "I can't wait to raise his babies while he's off making a difference in the world. It's been a dream of mine since I was little."

"Well, I think you're going to love this place. Come on, let's see the kitchen and you can tell me a little about what it is you're looking for."

The walk there was lengthy. Even in his socks now, Arthur stepped lightly on the flawless hardwoods. A stray bit of debris clinging to his foot, or so much as a toenail poking out, could lead to a scratch, and this flooring was more valuable than his entire net worth.

As they walked, Wren peppered Linda with absurd questions: "Now, does the house come with a service staff or will we need to hire our own? How big is the wine cellar? Is there a number I can call if someone yucky is walking around outside and I don't like the looks of them?"

Linda fielded them like a pro, then: "Dr. Peterson, what about you? What is it that gets you excited about your potential new home?"

He took the opportunity to speak honestly: "It's not so much features and looks that I really care about, but the feel of a place. I'm hoping we can find a neighborhood with plenty of young families with kids, good schools, friendly neighbors. Someplace that can feel like home." They reached the kitchen, finally, and found it was surprisingly modest, in both size and features. A simple white quartz countertop, a sink, plenty of open storage. It was the kind of kitchen he could see their family in, believe it or not, if it was detached from this monstrosity of a mansion and placed in a more normal dwelling. He could visualize the entire thing and it gave him hope and optimism for the first time that day. He could visualize it all: him clumsily chopping fruits into bite-size pieces on a cutting board, Wren trying to corral the baby into its high chair, both of them tired and disheveled and laughing, deeply joyful, sneaking kisses while the baby threw messy handfuls of raspberries all over the floor.

"Quite the butler's pantry, isn't it?" Linda said.

"I'm sorry, the what?" Arthur said.

"Butler's pantry. For food prep and storage."

"So this isn't the kitchen."

Linda laughed. "Of course not. That's through here." She pushed through a swinging door and they were off into the kitchen proper, the butler's pantry's big brother. It had the same aesthetic but was three times as large, outrageously spacious and grand. Arthur could envision Martha Stewart preparing a Thanksgiving feast in here. And the Peterson-Morris family was not invited.

"What do you think?" Linda asked.

Arthur looked to Wren, who was waving her hand under the automatic touchless faucet, turning it on as if by pure magic, watching it shut off, and doing it again.

"You know, Linda, seeing it in person, I think it might be a little too much house for us," Arthur said, feeling it was time to bring the charade to an end. "We're just two people, with one little tiny one on the way. In other words, we probably don't need the *two* swimming pools."

"Mm-hmm." She nodded. Arthur could see the look, the disappointment as she began to suspect they weren't the high rollers she initially thought. An urgent care doctor, perhaps, instead of private practice.

"But the place is beautiful," he quickly added. "A slightly smaller version would probably be exactly what we're looking for."

There had been some value in this visit, at least. There were bits and pieces of this place that spoke to him. The area, just maybe a part of it that was outside the confines of the golf course. The quiet roads with kids riding bikes; he'd seen them on the way in and couldn't help but smile at the memories it brought back of his own childhood.

"Well, hold on," Wren interjected. "It is a little cookie-cutter, don't you think? I mean, white much?" She gestured around the kitchen, at the white countertops, white backsplash, and white farmhouse sink. "I think we'd be open to something with a little more personality."

Linda jotted down notes. Taking the feedback to heart

even though this was all a farce. Even still, Arthur didn't want her to get the wrong idea about what they wanted.

"But school district is important to us, too. And being around other families like us. We don't want to be out in the middle of nowhere, or in the city."

"Who says we don't want to be in the city?" Wren said, now pulling out a cabinet drawer and giving it a little push, watching it glide back into place.

"Well, it's just that we'd have more space in the suburbs, but still be close by."

"Ah, right, and we can become obsessed with every blade of our meticulously manicured lawn."

"If it gives the kids some green space to run around, why not?"

"Kids can run around in the city. I did," Wren spat out, suddenly defensive. "And I didn't go to the 'best schools' and I turned out OK."

"It's a lot safer out here," he said, instantly regretting it. He knew how defensive Wren got about Baltimore's "reputation," fueled heavily by Fox News and people rewatching *The Wire*, as if there were a shotgun-toting drug dealer lurking around every corner.

"Is that what you think?"

"Come on, Wren." He lowered his voice, speaking only to her. "The city's got its problems, OK? This is just about giving our kid a nice place to grow up." Then he dropped to a whisper. "This is all make-believe anyway, so what does it matter?"

He hadn't meant to insult Wren with the schools comment, or by bringing up crime and safety. But he was also annoyed. He didn't feel like taking a principled stand right now, trying to prove he was cool enough to live in the hectic, crowded city when he preferred a much slower way of life.

And didn't every parent want the best for their kids, even better than what they had? He didn't appreciate her implying that growing up in a nice house in the suburbs meant you were devoid of personality or free will, just another cog in the capitalist machine. She hadn't said as much, but he knew she was thinking it. If she turned out OK despite her chaotic upbringing, he'd like to think he did, too, despite his milquetoast one.

"You're right," she said. "If we can just keep them completely safe, never expose them to any risk or anything different or remotely uncomfortable, then everything will be just perfect."

"That's not what I said."

"Arthur, I know you," she said. "Don't you remember when Charlie invited us to the pool and you refused to get in?"

"It said you shouldn't swim if you'd had diarrhea in the last two weeks. It was for everyone's protection!"

"Literally no one expects you to follow that rule!"

"Then why did they make it one?!"

Wren glared at him. He met her eyes. Linda blinked at them. She could sense the tension.

"So, do you guys still want to see the sauna, or . . . ?"

❑ ❑ ❑

It was time to go. Linda led them out, Arthur and Wren holding hands stiffly as they clopped down the granite stairs leading back to the driveway. He could feel her annoyance; it was radiating off her. Arthur had always had a sixth sense about her moods. It could also be that she was squeezing his hand in some kind of vise grip, contorting his thumb in such a way that she almost certainly meant to cause him pain. Yeah, the spirits were telling him Wren would probably be following up on this conversation later.

"Well, I'm sorry this one didn't work out," Linda said, folding her hands politely in front of her. "But let's stay in touch."

Arthur tracked her eyes. She was noticing their car for the first time. Putting together the pieces. Not a fancy plastic surgeon, not a free clinic doctor, no; just a big old phony.

"Could we have a card?" Arthur asked. Owning a home to raise their family in was still a dream of his, and he didn't know any other real estate agents.

"I gave you one, remember?" she said. Arthur shook his head no. "I'm certain I did. Check your pockets. Anyway, gotta run. Pleasure meeting you both."

"How do we get in contact with you?" Arthur yelled out as Linda literally sprinted away and peeled out in her golf cart.

"Google me!" she yelled in a cloud of dust. And then she was gone.

❑ ❑ ❑

When they got home that afternoon, Wren curled up in the bedroom and fiddled endlessly with her phone, popping in headphones to boot. A firm defensive position. Probably listening to music, fast-paced snare drums and anthems about being young and free—that was her go-to when she was pissed off or angsty.

Guess they weren't going to talk about it.

Arthur decided that if the mansion wasn't in the cards—and it most definitely wasn't; in fact, they didn't even have cards—he should get a sense of what they could actually afford.

He sank onto the couch. In front of him, a blue circle was

spinning jovially on his laptop screen with a Pixar-like bounce to it that implied this process was somehow fun and not incredibly nerve-racking. Like all his hopes and dreams weren't riding on the calculator's decision. He had found a little free online tool, filled out his and Wren's salary estimates, rough credit score, debts, and other pertinent information, and in a few seconds it was going to tell him what kind of mortgage they might quality for.

It was going to tell him if they'd be decorating and painting a beautiful nursery in the coming months, or if they'd be shoving a crib up against the entertainment center in the living room of their poorly lit one-bedroom apartment, right under the part of the popcorn ceiling that seemed to be flaking off at an alarming rate.

The circle spun and bounced. Spun and bounced.

When the text finally appeared, "According to our estimates, you may qualify for a mortgage up to . . ." Arthur could hardly bear to look.

It was at the moment that Wren called out for him. Well, not him specifically, but . . .

"TACOS!" she yelled.

And he understood immediately. He stalked over to their coupon drawer in the kitchen and removed one of the BUY ONE TACO GET ONE FREE vouchers from the stack of well over a dozen. He had the restaurant on the phone before he even reached the car, and when he arrived, the order was already ready—two pulled-pork tacos smothered in queso. But another text from Wren said simply, *SNOWBALL*, and off he went to rustle her up a skylite snowball with marshmallow filling. Once he'd procured it, another text came in: *BERGER COOKIES*. He sighed, desperately wanting to get home and keep researching houses, but he knew this was his penance.

His willingness to help her with her cravings was key to getting back in her good graces and them actually having a productive conversation when he got home. So he dutifully drove in the direction of Royal Farms to procure a box of the famous chocolate-drenched shortbread cookies. When all was said and done, he was gone for well over an hour, so long that he was forced to hold the snowball directly up to the air-conditioning vent in a desperate attempt to keep it from melting.

"Thank you," she said as he walked in and handed over the goods. "Now, about earlier—"

"I didn't mean to upset you," he cut her off, sitting down next to her on the sofa. "I was being crass and insensitive. I'm really sorry." It didn't mean he had changed his mind, or that he didn't mean any of what he'd said, but his delivery had been poor. They'd been together long enough for him to know that was at least half the battle.

Wren finished a bite of taco, washed it down with a scoop of light blue snowball, and leaned in. She began to rub his back.

"I forgive you," she said. Then she kissed him. Whatever it was, it had a little extra. Maybe some extra pressure and just a tiny bit of tongue. Maybe it was just the spicy salsa. It made his whole body tingle. "Isn't it great how we can forgive each other like that?"

"Yeah, I guess it is." They'd always been good about dodging fights. They disagreed, even bickered sometimes, but almost never had a knock-down, drag-out. Sometimes it was best to agree to disagree and both mutually agree to move on. At that, they excelled.

"I just love knowing that whatever life throws at us, we figure it out together. Always remember that. Because we're a team. And when you fall down, I pick you up."

"Um, OK."

"Also, very importantly, you pick me up, and you stand by me no matter what," she said, still going. "I've always loved that about you. It's one of many, many things that I love about you. Just like there are many, many, many things you love about me."

Arthur exhaled, the tension of a pending argument finally leaving his body. When he breathed in again, something struck him. He sat up.

"Why does it smell weird in here?"

And that's when he felt a long, rough tongue licking his ear.

10

WREN: *Rescue a Dog from Certain Death*

ARTHUR HAD BEEN FIDDLING WITH his laptop in the living room when Wren began to imagine their lives as they hurtled toward suburban monotony. It might not be right now, it might not be anytime soon, but they would eventually end up there. It was what humans did. Their migratory patterns were so predictable, like herds of wildebeests following green grass and fresh water. So, too, did humans have babies and gravitate toward the parks and the Blue Ribbon Schools and the family-friendly breweries.

She really had to stop watching so many nature documentaries. A side effect of her recent unemployment.

But this was exactly why the bucket list was so important, so urgent. And, at least so far, it had not been overly satisfying.

Her jar was right there on the nightstand, practically glowing under the warmth of her reading lamp. What could it hurt to pull something new out? She and Arthur were supposed to do this together, but he was right, the things in this jar were her dreams. Not everything she did had to be tied to him, all the time.

She snatched it and stuck two fingers inside, like pincers, immediately grabbing hold of one of the smooth slips of paper. She hadn't intended to actually pull it out, honest. It just happened.

And when it did, well, she figured she had to do it. Those were the rules.

❑ ❑ ❑

"I really, really don't see how I, quote, 'made you do this,'" Arthur said, picking bits of wiry fur off his slacks.

In all her years knowing Arthur, Wren knew that he was not the type to explode outwardly in anger. No, he would just get quiet and set his jaw, then eventually get over it. He was annoyingly healthy that way.

So she didn't see a huge problem with playfully antagonizing him.

"Well, you said I couldn't do any death-defying adventure sports, so what did you expect?"

In truth, she just wanted to make him laugh, and maybe if she could get him laughing he would see how awesome having a new dog was going to be.

"Wren, having a dog is a huge, huge—"

"Yes, yes, a huge responsibility. You don't think I know that? I've done all the research."

"Have you?"

"I've done some research. And this is something I've wanted for a long time."

She revealed the proof: her years-old handwriting on the slip that she'd pulled from the jar earlier. When she had first read "Rescue a Dog from Certain Death," it seemed impossible and wildly irresponsible. But it turned out that all it took was about five minutes of screwing around on Facebook Marketplace. Social media was, in many ways, a gigantic mistake by humanity. But it could certainly come in handy when you wanted to make a rash and impulsive decision. All sorts of magnitudes of mistakes were suddenly right at your fingertips.

She reached down and scooped him up, all eleven pounds of him: Ferdinand. He was the ugliest dog listed online by a mile, with crooked eyes and a tongue that permanently lolled out the side of his mouth. In her mind, the plan had been to adopt a puppy from an overcrowded mill, maybe spring the entire litter free and burn the place to the ground while she was at it. The plan had not been to save a weathered old sack of farts like Ferdinand. But the listing said that the foster parent had completely run out of options and was going to have to surrender him soon. No one else was ever going to adopt this ugly motherfucker, so he was bound to end up dead. The person was so desperate they were willing to come drop him off on short notice with almost no questions asked, which is why she'd sent Arthur on a wild-goose chase for food. Although, now that said food was here, she was thoroughly enjoying it.

"A long time? I've never heard you mention wanting a dog, not once."

"Well, it goes back farther than you. It was my dream as a kid, something I've always wanted to do. Wasn't that the point of all this?"

Bam. She had stunned him. Arthur had no response.

It was true, though, all of it. Without her parents, Wren had bounced around with different family members for years. She was lucky to have a network of aunts and uncles to take her and her brothers in, in various combinations at different times, but no one seemed to be up for the added burden of letting her adopt a dog, no matter how much she begged. Apparently having your brother and sister-in-law die unexpectedly and then being asked to care for their children was stressful, or something.

She could already see Arthur warming, ever so slightly, to the idea. Or maybe he was trying to fend off the beginnings of a sneeze. She hadn't bothered to ask, but she highly doubted the pup was hypoallergenic. Arthur looked the two of them over as Wren scratched an itchy spot behind Ferdinand's ears.

"He's pretty ugly. Did you pay money for him?"

"Just a few bucks for door-to-door delivery." The woman had been so relieved to be rid of him, of this burden, that she'd practically hurled Ferdinand out the window without stopping.

"I still think you got ripped off. They sold you a corpse."

She wanted to be offended, but he wasn't completely wrong. Ferdinand was extremely old and, if the smell was any indication, a little sick. If he were a human, his family would be telling him to get his affairs in order. But that was perfect for Wren, really, when she thought about it. Low commitment, temporary. She wouldn't get too, too attached. There wouldn't be time for that by the look of him. The crusty, weepy eyes. The foggy pupils. All the signs were there that he was not long for this earth.

"There are a few things you should know about him," she said. "One, he has arthritis. Two, he only eats raw foods—it keeps his skin from flaring up. And three"—here she lifted Ferdinand's little paws up into a playful begging pose—"he loves you already and really wants to stay."

Arthur and Ferdie—Wren had already decided on his official nickname—stared at each other.

After a moment, Arthur stood, as if to make a proclamation.

"Fine. But I'm not taking care of him, OK? If you want to do this, I support you, in the sense that I will be completely neutral and not involved at all. It's on you to feed him and give him his pills."

"Anal suppositories, actually."

"Oh, for the love of . . . And *you* are going to take him on walks and all that. And I'm not gonna do the thing where I slowly fall in love with him and he ends up becoming *my* dog, OK? So don't hold your breath. I've got enough to deal with being hopelessly unprepared for fatherhood."

"Yes, sir," Wren said, with a mock salute.

Arthur turned to head to the kitchen but caught himself. "Oh, and you'll have to tell the leasing office so we don't get evicted."

"Don't worry about him," she whispered to Ferdie as Arthur rounded the corner out of sight. "Now, come on, let's go get in bed."

She was sure Arthur wouldn't mind.

❑ ❑ ❑

The next day, it was time again for another exam. These goddamn exams had been multiplying like rabbits. First it was once a month, and now every week. But it was starting to feel like even more than that, as if Dr. Abadi were poking and prodding Wren every other day. As such, Wren insisted that Arthur sit this one out. It felt overly doting to have him always dropping everything to tag along. Admirable, but unnecessary.

Plus, leaving him at home was a good way to force him to bond with Ferdie. She imagined the two of them making awkward small talk over breakfast and eventually finding common ground in their shared love of bacon.

"So you're back," the doctor said flatly. "It's nice to see you again."

You would not have guessed it was nice by her facial expression and tone of voice. But she was always like that. Or maybe she was still pissed at Wren for suffering a totally avoidable fall at a sporting event she never should have attended.

"Guess I just missed you," Wren teased, standing there awkwardly in her gown, the cold room giving her flesh goose bumps all over.

"Come on, sit, let's have a look at you."

"I thought because I was just here the other day that maybe we could rubber-stamp this one. Whadya say?"

Dr. Abadi's face said no. Wren sighed and took her position on the exam table, and the doctor wheeled herself forward on her little stool and snapped on a rubber glove. Wren really hated these visits. They were tedious and invasive, and it was torture to endure the same thing over and over and over.

"I took a look at your vitals," she said as she applied water-soluble lubricant to her fingers. "Still not thrilled about your blood pressure. Have you been taking it easy? Staying at home?"

"Me?" Wren said, feigning shock. "I'm the ultimate homebody."

Dr. Abadi paused. "It's not a joke, Wren. You have to take care of the baby, and your own body, too. There could be serious consequences if you don't." She didn't belabor the point, just resumed the exam, the discomfort of which seemed to act as something of a punishment on its own.

Wren stared at the ceiling and tried to disassociate from her lower half. Feeling like this was all just a little bit unfair.

She *was* trying to take care of the baby; why couldn't anyone understand that? By trying to become the best version of herself, she would unlock her full potential as a mother. How was she supposed to accomplish that by sitting at home? Maybe her methods were, say, unusual. But it's not like anyone had ever been there to show her how to do it by the book. By all accounts, her mom was a screwup, too, just like her. Could never seem to hold down a job, thought extra-sweet jarred applesauce counted as a vegetable. So being irresponsible was embedded in Wren's DNA somewhere. And yeah, it was tragic and all, but sitting around crying about it wasn't going to change anything. So she had to keep moving.

She would try to be a little more careful, that much she could do. But she wasn't going to give up on the bucket list, no freaking way.

11

IT TOOK A LITTLE CAJOLING to get Wren in the car, but the promise of hitting the Wendy's drive-through on the way home proved to be enough convincing. (Though Arthur almost lost her when he suggested they stop off for toilet paper, dish soap, and bread on the way to the showing.)

Yes, he had scoured the listings, filtering out all the homes out of their price range and leaving behind a paltry, depressing selection. Horrifically outdated homes with visible water damage, total teardowns, and properties that warned of the gruesome crimes that had once been committed there. That was all that was left.

But there was one. Just one. And it was beautiful. Just the picture-perfect neighborhood. Gorgeous cream-white siding, old-fashioned country-style shutters, big windows, a front porch big enough for a rocking chair. The inside was even better—gorgeous hardwoods, an open floor plan, an adorable kitchen that reminded him so much of the one he grew up in, down to the high-top table in the corner where he'd eat his mom's homemade waffles every Saturday morning.

If they moved quickly, they might just swipe this one out

from under the noses of all the other young families looking. Maybe they could snatch it up before the sellers realized it was horrendously underpriced.

The drive over to see the Needle—that's what he'd been calling it, as in "the needle in a haystack"—was almost too perfect. Sunny and warm with a breeze to break the heat. A few clouds in the sky, but the pretty kind—fluffy and playful.

Their apartment was on the very outer edge of the city, in the no-man's-land between urban and suburban. A land of bleak strip malls and busy "stroads"—that's half street, half road—clogged up with gas stations and fast-food joints and unsightly power lines.

As they drove out farther into the suburbs, everything started to feel brighter, more open. The sky bluer, the air coming in through their open windows cleaner. They passed an adorable little elementary school, too cute to even believe. A hand-painted mural on one of the walls outside. A state-of-the-art playground with roller-coaster-like contraptions made of lime-green steel, seven different styles of swings, and full tunnel slides. And . . . was that a splash pad?

"How did it go at the doctor this morning?" he remembered to ask. "Everything OK?"

"Hunky-dory," Wren said, shooting him a thumbs-up.

Within a mile or so of the house, there was a shopping center with everything they could possibly need. A Target, a Starbucks—plus another Starbucks inside the Target—a grocery store, a lovely little boutique wine shop, and a couple of chain restaurants and ice cream shops. If they lived here, they'd never need to go far.

It reminded Arthur of his neighborhood when he was growing up, which, coincidentally, wasn't far away.

Before he even saw the house, it felt like home.

They turned onto the street in question. Like a perfectly composed photograph, each opposite sidewalk was lined with great, broad trees, branches forming a makeshift archway over the road, which was called Cherry Blossom Way.

"Would you look at this neighborhood? Gorgeous," Arthur said, gawking out the driver's-side window.

"Wonder what it's like at rush hour. Lot of through traffic, I bet. Maniacs speeding by, mowing down innocent children. Would it kill them to add a few speed bumps?" Wren quipped, holding tightly to Ferdinand, whom she'd brought along for the ride, his tongue flapping in the breeze.

Arthur rolled his eyes. "You said you'd have an open mind. I really think if you give it a chance, you'll see how great it could be to live somewhere like this."

That had taken some convincing, too. But Wren had said she'd try to see it his way.

"This is me having an open mind. But I'm a safety nut, you know that. Can't turn it off."

"OK." He laughed.

They pulled into the driveway next to another car and hopped out. The house matched the pictures, which was a good sign. It was in terrific shape, smaller than he expected, but infinitely more charming. The perfect size for their family.

"Spacious driveway," Arthur noted. "Big enough if we decide to upgrade to a minivan."

"Crack," Wren said, pointing one out. "Crack, crack, crack."

She kept jabbing her finger at little hairline fractures in the cement.

"Just cracks," he reassured her.

"Yeah, for now. But this thing is a ticking time bomb. Could be on top of a sinkhole for all we know!"

"I really doubt it."

"Don't say I didn't warn you when the ground collapses one day and we end up in China."

"It doesn't work like that; that's a myth."

"I'm just saying I wouldn't want to find out the hard way."

Linda Kellerman, teeth somehow even whiter than the last time they saw her, greeted them with something resembling a smile.

"Doctor," she said cheekily when she saw him. Arthur turned red. His phone call to her apologizing, coming clean, and begging her to keep working with them had not been a fun one. But business must have just been slow enough, because eventually, after a long lecture on professionalism and respect, she agreed.

She threw him a wink and then began walking them around the property.

"Three-quarters of an acre," she said. "Really a great lot. Fenced-in yard, as you can see. Flat. A lot of room for a pool, maybe a play set or a fire pit or whatever you can dream up! Personally I think a hardscape with a brick pizza oven would be a lot of fun."

"A brick pizza oven?" Wren said, aghast. "Sounds like a death trap to me."

"We love the fenced-in yard. Don't we, Ferdie?" Arthur cut her off, gave Ferdinand, whom Wren was carrying, a little chin scratch.

The agent smiled and continued.

"Did you just baby talk Ferdie?" Wren whispered.

"I'm just trying to look like a respectable, dog-loving suburban homeowner. It would be super awesome if you'd do the same. Speaking of which, would it have killed you to adopt a golden retriever like a normal person?"

They sped up, caught up with the Realtor, who spun around jovially to face them.

"So, what do you think?" she said.

"It's stunning," Arthur said. He truly didn't get it, didn't see how this all added up. Why was this place so, well, cheap? Dirt cheap compared to the competition. The mortgage would be tight, but the prequalification he got online said they could hypothetically afford it, and hypothetically was good enough for him. Even better if Linda Kellerman could live up to her name tag and GET THEM A GREAT DEAL—and how had it not been scooped up already? "We'd love to see the inside, obviously."

The agent cocked her head, confused. "Not much to see," she said. "But why not?"

Wren shot Arthur a look of concern, which he deflected with an *It's all good* smile. The inside was probably flawless as well. As crisp and bright as the photos, with Glade PlugIns pumping mouthwatering scents throughout. Just a formality to give it a once-over.

They looped back around to the front porch, climbed the wooden steps, and approached the door. Linda fiddled with the lockbox on the door handle and removed the key.

"Can I ask"—Arthur finally gave in—"what's the deal with this place? The asking price is shockingly—"

The agent swung the door open, and Arthur immediately had his answer.

"Low."

That's because, he realized, there was no house. Just a beautiful exterior facade. The inside was completely empty, barren. Wooden boards framing out the spaces where, theoretically, there might one day be rooms. Raw subflooring where there should be planks of gorgeous hardwood. Exposed pipes poking out waiting to be attached to a toilet or farmhouse sink.

"Be still my heart," Wren cooed. "Someone call *Country Living*."

The Realtor ignored her and read Arthur's face.

"As you can see, bit of a fixer-upper. It was a new build and the previous owners ran out of money midway. But, gosh, can't you just see the potential?"

❑ ❑ ❑

Back in the car, Arthur waved and smiled as Linda backed out and drove away, then laid his head down on the steering wheel.

"Is it weird that I like it more now?" Wren joked. "Place is fucking metal. Like something out of the *Saw* movies."

"Don't even joke about those."

He'd watched one with Wren begrudgingly, just the once, and had nightmares about it for weeks. And besides, he wasn't in the mood. She reached over and rubbed his back.

"Hey, it's OK. This one wasn't meant to be."

"I can't believe the photos were all AI fakes." He was fuming. Sure, it had said as much in the fine print at the very bottom of the listing, that the AI-generated interior photos were simply there to illustrate the home's possibilities. But he felt duped, and furious.

"The upstairs bathroom having three toilets didn't tip you off?"

"I just thought whoever built it really loved pooping."

"We'll keep looking," she reassured him.

"There's nothing else. They're all like this. It's either a shithole death trap or it costs half a million dollars."

Wren didn't have an answer for that one.

"I just feel stupid," he said.

"Why?"

"Because. I'm a public school teacher. We've had to fight and scratch and claw just to be sort of not broke. Like, of course I don't belong here, in a neighborhood like this. What was I thinking?"

Arthur winced at his own words. He had grown up in a neighborhood like this. Of course, then it wasn't a place for elites with generational wealth. It was just a neighborhood where normal families lived. But still, how was it possible that he was actually going *backward* in his life?

He lifted his head up, caught sight in the mirror of an impression of the steering wheel pressed into his forehead. "Great."

"You know what?" Wren said. "Fuck 'em. We don't need 'em."

"We have to live somewhere."

"Yeah, but here, with these pretentious assholes? You just know this is one of those neighborhoods with a psycho HOA—quiet hours, fines for visible trash cans, palettes of approved mulch colors. Is that really us? I don't know about you, but I don't want to be one of those people."

She was ever so gently rubbing it in his face that she had been right all along.

"I know how you feel about the burbs. And you're not wrong about the HOAs. But sometimes you have to put up with it to be around other families with young kids. That's what we need, what the baby will need. Friends, comfort, normalcy."

"We have kids in our apartment building."

"That weird guy who claims to live with his mom upstairs does not count. He's, like, our age and I've never seen this mom of his. I'm starting to think it's a Norman Bates situation."

Wren paused, thought for a moment, and then spoke. "Either way, we agree that this one isn't right for us?"

"Not unless you're OK living in a zero bed zero bath."

"OK, good. Because I just remembered something that I've always wanted to do and never had the chance to."

She yanked on the handle and flung the door open, then stepped outside.

"Where— What—" Arthur called out, but she was moving too fast. Before he knew it, she was behind the car, rummaging around in the trunk.

"Oh no."

He clambered out to try to stop her.

By the time he got there, she was already armed with a roll of toilet paper in each hand.

"No, no," he said, placing himself between her and the house. "We are not doing this."

"Why not? No one lives here, obviously. Who cares?"

"I care! Maybe this house isn't for us. But I still think this is the kind of place I want us to eventually end up. I don't want to spit in the face of that."

"Have you ever tried spitting in someone's face? It's incredibly satisfying, especially when they deserve it, and I'm pretty sure the people who live in houses like this deserve it," she said, offering him one of the rolls. "Now, come on. You with me?"

He looked at her hand, at the free end of toilet paper flapping in the gentle wind. It was cocked and ready to go.

"Is this on the list?"

"Not officially," she said. "But if you say no, I'm still naming our child Princess. Even if it's a boy."

"All right," he groaned. "Gimme."

Maybe she was right, but for the wrong reasons. Maybe they *didn't* belong here, but not because they were better than these people, but because they weren't good enough. *He* wasn't good enough.

In another world, another time, they would have bought a house like this in their early twenties. He'd have been a wildly successful door-to-door vacuum salesman, and she'd have been—an operator, or something? He supposed that the sexism was a pretty good reason not to idealize the past. That and the rampant racism, and the war.

He was tying himself in knots. There was no one to blame but himself.

Wren launched her roll of toilet paper. It fluttered through the air and unraveled beautifully, looping just over a branch of the big tree in the front yard and landing on the ground on the other side, leaving a perfect arc of paper behind.

"*God* that felt good," Wren cried, looking down at her hands like she had just been granted infinite cosmic power. "That must be what people feel like the first time they do cocaine. I'm getting another one."

Arthur lined up his own shot. He wanted to TP the house itself. The arrogant Realtor and her *Gosh, can't you just see the potential?* rang in his ears. Yeah, people used to say that about him, too. To hell with all of them.

He unfurled a perfect throw, which arced over the roof and just to the right of the chimney, streaking the entire front of the house with a long trail of paper.

"Nice one!" Wren said. "You're a natural."

He looked back at her. She was balancing the rest of the eighteen pack of rolls in her arms.

"Woah, you're not screwing around," he said. He looked around nervously. This was insane. It was broad daylight.

"One day I'll be someone's mother, a self-respecting member of the community who doesn't resort to petty revenge and vandalism," she said. "But today is not that day. Now, come take some of these."

He grabbed a few, then felt the beginnings of a light drizzle. At some point, a few clouds had rolled in without him noticing.

"Oh, this is gonna be an absolute mess," Wren said with glee, tossing another roll, which clanked off a window.

Arthur lined up another shot himself, cocked his arm back, and felt his phone buzz right as he was about to let go. He paused to check the screen and let out a little yelp when he saw the name.

It was Linda Kellerman.

"You OK?" Wren said, still tossing.

"All good, just a sec." He wandered across the yard to take the call. "Hello?"

"Arthur," she said, all business. He gulped. Was she watching them from down the street? Had a neighbor spied them and called her to tattle? "I feel a little bad about the showing. You seemed a bit . . . blindsided."

He breathed a sigh of relief. "Yeah. Yeah, I guess a little."

"Even still, I wanted to encourage you not to give up on the property. Maybe it's not the ideal fit for a young couple expecting a baby—and you two are adorable, by the way—but if you're serious about getting into the area, it could be a huge opportunity. Will it take a lot of work? Yes, of course. But for the price, you can't beat it."

"We're about to have a baby and there are no bedrooms. It can't work."

"Can't it? If you move quick enough and are willing to live

in a construction zone for just a few weeks, boom, you've got your nest egg. It's an absolutely incredible investment."

"I don't know. My girlfriend's not sure she wants—"

"Oh, she doesn't know what she wants," Linda scoffed. "She's about to pop; her hormones are going crazy. She can't be held responsible for anything she says and does, OK? It's your job to make this decision. She has enough to worry about. Take this off her plate. And, wait—did you say girlfriend? You're not married?"

"No, we're not."

"Well then. All the more reason to follow your gut on this."

Arthur turned around and watched Wren chucking rolls of toilet paper with a demented glee in her eyes. The lady had a point. Wren was certainly making some rash decisions lately.

"Just think about it," the agent said. "And call me, OK? Just give it some thought before you let this one get away."

After, Arthur and Wren surveyed the damage. It was pretty impressive. The house was nearly mummified.

"We should probably get out of here," Arthur said, amazed that no one had walked by yet. "Returning to the scene of the crime is one thing. Never leaving in the first place is another."

"Sorry, it's just—" Wren sniffed, admiring her work like a canvas masterpiece. "It's beautiful."

He couldn't help but laugh.

"I know it sounds ridiculous," she said. "But I was never allowed to be the troublemaker, to screw around a little, you know? I mean, I had a short phase, don't get me wrong. But I was already a big enough burden to everyone as it was."

Just as quickly, he felt guilty for laughing. Until she looped her arm through his and tugged him toward the car.

"Let's go. Can we pretend we hear sirens and we're making our getaway?"

"Sure."

"Can we just barely sneak under the railroad crossing arm right before a train whizzes past?"

He rolled his eyes. There was a lot rattling around in his head. The real estate lady had made some sense, but the truth was that he wasn't going to lie to Wren.

Arthur wasn't sure where that left them. But he knew one thing. Somehow, he was smiling. Because of her.

"Fine. Get in," he said. "Buckle your seat belt and I will consider plowing through one sidewalk fruit stand."

"You're the best."

In the car, Arthur pulled up directions to Home on his phone and plopped it in the cupholder. Was it the world's safest setup? No. One day he'd love to have a minivan with a modern touchscreen, where Google Maps and Spotify and all sorts of other goodies would be at his fingertips. A flip-down screen in the back for the baby. But that was starting to feel very far away. For now, he'd have to settle for viewing the map at this harsh and confusing angle that required him to take his eyes completely off the road.

"Where do you think you're going?" Wren said, snatching the phone and canceling the navigation.

"Home? I'm hungry."

"No, no, no. First," she said, "you need a redo."

12

ARTHUR: *Make a Difference in a Kid's Life*

"WHAT, ARE YOU JUST CARRYING the jars around with you everywhere now?" Arthur asked. He'd been driving full speed down the road when she'd produced his out of nowhere and forced him to draw. She was like a magician, this one, a sleight-of-hand master.

Or maybe she just kept it in her purse.

"I've got to say, Arthur. This one's a little corny."

She wasn't wrong. It definitely gave "late 1990s DARE presentation" or "very special episode / after-school special" or even "The More You Know." Maybe those early TV years when he was little were where he got his idea of what it meant to be a teacher. He was just old enough to have caught some reruns of *The Magic School Bus* and even, later, a little bit of the tail end of *Boy Meets World* thanks to the wonders of streaming. Those programs made teaching seem like this magical, all-rewarding thing.

He missed thinking that it was.

"It *is* corny," he said. "And it's also vague. It's something an idiot college kid thought up."

"Not an idiot, an optimist. Come on, tap into that part of yourself."

They were stopped at a red light, and Arthur took the opportunity to shut his eyes tight, racking his brain for an idea of how he could bring this one to life.

"It's not in your brain," Wren said, reaching over and touching his chest with a jokey seriousness. "It's in here."

"Who's being corny now?"

He thought of his students. They'd called him corny more times than he could count, or more frequently, they called him *cooked*. Especially during the TikTok debacle, but also every other day. He was always doing something cringe that meant he was cooked, like wearing a tie, having the wrong color socks on, or trying to educate them. He wasn't the worst teacher on the staff. They didn't hate him, but they didn't particularly seem to like him, respect him, or think they needed him in any way. How exactly was he supposed to "make a difference" in one of their lives? Whatever that even meant.

"There is one kid . . ." he said, trailing off and remembering.

"Yeah? Go on," Wren said.

"It's . . . No. Well, maybe. I mean . . . I guess it's worth a shot."

"I don't know who or what you're talking about, but I one hundred percent agree."

❑ ❑ ❑

After a quick stop to hit the ATM and give Arthur a chance to access the school directory, they found themselves outside Martin Lamb's listed address with three hundred dollars in cash. And a Snickers bar, but that was for Wren.

"So, what's the plan?" she asked between bites.

"Well, with any luck he's still really bummed out and needing money for band."

Wren crossed her fingers sarcastically.

"He wouldn't let me buy the trumpet for him before, but I don't know, maybe I can get him to change his mind."

"'Oh, I don't know, maybe . . .'" Wren mocked. "Where's your confidence? Don't you think you can do this?"

Arthur was tired. "I don't know, man. I just work here."

"Well, you're never going to make a difference in anyone's life with that attitude."

Arthur knew she was busting his chops, but he couldn't help but think she was right.

"You know who's good at this stuff? Tristan," she said. Before Arthur could protest, Wren was already dialing on her cell phone.

"He usually talks people into giving him money."

"So just take whatever he says and do it backward," Wren said.

"Go," Tristan answered, and Arthur rolled his eyes so hard they almost got stuck back there. Tristan was a *go* guy.

"Hey, Tris," Wren said. "Got a little bit of a sitch-ee-ation here that we could use your expertise in."

"What's up?"

"Arthur wants to help this kid at school who needs six hundred dollars for a bassoon, but the kid won't take the money. Too proud or something."

Arthur leaned in, feeling the need to correct her: "That was only half right, but . . . yeah, that's basically the gist. I have to get this kid to let me help him."

"Hey, hey, hey," Tristan said. "You don't have to. You *get* to."

"Yeah . . . right. So, any advice?"

"Well, it's like what Wren said: Anyone with pride isn't going to want to take a handout. You've got to make it seem like he's doing you a favor, or even better, like he really *deserves* the money."

"OK," Wren said. She turned to Arthur. "That makes sense."

"Yeah, and if all else fails, just slip him the money and run. Ask for forgiveness, not permission."

"Tristan, you are a national treasure."

"Thanks, Wren. Now I gotta run. You guys good?"

Wren nudged Arthur with her eyes and tilted her head toward the phone. *Say thank you!*

"Uh, yeah, thanks, man. You're a lifesaver and all of that."

"All right, cheers." Tristan hung up. *Cheers.*

Arthur paused for a second and tried to check his attitude. He'd been thinking about Martin, remembering when he'd been in his class. The kid was aways drumming with pencils, tapping his foot to a beat, and humming. It irritated the kids sitting next to him to no end, but now it was all making sense: He just loved music. It would mean a hell of a lot to Arthur if he could enable Martin to actually pursue his passion. It was ridiculous that a few hundred dollars should stand in the way of something so important.

"OK," Arthur said, steeling himself. "I'm ready."

"Let's go, then," Wren said, opening the door, then thinking better of it and shutting it again. "Actually, I just got hit by a tsunami of exhaustion, so maybe I'll just wait in the car."

❑ ❑ ❑

The house was nice, or, rather, was probably nice at one point, but now was in desperate need of repairs. As he walked up the front steps, Arthur felt as though his foot might go through one of them at any point. Gutters were falling down and the windows were permanently smudged. The place was probably somehow worth five million dollars, Arthur thought bitterly.

After a knock on the door, Martin himself answered, wearing an oversize T-shirt.

"AP? What are you doing here?"

"Hey, bud. Can I come in?"

A confused Martin nodded and stepped aside. Inside, the TV was blaring. An elderly woman was sitting on the couch watching some talk show at an extraordinarily high volume.

"That's my grandma," Martin said. Arthur raised his hand to wave, but Martin quickly grabbed it. "Don't draw attention to yourself. She gets confused and she'll probably think you're here to rob us."

"Understood. I don't want to frighten her."

"Oh, it's not her I'm worried about," Martin said ominously.

Arthur shook the comment off. "I'm actually here to do the exact opposite."

"Why are you being sus? You're freaking me out."

Come on, Arthur, just come out with it already. He led Martin into the kitchen, out of Grandma's sight, and took a look around as they walked. The inside of the house was no better than the outside. It looked like someone had made a valiant attempt to keep things clean—probably Martin—but there were a number of burned-out lightbulbs, blinking appliances, and loose floorboards. The place was in dire need of a handyman.

"Is it just the two of you here, you and her?"

Martin nodded. He remembered now, hearing a rumor

last year that Martin's parents weren't around. Kid always got his work done, never acted out, never let it show. But now it was all too painfully obvious. From what Wren had told him, she had spent a lot of time in a house not too unlike this. It was a tough and lonely way to grow up.

"Well, listen," Arthur said. "I know it's not much, but I really wanted you to have this. No strings. No paying me back. You can get that trumpet if you still want, or anything else you might need."

He pulled the wad of bills out of his pocket and held it out.

Martin just shook his head no.

"I can't take that."

"It's for you. It's really OK."

"Nah, my grandma will kill me if she finds out I took a handout." An elderly boomer. Of course she would. "She says people should work for their money. What I don't get is why it's OK for her to get checks from the government, though."

"Don't waste your brain power, it'll never make sense. Listen." Arthur thought. He considered just accepting the boy's answer and leaving. But no. He was here on a mission. He needed to be confident, have the right attitude, like Wren said. No one was ever going to look up to him if he couldn't project strength and authority. "If she asks, just tell her it's an investment."

"An investment? In what?"

"Anything. You're a smart kid. I did all kinds of stuff when I was your age. I mowed lawns, washed people's cars. You get a bucket, some soap, and a sponge and you can make yourself a good little allowance."

Martin pressed his lips together, thinking, staring at the money. But he still wasn't moving to take it. Arthur decided, even though it physically pained him, to try some of Tristan's advice.

"You know, when I was a kid, I really wanted to go to this chess tournament that was out of state. My parents said I could go, but I had to pay my own way."

"That sucks."

"Yeah. The difference was, I had the money. I told you, I worked all the time when I was a kid. I could have afforded it. But I was so uptight and scared to let it go that . . . well, I still think about what I might have missed out on."

Martin nodded, understanding.

"It would really help me out if you'd take this, so I know my mistake wasn't for nothing."

Damn, Arthur. That was good, he thought. He was proud of himself, and especially so because every word had been true.

Finally, Martin reached out and took the cash.

"OK. But just as an investment."

They shook hands.

Suddenly, Arthur realized—"Why don't I hear the TV anymore?"

❑ ❑ ❑

Moments later he came sprinting out of the house, Grandma behind him, swinging a bat over her head like a helicopter propeller.

"Wren, start the engine!" he yelled. Wren, just waking up from a car nap, eyes wide, did as she was told. Arthur made a mental note of how quickly and smoothly she shifted into Getaway Driver mode. He would have to ask her some additional questions about her past.

But only if they survived this.

Arthur stumbled down the stairs, sprinted across the front lawn, and dove in. In an instant, they peeled away, just in time to dodge the bat, which Grandma had hurled at them like a tomahawk.

"So . . . how did it go?" Wren asked.

13

WREN: *Have a Birthday Party at Chuck E. Cheese*

WITH LESS THAN THREE WEEKS now left until baby, until parenthood, until full life upheaval was upon them, Arthur was driving blind.

Wren would have driven herself, but squeezing in behind the steering wheel was getting more than a little uncomfortable. Plus, it was more fun this way.

"Right at this light," she called out at close to the last second, reading off her phone's GPS. Arthur just barely made the turn, sending the loose car seat in the back tumbling. He was really going to have to get around to putting that in, or they'd never let him take the baby home. Worse, he'd be the laughingstock of all the other new dads at the hospital.

"You could just let me see that map; that would be easier. And safer," he said.

"It'll ruin the surprise. A left up here."

"You said this was an experience for *you*," he said, jerking the wheel again, "so why do I need to be surprised?"

"Because it's clearly annoying you."

Wren gave his leg a squeeze above the knee, then another

high up on his thigh. Arthur let out a yelp and jerked the steering wheel.

"Woman, what are you doing?! You know driving in the city stresses me out; you're not helping."

"I know," she said, beaming. "I'm just excited."

So it hadn't gone great with Martin. But at least it had gone at all. Maybe getting right back on the horse was the smart thing to do.

A few minutes later, they arrived, pulled into the parking lot, and stepped out. Wren needed an extra hand from Arthur to make it all the way out of her seat. Her legs were feeling like jelly and her energy was low. She knew Dr. Abadi would tell her she should be at home resting. But she wasn't going to pass this up, not a chance.

Before them was one of the few remaining Chuck E. Cheeses in the greater Baltimore area, and even though it had seen better days (the *H* had fallen off of the sign, making it just C UCK E. CHEESE), it lit Wren up on the inside like Christmas morning.

"This is what you drew out of the jar," Arthur said. "This is what you've been so secretive about today?"

"Not just today," Wren said wistfully. "I've been waiting for this."

❑ ❑ ❑

Inside, the place was dark, a little damp, with flashing neon lights and upbeat synthetic music pouring out of all the machines. A children's casino. They walked up to the front desk, where a bored-looking teen girl twiddled on her phone.

"Welcome to Chuck E. Cheese," she droned.

"Hi," Wren began. "I'd like to book a birthday party."

She could feel Arthur looking over at her now, no doubt wondering what the hell she was doing. Wren's birthday wasn't for another two months. But by then, she knew, no one would care. The day would be like any other, going by in a haze of diapers and bottles and all the day-to-day tasks that couldn't be paused just because Wren wanted to feel special. God, being a grown-up sucked.

"What day?" The teen still wasn't looking up.

"How's about right now?"

That got her attention. The girl looked at Wren, looked at Arthur, looked around, looked at Wren again.

"You usually have to book in advance."

"Usually, OK. But maybe you could make an exception?"

"Sorry, it's policy."

"Come on," Wren pleaded. "The place is dead. I promise you can go right back to posting TikToks for your twelve followers."

"I'm actually an influencer."

"And I'm an artist. Now, what do you say?"

It was true, the place *was* dead. There wasn't another paying customer in the place at midday on a weekday, except for maybe one sad-looking child playing on an iPad in the corner. Probably an employee's kid, Wren guessed.

"How many in your party?" The girl sighed. "We offer an all-inclusive six-child package for ninety-nine dollars."

"Just two adults—wait, ninety-nine dollars?" Arthur said, aghast. "Are you kidding?"

"If you don't like it, you're welcome to go down the road and try your hand at Boing Trampoline Park. Their party packages *start* at four hundred dollars."

"That's completely unreasonable! When I was a kid—" Wren shot him a look, signaling to get on with it. He promptly bit his tongue.

"Whatever, fine. Just two adults," Wren said.

The teen groaned, looked at the ceiling like *Come on, lady.* "I don't have a button on my computer for that."

That's when Arthur stepped back in.

"Look, we'll pay the"—he swallowed hard—"ninety-nine dollars. Can you just give us a pizza and some game cards and get the mouse guy to sing to my girlfriend?"

In that moment, Wren could not recall ever loving him more.

"Girlfriend?" The teen couldn't help but eye Wren's belly.

"Hey, up here," Wren snapped, pointing to her eyes. Arthur put a hand on her shoulder, *Down, girl.*

"So can you help us out?" Arthur asked.

The employee sucked her lips, then hit a few buttons on the screen. A moment later, she handed over a few game cards.

"These are loaded up. Your pizza will be in the party room in about twenty minutes. What's the name and age of the birthday boy or girl?"

"Wren, that's *W-R-E-N,* and . . . twenty-nine," Wren answered.

"This is amazing, thank you," Arthur said, grabbing the cards before the employee could change her mind. "And what about the mouse?"

"No one sees the big man without an appointment," she replied, stone serious. For some reason, Wren gulped. "I mean the guy that plays him doesn't get here until five. Now, if you had booked ahead, like you're supposed to . . ."

Wren, light on her feet with glee, grabbed Arthur by the

arm and dragged him toward the games. "Come on, let's go!" she said, before yelling back, "Thanks again!"

"Hey," Arthur said, "you're sure Ferdie will be all right if we're gone a few hours?"

"He's nine thousand years old and totally housebroken, what's he gonna do? Have a kegger? Now, hand over the game card."

They reached the center of the establishment, arcade and midway games and ball pits and trampolines surrounding them. Wren took a moment just to soak it all in. The lights, the sounds. The stale odor of pitchers of Coke spilled many years ago. It was pure extract of childhood, and she let it wash over her, trying to absorb it into her soul like a witch trying to stay young.

"Charles Cheese, you magnificent bastard," she said. He really was the best celebrity mouse. "Mickey Mouse can eat shit."

"I don't mean to interrupt this spiritual baptism for you," Arthur said. "But . . . what did the slip of paper say, exactly?"

"It said 'Have a Birthday Party at Chuck E. Cheese.'"

"And you're sure you didn't mean have a *child's* birthday party? Because that, I think, we can do."

Wren supposed that, to him, this all seemed ridiculous. That maybe she owed him at least a brief explanation.

"We can do it, and we will. But it won't be for me," she said bluntly. "Look, I can't wait to be the mom handing out floppy plates of pizza and leading the chorus of 'Happy Birthday,' really. But is it so bad to want to be the star? To be the birthday girl, one last time?"

Last time, first time. Who was counting? Family had done their best when she was young; she remembered a few Funfetti cakes with cheap numbered candles, a handful of presents unwrapped at kitchen tables. But never the big party all the other kids at school seemed to be having—and not inviting her to. And why would they? She was never in one place long enough to make good friends, birthday party friends, Chuck E. Cheese friends.

Except there had been one girl in fifth grade, Emma. She and Wren had become close pretty quickly, close enough for Wren to get the coveted invite to Emma's Chuck E. Cheese birthday. It was everything she had ever wanted, and it was all finally happening. But her uncle had an unexpected work trip come up and sent Wren away for a couple of weeks to stay with his sister, who lived far on the other side of town, and she wasn't able to go. Worse, everyone who went brought in all their winnings from the Rat Casino the next day, to show off: little plastic army men, slap bracelets, candy necklaces. Flaunting all of it right in front of Wren. Those traitors.

Arthur smiled, understanding, and took her hands. "No, no, it's not so bad."

He looked like he wanted to kiss her, but she had her sights set on something else.

"I see Skee-Ball, get out of my way!"

And she was off.

❑ ❑ ❑

After a dozen rounds of Skee-Ball and three sweaty, profanity-laced games of air hockey and a down-to-the-buzzer basketball shootout, Arthur and Wren's party room was ready.

The influencer led them to the Yellow room, where they were seated next to each other at one of several long, cafeteria-style tables draped in cheap confetti tablecloths.

There were two paper plates in front of them and a piping-hot, golden-brown pepperoni pizza sitting on a silver stand.

"Happy birthday," the teen deadpanned. "Do you want a cake? It's an extra charge."

"Yes," Arthur chimed in. "We'll take your finest cake."

"There's only one kind."

"Then that's the one we'll take."

The girl rolled her eyes and turned to leave, but Wren stopped her.

"Sorry, no chance the costume guy decided to come in early, is there?"

"Not yet, but I'll page him. Let him know there's an emergency."

"Really?"

"Oh sure, right away." And then she left.

"You know." Wren frowned, donning a cone-shaped party hat from a stack on the table. "I'm beginning to think these people aren't taking their job seriously enough." She blew loudly into a paper party horn.

"So," Arthur said, ignoring her and serving them each a slice of pizza. "Is it everything you dreamed of? I'm sorry you won't get to meet Chuck."

"Yeah, that part is a bummer," she said, a little embarrassed by how disappointed she was. "But, on the plus side, we have *so many* tickets!"

"Wait, we do? From Skee-Ball and basketball?"

"When you were in the bathroom I *might* have played a few ticket games. What took you so long, by the way?"

"I accidentally wandered into an employees-only area, took forever to actually find the bathroom. This place is a maze."

"Well, you being gone was obviously my good luck charm,

because I hit it big, babe," she said. No jackpot, unfortunately, but she had gone on a hot streak on the Stop the Light game and racked up some big numbers. "We might even have enough tickets to get a Chinese finger trap."

"Whoa, whoa. Let's not be too ambitious. I'd be more than happy with a single stale Tootsie Roll."

She laughed and dug in, taking a bite of the gooey pizza and immediately feeling like she was in a food commercial. The steam still coming off of it, the way the cheese strung out in delectable little strands, the just-so crispiness of the crust. It was salty and chewy and warm and perfect. It was everything ten-year-old Wren had ever hoped it would be.

After the first bite or two, she sat and waited for the nausea and heartburn, but none came. Damn it, this place ruled.

"While we're here," Arthur said, pulling out his phone, "I wanted to show you something. Look at this."

She leaned over. "What am I looking at? All I can see is an ad for sexy singles in my area."

"What? Hold on." He x-ed out of a full-screen pop-up. "Now look."

"It's . . . a house."

"I think I found some new listings that might work for us. They're a little rough around the edges, but if you just keep an open mind."

"Arthur," she stopped him. "I did have an open mind. And you took me to some kind of weird suburban sex dungeon."

"It wasn't a—" He caught himself, took a breath. "You know what? You're totally right. I'd love to see the kind of place *you* imagine us living in."

"Don't get defensive, now."

"No, I'm completely serious. I think you should pick the next place we go see. I promise to keep an open mind."

"Really?" She cocked an eyebrow at him, trying to gauge how serious he was. Was he genuinely interested in her perspective or just trying to prove a point? "Because I've got some ideas."

"It can't have heated floors or an elevator. It has to be in our realistic price range."

"Aw, no fun."

"Wren, I'm serious," he said. "We can't stay in the apartment forever. So we've got to figure this out, one way or another. Preferably together."

He kissed her on the cheek before she could say anything else, then stood. "Sorry, bathroom. Way too much Sprite. I'll be back before the cake. Just promise me you'll think about it?"

"OK, I will," she said as he stood up and walked out of the room. Arthur's head swiveled back and forth as he tried to get his bearings, before he seemingly decided on a direction and walked out of view.

She didn't know why she'd just agreed to get involved in this process. Just to placate him, not have a fight right here in the middle of her fictitious thirtieth birthday party? Because the more she thought about it, she wasn't even sure she wanted to buy a house, in the burbs, the city, or otherwise. No matter where they ended up it would be the same. Volunteering at the PTA, making cookies for the bake sale, having dinner parties with neighbors that ended at 8:00 p.m., a thirty-year mortgage. It was everything she was supposed to want, and yet, there was a knot of dread sitting right there in her stomach, refusing to be ignored. It was like she could predict exactly how the rest of her life would play out once they signed on the dotted line, and that terrified her. The apartment wasn't much, but it was temporary by design. It meant that whatever came next was still unknown and full of possibility.

Sitting in that uncertainty felt good, and she wasn't quite ready to leave.

Her rumination was cut short moments later when the speakers in the Yellow room clicked on. An upbeat acoustic guitar ditty piped in, along with rhythmic clapping.

"Oh my God, it's happening," Wren said.

The voice of Chuck E. Cheese came in next: *"We say Happy, you say birthday! Happy—"*

"Birthday!" Wren shouted.

"Happy—"

"Birthday!"

She clapped along and then quickly decided this was the best moment of her life. Sure, she would tell people later on that it was finding out she was going to be a mother, but really, it would be this.

She just wished Arthur was here to enjoy it with her and that he would hurry back.

And then, in the doorway, she saw the very edge of a large, brightly colored birthday cake. The hands cradling it from underneath were large, much larger than a human's hands should be, and they were furry. The figure carrying the cake rounded the corner, and Wren's jaw hit the table.

It was Charles motherfucking Cheese.

The giant mouse placed the cake down on the table in front of Wren and began to dance along to the birthday song.

"Happy—"

"Birthday!" Chuck pointed at her animatedly, then gyrated his hips and waved his hands in the air.

Wren changed her mind. *This* was the best moment of her life.

"Arthur!" she yelled out. "You're missing it!"

Mr. Cheese pulled out an assortment of dance moves

cribbed from, as far as Wren could tell, the YMCA, *Boogie Nights*, and the Macarena. Finally, she couldn't bear it any longer, scooted her chair out, and stood, waltzing over to him and dancing right along. It was harder to dance than she remembered, her movements slower, but everyone got the general idea. Chuck even took her hand and twirled her in a circle, then gave her just the slightest dip without allowing her to fall. His grip was firm and protective. She couldn't believe she was thinking it, but the whole thing was almost romantic. No, sexy. If it hadn't been for Arthur, and the fact that Chuck E. Cheese was a mouse and this was a children's establishment, things might have gotten steamy right there in the Yellow room. All the right hormones were firing in that moment.

Wren stopped and stepped away to fan herself and catch her breath.

"Whoever you are under there," she said, "thank you."

"Anything for you," he said.

Wren knew that voice.

A moment later, the furry hands pulled off the head of the costume and the sweaty, panting smile of her boyfriend confirmed it.

"How—"

"Saw it hanging on the wall in the back." He smirked. "Guess I couldn't help myself."

No, no, no. Hands down, final answer: This was the best moment of her life. But she didn't have long to enjoy it.

"Sir!" It was the teen employee and another worker, a much larger man, hurrying their way from across the arcade.

"OK," Arthur said. "Probably time to go."

"What about the cake?"

"Grab it and come on!"

He tossed the head aside and began fumbling around under

his shirt (purple, with a bright yellow *C*) for a zipper pull. The suit's gloves were just nimble enough that he was able to grab it and begin to remove the top portion of the costume. Wren grabbed the cake and they made their way toward the exit.

Of course, between the two of them—Wren waddling along holding a giant cake, Arthur shedding pieces of the Chuck E. Cheese costume behind him—they weren't moving very fast. The workers caught up quickly.

"I don't get paid enough for this," the girl whined.

Arthur, hopping along and removing one of the oversize red shoes, was red in the face.

"Sorry, sorry, I'm really sorry," he said.

"I hope it was worth it," the large man said. "Because you two are officially banned from Chuck E. Cheese for life."

"All locations!" the girl added. Wren hoped this wouldn't have any ramifications for her future child. But she could always use a pseudonym if they ever wanted to come back. How advanced could the security possibly be at Chuck E. Cheese?

Arthur finally removed the final piece. The pants. And handed them over gently.

"Totally get it," he said.

"Would it help if I told you this was my dying wish?" Wren asked. She got a look of no sympathy. "OK, I'm not saying it is, just asking if it would help. Sorry again and thank you!"

The employees stared daggers at them as Wren and Arthur hurried out the door, Wren careful not to drop the cake on the way to the car.

❑ ❑ ❑

When they arrived home, they were immediately greeted by the smell of vomit. Sadly, it was not fresh. It was stale, the smell having dissipated somewhat and permeated the cushions and walls. It was cold, and lived-in, and that was somehow worse than discovering a hot, steamy pile.

"Ferdie, what happened, buddy?" Wren cried out, spotting the yellow crust on the carpet, Ferdie looking up at her with utter humiliation in his eyes. "Are you OK?"

She dropped to her knees and scratched behind his ears. He seemed OK, his tail perking up somewhat.

"We can't leave him alone for so long," Arthur said.

"Relax, it was just a fluke. A fluke puke. Just an upset tummy. He's all better now, see?" She pulled Ferdie's lips into something resembling a smile.

"I'm just saying, if we're going to be out, we should find a dog sitter who can come check on him."

"Great idea! Because if only someone was here at the exact moment he began to feel sick, this whole tragedy could have been avoided."

Arthur rolled his eyes. "Will you just relax?" Wren continued. "I'll clean it up, don't worry."

She put out a hand, signaling Arthur to help her up, which he did, and then retrieved paper towels and cleaning solution from the kitchen. But once she knelt next to the soiled spot on the carpet, she felt like she was going to experience her Chuck E. Cheese pizza in reverse.

"Never mind, I can't." She gagged. She could taste the pepperoni coming back up already.

"Oh, how convenient," he replied, having already settled onto the couch with his laptop.

"Seriously, I need you to take over. Whatever you want. I'll cook for you, I'll grade papers for you, just please don't make me stay here and smell this."

"I'd be happy to just get you to stop snoring."

"Done, OK? I'll get that weird mouth tape or whatever, just please get me out of here."

Arthur looked up at the ceiling and inhaled. Wren knew he was reconsidering his dedication to being a good guy, a decent boyfriend and future father. Probably wondering how much easier it would be to be downing cheap beers with friends at a sleazy bar right now and ignoring her texts.

"Here," he finally said, hoisting himself off the couch and taking her place. "Give me that."

"Thank you. Look, I'll even give Ferdie a bath."

"What, in our tub?"

"Where else?"

Arthur sighed and said nothing else, just dutifully began sopping up the mess with paper towels and scrubbing the remaining stain with carpet cleaner. Wren almost felt bad. He hadn't asked for this. And yet here he was, showing up for her, picking up the slack without complaint. OK, maybe with minor complaint. But that was all she could ever ask for, more than anyone else had ever done for her. Certainly no one else had ever dressed up as a mouse for her entertainment and been nearly arrested for it. The closest thing that came to mind was one of the few photos of her with her dad, who had dressed up as Spider-Man for her superhero-themed first birthday party. She sat bewildered in a high chair, staring at him in awe, her tiny face covered in cake. She hated that she couldn't remember it outside of the one grainy, poorly lit photo she'd found in an album as a kid. It would be asking a lot of a one-year-old, but it sure would have been a good thing to remember.

Then there was Arthur. She appreciated him deeply in that moment, and even found herself lustily watching the tendons flex in his forearms as he scrubbed. Didn't think she'd ever noticed those before.

In the bath, she lazily doused a stiff and confused Ferdie with warm water; he looked rail thin with his fur matted down. Poor guy. She'd only left him home for a few hours, tried to do one thing for herself, and all three of them had paid a price. Was this what it was going to be like all the time soon? No, it would be worse. Can't leave a baby unattended even for a second, not to run to the car because you left your leftovers baking in the sun on the passenger seat, not to pee, not even to take the dog out! The little rascal would be strapped to her at all times, like one of those obnoxious weighted vests, tagging along and slowing her down everywhere she went, when it didn't stop her from going at all.

Ferdie reached over the ledge of the tub and licked her face, snapping her out of her thoughts. He did it again. It tickled and she couldn't help but laugh.

14

ARTHUR: *Become Independently Wealthy*

"IT'S YOUR TURN," WREN SAID.

"I'm tired."

"Just stick your fingers in the hole and grab something."

He did as instructed, trying to remember that hazy night that just refused to come all the way back to him. What had he said at the time? Who had he wanted to be when he was a bright-eyed college kid?

Standing there in the living room, he pulled out the first slip that brushed across his fingertips and read it aloud.

"Well, I'm nothing if not consistent. Another impossible task that, under the best circumstances, would take decades. And we've got . . . less than three weeks."

"Are you chickening out?"

"No," he said defiantly. "No, I'm not."

In truth, he was feeling pretty good after his encounter with Martin. I mean, come on, he had potentially changed that kid's life. Martin could go on to become a famous musician or songwriter, or maybe get a scholarship to a prestigious arts school, and it would be, in part, because Arthur made it possible.

That . . . was an amazing feeling. It was what he'd been searching for, for years.

"I have to ask," Wren said, rattling the jar in small circles as if it were a whiskey on the rocks. "How had you initially planned to pull this off?"

Now some of the thinking was coming back to him.

He'd figured he'd get an entry-level teaching job, for starters. But he'd subsist pretty frugally. Maybe even live at home with his parents for a few years, or split an apartment with a roommate or two (or three). He estimated he could scrimp enough to save at least 20 percent of his salary, like the experts recommended, but ideally 30. That wouldn't be much at first, but he'd make smart, aggressive investments. During the summers, he'd work on side hustles—doing freelance writing or tutoring . . . He hadn't totally figured it out yet. But he'd pour the extra money into his investments and the compound interest would do the rest. He'd grind hard for a few years, forgoing as much sleep as humanly possible, living off Cup Noodles and 5-Hour Energy drinks, before investing big in himself and starting his own business. Something boring but stable, a sure bet, like junk hauling or power washing. Now, did he know the first thing about how any of that worked? No. But he'd figure it out. That's what YouTube was for. And he'd design it to be hands-off so he could have time to write again and continue working with kids when he wanted—that part he had always enjoyed—and when he was finally an honest-to-God millionaire, he'd be ready to meet his wife and start a family.

It was a foolproof plan.

But then he had to go and screw around and fall in love young. After that, he wasn't sure exactly where the time had gone. Having two roommates had turned into having one (although she was very pretty). Teaching, and working in general, had turned out to be a lot harder than he thought. Instead of dreaming up side hustles in the early mornings, he was always scrambling just to make it out the door on time. Rather than cook up lofty business ideas in the evenings, he was fighting to keep his eyes open during Netflix documentaries because his brain couldn't handle much else after the long days. Someone had once told him to work hard for eight hours, sleep for eight hours, and spend eight hours with the people he loved—but he must have been doing something wrong, because the math never seemed to add up. Plus, it was so hard for him to get out of bed when there was a warm body pressed up against his, soft skin to lay his hands on, the curve of his palm fitting just so perfectly on her hip. That had never been part of the plan. Summers came around and he was burned-out and totally unprepared to capitalize on the extra time. It felt good to veg with Wren, read books, sneak into neighboring tennis courts, and eat coupon tacos on warm patios. The years got away from him in a hurry. The best he'd managed lately was his idea to go to grad school, which would allow him to make a *little* more money—on the order of dozens, not millions, of dollars. But he hadn't even made much progress at that.

Maybe it was finally time for that to change. Time to finally take action. But first . . .

"I had concepts of a plan," he admitted, trying to refocus on the present moment, the task at hand. "The question is . . . how can you become a millionaire in a single day? Got any ideas?"

"You act like you're the first person who's ever wanted the instant gratification of immediate wealth. There's a societal mechanism for this. But I don't think you're gonna like it," she said.

He cocked an eyebrow at her, not getting it. So she began

singing the Maryland Lottery jingle from his youth, twirling around and shaking her hips, ending the number with finger guns pointed at him and belting out the lotto's signature catchphrase: *"It could be youuuuuu!"*

"No. No, absolutely not. I won't do it," he said. "I won't."

❑ ❑ ❑

They walked into the Royal Farms convenience store, about a three-minute drive from their front door, and the door chimed behind them. Instantly, they were met with the scent of crispy fried chicken, or not so much met as they were drenched with it. Arthur knew the clothes he had on would need a good washing or two before they smelled normal again.

"This is ridiculous. We could have just lit a five-dollar bill on fire at home and saved the gas money," Arthur huffed. He'd never been a fan of gambling. Not that he looked down on it ethically, but he viewed it as a colossal waste of money, which it objectively was. They'd been able to save as much as they had specifically because he'd avoided frivolously throwing money away on impossible pipe dreams.

"If you've got a better idea, I'd love to hear it," Wren retorted. He didn't. "Now, should we play the Powerball or the Mega Millions?"

"How much is the Mega Millions jackpot?"

"Three hundred forty-eight million dollars."

"Jesus Christ," he said. That was a number he couldn't even fathom. His goal was to become independently wealthy, not to get invited to Jeff Bezos's next yacht-based wedding. "And the Powerball?"

"One hundred fifty-five million," Wren sneered. "Gross. That's not even worth it. Let's go for the big'un."

"Sure, why not." He pulled out his wallet and prepared to hand over the cash. It didn't matter. They weren't going to win, but at least he could say he gave it a go, and then he could get to thinking about more realistic ways to secure their financial future together. Stocks and bonds and CDs. And real estate.

"Wait," she said, stopping him and squinting to read something behind the counter. "Says here the drawing isn't until next week. That might be too late."

"OK. What about the scratch-offs? How much can you win on those?"

They perused the little glass display case of scratch-off tickets, like looking over the desserts sitting out by the hostess stand in a diner.

"This one says you can win two million," Arthur pointed out. It was a Monopoly-themed ticket with the mustachioed Mr. Monopoly skipping jovially across the face of it, carrying a sack of coins. He'd always liked the game. He'd been good at it, liked the strategy of buying aggressively, depleting his cash reserves, and playing to win. It was the opposite of how he lived and was a fun escape. Of course, Wren had only played with him once and then vowed to never do it again, accusing him of being a "dirty slum lord" after he'd scooped up a murderers' row of cheap light blue and purple properties that was impossible to bypass, slowly and agonizingly bleeding her out over the course of several hours. By the end, the light had all but left her eyes, until she demanded they play Yahtzee instead and promptly destroyed him. "So with taxes we'd walk away with maybe a million? I guess I could live with that."

Wren smiled and flagged down the attendant to make the purchase. Then she swiped a coin from the take-a-penny, leave-a-penny tray—a nickel with concerning black marks covering most of its face—and handed it over to Arthur. "Do the honors."

He found his heart speeding up as he began to scratch away at little colored stacks of money on the card, the sticky rubbery coating peeling and flaking away. Behind the coating were numbers, each attached to a different prize amount. At the top of the card was a row of six winning numbers: 17, 3, 45, 66, 11, and 49. The legend also included special symbols that would make him an instant winner if he were to find them on his card. Arthur scratched and scanned, scratched and scanned.

"So?" Wren asked impatiently.

"Give me a second!" He felt ridiculous, of course, the way he was ever so slightly getting into it. There was a small chance they'd win, but probably just enough to buy another ticket. That was how they got you. The odds of winning the grand prize were infinitesimally small. Even still, he couldn't help but imagine what might happen if fortune were to strike. They'd have no trouble affording a house, one that actually had rooms. Could trade in the sedan and get a new SUV or minivan. Go on proper family vacations without guilt. It was just a fantasy, though, a daydream to keep him busy while he tediously scratched away. Never going to happen. But scratching and revealing the numbers was kind of fun, he had to admit. Was there value in that? Fun, excitement, and a brief flicker of hope? Was that worth a couple of bucks? No, he decided. It was a cheap, hollow dopamine hit, like getting a notification on Instagram.

Then again, the lottery revenue did go to support Maryland's schools. At least, in theory. So, he supposed, without vulnerable suckers like himself, he'd be out of a job.

"Um, Wren?" he exclaimed suddenly. One of his numbers was a match.

"What, what is it? Did we win?"

He looked back and forth, his number, 17, and the winning number at the top, also 17. He didn't trust his eyes, was probably just a little overexcited. It couldn't be right. But no, sure enough, his card was a winner.

"We won!" he shouted.

"We won!" Wren echoed.

"We won!" they said in unison.

"We won five hundred bucks!"

Wren's face fell a bit. "Oh," she said. "That's it?"

"Wren." Arthur grabbed her shoulders, held her like he was giving her an urgent, dying message. "This is huge."

Now he was getting legitimately excited.

"I guess, yeah," she mumbled.

"Five hundred dollars is a lot of money."

"But it doesn't make you wealthy," she pointed out. "It's barely a run to the grocery store." Not the way she did it, mindlessly swiping random items off the shelves and into the cart if they were shiny and interesting, like a bored cat. It was plenty if you shopped the sales. But that was beside the point right now.

"No. But we can save this. If we put it away in our investment account and stay patient, in thirty years this five hundred dollars could be worth . . ." There was a twinkle of adrenaline in Wren's eyes as she imagined the end results of Arthur's quick mental math. "Nine thousand dollars!"

"OH MY GOD!" she yelled. Arthur could immediately sense the dripping sarcasm as she slipped into an overexcited Valley girl accent. "Nine thousand dollars! And we only have to wait thirty years? Why didn't you say so?! Oh my freaking God!"

"OK, I get it. You're not psyched."

"No, I'm not psyched! Nine thousand dollars will barely buy us cat food in thirty years."

"I don't understand. Are we getting a cat?" Multiple cats?

"No, we'll be living off it ourselves at this rate. Come on! Where's your ambition, Arthur? Where's your sense of adventure? Why are you settling?"

He couldn't imagine what it would be like to not see this as a huge win. Wren hadn't grown up with a lot of money, he knew that, so he couldn't understand why she wouldn't be over the moon about anything that could help them give their baby some of the things that she never had.

"Being with you when I'm eighty. That's the adventure, that's what I want more than anything," he said quietly. "I know it's not always sexy and exciting, but we have to put in the work now to get there."

"I know," she said. "But even if we do everything right, nothing is guaranteed, is it? I don't know where I'll be, or *if* I'll be, in thirty years. What I know is I'm here with you right now, and I want to make this life worth living."

It sounded romantic and incredible when she said it. Heartbreaking, too, remembering that her parents had been ripped away from her far too young. She didn't grow up with a good picture of two people who had worked hard to build their future together and lived to see it through. Her uncle did his best, but he was a sad and distant man. Everyone else rotated in and out of her life, much too focused on their own problems to be anything resembling a role model.

"OK, so what . . ." he said. "What do we do with our winnings?"

"We turn it into more."

"More lotto tickets? I don't think so. We got lucky once. I'll be physically sick if we blow this trying to capture lightning in a bottle again."

"Come on." She nudged him. "Think bigger."

He did. And there was only one place he knew where you could quickly turn money into more money, or, far more likely, lose it all in an instant.

❑ ❑ ❑

It was sunset by the time they reached their destination: a hulking beige building illuminated by golden lighting. The sky behind it was pink and purple, Ravens purple, Wren pointed out, and the name on the side of the structure read simply: HORSESHOE.

Yes, they had arrived at Baltimore's one and only casino. A glitzing money grab near M&T Bank Stadium that was supposed to revitalize the entire neighborhood, creating a vibrant arts and entertainment district, not to mention pour hundreds of millions of dollars into the public school system. Arthur had not seen evidence of any of this actually happening, but he did see an abandoned structure in the near distance covered in graffiti, and an intoxicated woman hurling her guts up just a few feet shy of a trash can.

Wren breathed in as they stood outside the door. "Smell that, Arthur? It's crab cakes, it's championship football, it's art and history and culture. It's the *city.*"

"Is that what you smell?" He gave the air a whiff. Urine, polluted seawater, and more urine is what he got. But never mind that. "Shall we?"

They pushed through the glass doors and the noise was immediately overwhelming. Digital trills and chimes, pumping music, chattering people, the occasional "jackpot" noise of endless coins falling into a metal bin. It was an assault on the senses. It was Chuck E. Cheese on performance-enhancing drugs, or maybe just actual drugs, if Chuck E. Cheese could ruin your life in an instant.

Arthur grabbed Wren's hand and they began walking the floor, taking in the sights.

"I read somewhere that the best odds are actually at the blackjack table," Wren said. "Do you know how to play blackjack?"

"Kind of. Not well enough to win big."

"Let me see your phone," she said. "I got too excited and left mine at home." She had been a little more forgetful lately, playfully throwing the phrase *pregnancy brain* around a lot more frequently. Just the other day, she'd left the oven on for hours. And open. He handed his phone over and she tapped in his password, which she knew, and began typing furiously.

"What are you doing?" he asked.

"Just googling 'how to count cards' real quick."

He snatched it back from her. "Don't even joke about that!" His eyes flitted to the ceiling. Black, spherical cameras everywhere. They were being watched and listened to. He didn't want to end up getting pummeled in a back alley by some casino goon.

In truth, Arthur couldn't believe he had been reduced to this. If playing the lottery was for suckers, who was this place for? For the life of him he couldn't figure out how losing hundreds or thousands of dollars in a single evening could qualify as entertainment. And for what? Did the people sitting at the slot machines like zombies really think they had a chance to hit it big? Honestly, though, they were probably people who had tried it the other way and found it was a road to nowhere.

Working hard, being a good person. Where did that ever get anyone? Maybe the new American dream was just to hope you got extremely lucky.

All he really wanted to do was to take the crisp five hundred dollars the cashier had pulled out of the Royal Farms cash box immediately to the bank. But he could see the electric look in Wren's eyes, the adrenaline coursing through her, and he remembered the purpose of the bucket list. For him, it was about being the man and father his family needed him to be. They needed somewhere to live, somewhere for the baby to grow up, and thus far he had been unable to provide that for them. The apartment was completely unsuitable in the long term, and to date he had not come up with a better solution than gambling, which was really saying something. This—all of this—was an incredible long shot, but maybe it was still a shot worth taking.

Still, he didn't want to drag this out.

"No, I'm not going to sit here all night." The thought of watching his pile of chips go up a little, then down, then up, then down, getting just a little bit smaller over time, would surely send him into a panic attack. His chest stung with heartburn just thinking about it.

"One big bet. The whole five hundred. I'd rather take my chances that way."

Wren looped her arm through his and gave it a squeeze. "Now you're talking. Lead the way."

❑ ❑ ❑

After a bit of internet research, they found themselves on the outskirts of the high-limit roulette table. They watched a few rounds. Gamblers leaned over the green felt table with shiny wooden edges and placed chips on various numbers or other tiles marked on the felt. The dealer spun the wheel, a small metal ball whirling in the opposite direction. People chanted and cheered, held their breath. After the ball landed, a few sighed, pounded fists on the table, or clapped excitedly. It all happened so fast, was so chaotic—Arthur wasn't sure he'd have the nerve to step up to the table.

That is, until Wren shoved him up there as the next game was beginning.

They'd studied the odds and knew that the biggest bet was to place all their money on a single number, 1 through 36. On the rare chance their number hit, the payout would be 35 to 1. In other words, seventeen thousand five hundred dollars. Now, that would be life-changing money, not in thirty years, but right now. It could open up the next bracket of homes to them, neighborhoods Arthur hadn't even considered before.

Or go a long way toward finishing the one that had everything he loved but an interior.

There were other bets they considered, too. There was red or black, which would pay even money, and was far more conservative. Same with odds or evens. They could also bet various combinations of two or three or even six numbers, with ever-decreasing odds. But no. They were here to go big, and then go home, in that order.

"Our anniversary is the twelfth," Wren whispered in Arthur's ear as he handed the cash to the dealer, the "croupier," not quite wanting to let it go, and received one purple chip in return worth five hundred dollars. It had an impressive and somehow very satisfying heft to it, and Arthur found himself twirling it in his hands and staring at it. "There are also three sets of twelve numbers on the board. And today is the sixth, which multiplied by the two of us is twelve. It's too perfect. Bet the house on twelve."

Arthur wasn't sure when Wren had become a faux numerology expert, but he considered it as other players around him stacked their bets. A busty woman in a low-cut dress. A guy in a hoodie and sunglasses who looked like he belonged at the World Series of Poker. An older lady who could barely see over the edge of the table. Impossible, stupid, reckless—but utterly life-changing, that's what this could be. And more, it was a bet on himself and Wren, on their love, in a weird way. He liked the sound of that. It had a certain ring to it.

"Final bets?" the dealer asked.

But he couldn't do it. He wanted to, but his hands simply would not cooperate. It was too risky. To Wren, this was a game, just an adventure. To him, the stakes were real, and they were ugly. The odds were so long they might as well not exist. No, the smart move, the calculated move, was to play more conservatively and walk away a winner. Everything in his body and brain was screaming at him not to be so risky.

He placed his chip on black.

"What the hell?" Wren shrieked.

"I know what I'm doing." The last couple of rounds they watched had all landed on red numbers. Black was due. Overdue. This was called playing the odds.

"But you could still lose it all in one spin and it wouldn't even be worth it!"

"We've got a fifty percent chance of turning this into a thousand dollars and walking out of here."

In thirty years, that could be almost the same amount of money as miraculously hitting a 35-to-1 bet, with far better odds of actually coming true. He imagined his dad would be proud of the quick analysis and strategic decision-making. Hey, crazier things had happened than getting a genuine compliment from his father.

"Sir," Wren overruled him, speaking directly to the croupier. "We'd like to change our bet."

"I'm sorry," the vested man said, waving her off. The bets were locked. The game was starting. The wheel, with a flick of the man's wrist, was spinning.

"You chickened out," Wren scoffed. "I can't believe you."

"Shh, just watch," he said. She'd see. She doubted him now, but she was going to have to trust him. He watched intently as the wheel spun with a satisfying click, the metal ball whirling around the outside ring in the opposite direction, like a person stuck on one of those centrifugal carnival rides. Gradually, the spinning slowed, the ball hopping in and out of the numbered divots. Arthur's heart was going to explode, and as the wheel came to a stop Arthur suddenly regretted everything, all his choices leading up to this point. So much on the line. Not only the money, but Wren's respect. Admiration even. His dad's, too. The old woman and the busty lady and the hoodie guy watched with bated breath; no one made a peep.

The ball landed on a black number, sending Arthur's heart rocketing up through his throat, his eyes popping wide in excitement. He couldn't make out the specific number, no, because in less than an instant, the ball hopped once more, spinning and bouncing, then finally coming to rest elsewhere on the wheel.

Right there on red number 12.

His heart dropped, from his throat into his stomach. He thought he was going to be sick, or at least faint. Fight-or-flight adrenaline shot directly into his brain, making him woozy, giving him tunnel vision. He watched helplessly as the croupier reached out with that stupid little stick and dragged away his chip, his five hundred dollars. His hope at a shortcut to the life he'd always dreamed of shattered.

"Nice going," Wren said helpfully.

"I can't believe it," was all he could say.

"Told you to bet on us."

"I seriously cannot believe it."

Five reds in a row, what were the odds? Mister Smart Guy didn't have an answer for that one.

She sighed and placed a hand on his back, rubbed it lovingly. "Well, that was fun while it lasted. Will you just listen to me next time? Haven't you learned by now that I'm always right?"

"Where are the people with the free drinks?" he said. Now was not the time for his pregnancy solidarity pledge. He needed a cold beer, or something much stronger, in his mouth that instant. And he was pretty sure Wren would understand why.

"They don't do that here."

"Oh," was all he could say. Totally numb. "Perfect."

❑ ❑ ❑

At home, Arthur decided to check the mail. That was what being an adult was mostly about, he had learned. Continuing to plod your way through administrative bullshit while ignoring the constant existential devastation you were feeling inside. No matter how much of a failure he felt like, the mail needed to be checked, bills paid, trash taken out, dog walked, dinner made, dishes cleaned, the apartment then readied to do it all again the next day. He dutifully inserted his key into the mail slot and turned. He took out a stack of crap. Nine flimsy cardboard mailers that he would take inside and recycle like a good little grown-up, a bank statement, a car insurance bill, and one of those advertisements in an envelope that looked handwritten enough to trick you into opening it. He was certain that he'd switched to paperless statements with the bank, and he'd paid the car insurance online weeks ago. This entire errand could have been an email.

But upon closer inspection, the envelope really *was* hand-addressed to him.

It was from Martin Lamb, the name inscribed in the wrong corner, handwriting jagged and barely legible. He ripped it open and a floppy pile of twenty-dollar bills fell out, along with a handwritten note:

> *Mr. Peterson—Busted by Grandma. She said Absolutely No Handouts.*
> *Also, she kept a 20 for the cost of mailing this.*

Arthur just stared at the cash on the floor. A part of him didn't even want to pick it up.

He had failed at this, too, and he should have known he would. He couldn't make a difference in someone's life—what was he thinking? He couldn't be a memorable role model for this random kid, and he doubted he would be one for his own.

He wanted to be gutted, but at least he was consistent in his inability to do anything good in the world. Succeeding would have only confused him more.

❑ ❑ ❑

Inside, Wren was checking on Ferdinand. They'd paid Norman Bates from upstairs ten dollars to take him out for a quick pee while they were out. Ten dollars for a single pee! Insult to injury. Arthur winced. But hey, at least he had some cash burning a hole in his pocket now. Wren peppered Ferdie with questions about how it went, whether he liked his new unofficial dog sitter, as if he could answer. When Arthur came in, she grabbed his attention: "Hey, watch this. We've been working on it and we're finally ready to show it off."

"OK."

Wren sat up on her knees in front of Ferdie, who stood rigor-mortis stiff on the carpet. She held up a treat. "Ferdie, paw."

He stared at her, at the treat. She tried again, more commanding. "Paw!"

Ferdie unenthusiastically lifted an arthritic paw what would be generously called two inches off the ground to appease her, then flopped down into a more comfortable position. Wren began clapping gleefully.

"Good boy!" She scratched behind his ears, celebrating him as if he'd just split the atom. "Who's my Mr. Smarty-Pants?"

"Wow," Arthur said. "What a feat."

From there, he wasted no time flopping directly into bed, his head spinning.

The bucket list wasn't working. He wasn't getting any closer to feeling like he was ready for fatherhood. If anything, he felt farther away than ever, his shortcomings becoming more and more apparent. His judgment and overall competence, too.

He stared at the ceiling. A stain here. A mummified cockroach in the corner. A flicker of light that came from his bedside lamp, which had a tendency to short in and out randomly, not because of the lamp or the bulb, both of which they had replaced, but because of some inherent and probably hazardous wiring problem hidden deep within the walls. He hated this place, hated the idea of feeding and rocking his newborn child to sleep in this awful cave, and worse, he had not a single prospect for getting them out of this mess.

"Oh God," Wren interrupted. "Oh no, no, no, no, no."

"What is it?" He sat up as Wren entered the room, staring at her phone now, sheer horror and panic in her face. Her giddy mood from just moments ago was cratering fast.

"I left my phone here today and I've got half a dozen missed calls from Charlie."

"Is she OK?"

"Today was the cake tasting. I was supposed to be there. No, no, no, no, no," she repeated, as if saying it enough times would allow her to go back in time.

She typed something, deleted it, typed and deleted again, held the phone up as if about to make a call, then decided against it and dropped the phone in resignation. No way of making this right, not right now. It was too late.

Wren flopped into bed beside him, and soon Ferdie joined them, creaking his way up the little doggie stairs cushion Wren had purchased. The little purchases like that were adding up, and their savings had really plateaued. They really could have used that seventeen grand.

"I completely forgot," Wren said, now also staring at the ceiling. "I'm the worst friend. The one thing she asked me to do, and I couldn't be bothered to do it."

Arthur turned to face her, placed his hand on her belly. He felt it go up and down with her breathing, and while he waited for a kick to come, he could definitely feel some movement in there. Wriggling and repositioning. The little guy trying to get comfortable. Couldn't have been easy; he or she was getting really big in there and running out of room. He wondered if the baby knew how miserable Mom and Dad were out here, if they could sense it somehow.

"You're not the worst," Arthur exhaled. "*I* am. If I was more like you, our life would be so much better. If I could take some chances, live in the moment, not be so scared to fail."

"I think sometimes I'm so busy living in the moment that I'm actually missing out on the things that really matter. Like this. Lying here with you and Ferdie. Like being there for my friend. Not chasing adventure all over the city. What am I doing?"

They weren't talking to each other, not really, but to the heavens. Some kind of higher power that could take pity on them and do something meaningful to change things.

Arthur wondered: Had he always been such a chicken-shit? Surely not. He'd always been a little more shy and reserved. A conservative, goal-oriented person. But he'd always had the courage to go for those goals before. What had happened to him in adulthood?

He looked over at Wren, who was lying higher than him on the bed. Something about the angle, viewing her face from below, triggered a memory. Suddenly he was at the National Aquarium with her years ago, in the dark and moody exhibit called Shark Alley. They'd walked down spiraling ramps and taken in the sights of tiger sharks, sandbar sharks, and great hammerheads in massive, glowing blue tanks. At the bottom, they paused, and Arthur had decided it was the right moment. He was so excited to get down on one knee and ask her to marry him, to the point that he was shaking and stumbling and could barely get the words out.

Most of all, he remembered the look on her face, and the way she looked over at the sharks, as if hoping one of them would climb out of the tank then and there and eat her in a single gulp. It would be painful, but not as painful as what was going to come next.

Then he remembered her saying no.

That was the last impulsive thing he could remember doing.

She loved him, she'd assured him, but wasn't ready for the commitment. They were young. Fresh out of school and twenty-two years old. Living together, broke, scraping by on their love and not much else. At least that much hadn't changed in the years since. He remembered not knowing what to do after that, exactly, if he should gather his self-respect and leave, or if maybe she was right and it was too soon. In the end, he decided that, whatever her real reasons were, it was probably his fault. If he could just be perfect, make everything just right, never make a single mistake, become a man she could be proud of, maybe things would eventually work out and he'd be able to try again one day.

That kind of courage never came to him. He held his chin up high and never let on how much it devastated him. And he never let on that he knew he'd always wonder how much she really loved him, if the day would eventually come when she'd realize that she didn't and head for greener pastures.

"I don't want to waste any more time playing it safe, Wren," he said finally after the long silence. He grabbed her hand and ran a thumb along its side. Whatever else had happened before, and whatever would happen, he was so glad to have her here and now. He felt maybe if he wrapped his body around hers and locked his arms together that they could just stay right here in the safety of this moment and not have to face whatever would come next. Whatever it was, they weren't ready for it.

“And I have to figure out a way to take it easy,” Wren said. He could tell in her voice, she was exhausted. They’d been out all day, she on her feet the entire time. Arthur couldn’t help but think that, too, was his fault. “Dr. Abadi said if I don’t . . .” She didn’t need to finish the thought. “I’d never forgive myself.”

Arthur squeezed her hand even harder. To let her know it was OK, that they were still in this together.

“So what do we do? Do we abandon the bucket list?” she asked.

Arthur got an idea then. He began to think—but he stopped himself on the spot. He wasn’t going to think. He was just going to say and do.

“No,” he said. “We’re not going to abandon it.”

Before he could pull his hand away and sit up, the kick came, powerful and crystal clear. The baby, whoever they were, or were going to be, approved.

15

WREN PULLED UP AT THE curb, bumping it slightly and really hoping Arthur wouldn't notice the scuff. She was outside Charlie's building, a high-rise condominium with stunning views of the harbor and city skyline. The whole street was posh and beautifully well-kept. Immaculately trimmed trees lined the sidewalk like watchful little soldiers. Dirty street pigeons were nowhere to be found, but beautiful doves seemed to be everywhere, as if someone were manually replacing one for the other 24/7 to maintain the aesthetics of the area. A trash can on the corner was disguised as a bush.

But the plan was not to go up and knock on the door, beg her friend to forgive her. The plan was to lure Charlie down.

It started with a phone call.

"Yes?" Charlie answered tersely.

"Thanks for picking up."

"What do you want? Very busy up here."

"Doing what?"

"Stewing, mostly. Also brooding and ruminating. I've got my hands full, clearly, so if you've got something to say, let's get on with it."

It stung Wren to hear her friend so angry at her. Their relationship had always been full of playful banter, teasing, and even bickering like an old married couple. But a full-on fight was a rarity for them.

"I'm outside your place, but I have something for you. A token of my apologies. Can you come down? I can't carry it up on my own." Wren feigned a pregnant, back-aching groan. Whatever it took to play on Charlie's sympathies.

Charlie huffed, sounding offended that Wren could even think to buy her off with a simple gift. But her curiosity got the better of her. "What is it?" she asked, failing miserably to disguise the hope and excitement in her voice.

"Come down and see."

Then Wren hung up. With the bait set, there was nothing more to say, and she knew Charlie wouldn't be able to resist. Sure enough, her friend soon appeared on the sidewalk, dressed casually in leggings and a tank top. Tristan was with her. That was also part of the plan and had been prearranged.

Charlie opened the passenger door. "This better be good. Our elevator is out so I try to limit my visits to the ground floor."

"Hi, Wren," Tristan waved from behind his fiancée, not even pretending to be angry on her behalf. "Heard you might need my brute strength." He jiggled his pecs through his shirt. He could do that. While Charlie scanned the interior of the car for the so-called present, Wren threw Tristan a wink, which he returned.

"I got you your favorite," Wren said, revealing a white cardboard box filled with fresh-baked cookies, whoopie pies, and glistening sticky buns.

Charlie tried to remain stoic, not showing her excitement.

"Are those"—she couldn't help but lick her lips to prevent visible drool—"from the Pennsylvania Dutch Market?"

"The one and only." Wren grinned. It wasn't too far from Arthur and Wren's place, despite the name, and it was always well worth the trip. "Why don't you grab one?"

Charlie eyeballed them, looked around as if this were some kind of illicit transaction, and took a hesitant step closer.

"That's it, come on. Just reach in and take whatever you'd like. Atta girl," Wren said, holding the box out a little, just out of reach of Charlie's fingertips.

"Is that a . . . red velvet whoopie pie?"

"You mean this, right here?" Wren picked it up, held it out, agonizingly close to Charlie, who was now bending down through the passenger doorway, reaching, ready to grab it. With her free hand, she made sure to angle her air conditioning vent Charlie's way, wafting the fresh bakery scent in that direction. With one more forward lean, Charlie's fingers grasped the dessert, and at that, Wren shouted, "Now!" On cue, Tristan gave Charlie the lightest of shoves from behind, sending her tumbling into the car, and he slammed the door behind her. In an instant, Wren peeled off, trapping her friend inside.

"Are you out of your mind?! You're kidnapping me?!" Charlie righted herself in the seat and, one hand occupied by the pastry, buckled herself in as Wren sliced through traffic.

"I needed to make sure you'd talk to me and really hear me out."

"Yeah, well, you don't deserve it. Where the hell were you yesterday?"

"I know. I'm so sorry I wasn't there to help with the cake." Then, tentatively: "How did it go?" Wren never really understood big, lavish weddings, but she knew enough to know that little things going wrong could pile up and become massively stressful for brides like Charlie. And she knew how important the cake was. It was the final event of the night, the grand finale, and a centerpiece of a lot of the best photos. Charlie, she was certain, cared desperately about the photos.

"The cake is whatever; I don't care about the cake."

"Then why are you so pissed?"

"Because I wanted to spend time with you! We've barely seen each other and you totally bailed on me."

Wren nodded. "I did, and I'm sorry. It's just . . . I spaced and got major pregnancy brain. I left my phone at home and completely lost track of time."

"Uh-huh." Charlie wasn't buying it.

"I know we said we wouldn't let this push us apart—"

"We're not growing apart because you're pregnant, Wren. We're growing apart because you're an asshole."

That stung, too. But, again, it was well deserved. Wren hadn't bailed because of a medical emergency, false labor, or feeling ill and exhausted. She'd bailed because she was too busy thinking about the bucket list, about cramming in as much as she could before the baby arrived. At the expense of the things that really mattered. That was not the kind of person she wanted to be. Not anymore.

"Well, I'm here now," Wren said, laying herself at the mercy of the court. "I screwed up but there's nothing more important in the entire world to me than a good hang with my best friend."

"Not important enough to ask for my consent first."

"I couldn't risk it."

Charlie sighed, then finally took a bite of the whoopie pie she'd been holding this whole time, which had begun to dissolve into her fingertips. "Fucking Mother of God," she moaned. “Those Amish don’t miss.” She devoured the entire thing seconds later.

“Now that I’m here, against my will,” she said as she swallowed the final bite, “where are you taking me?”

“You’ll see.”

“They say you should never allow yourself to be taken to a second location. If you don’t tell me, I’m gonna scream.”

Wren smirked. “Someplace we haven’t been in a long, long time.”

❑ ❑ ❑

Wren dragged her friend through the door of Walt’s Inn.

“Wren, stop, we’re too old for this,” Charlie whined.

The bar was like all of Baltimore’s best. Long, extremely narrow, and smelling of spilled Natty Boh and buffalo wings. It wasn’t much to look at, at all. But it was known as one of the best karaoke spots in the city. Not renowned for its flashy lighting or slick auto-tune, no. This was a place for the diehards who wanted to sing raw and loud.

Except this was a Tuesday afternoon and the place was empty except for one hardened, potentially toothless older man at the end of the bar downing pints.

“Exactly. We are most definitely too old for this,” Wren agreed. Karaoke at Walt’s was a staple of their nights out in college, but the tradition died out quickly after graduation. Of course there were the stubborn years, the two friends yawning as they pushed their way through the crowded bar and tried to pretend they weren’t too tired from work to party. But by twenty-five they had given up even pretending. It was a decision that Wren deeply regretted.

“So what are we doing here, then?” Charlie asked, leaning

against the bar. A bald, flannel-wearing bartender approached and gave a subtle flick of his head, *What can I get you?*

"Two seltzers with lime," Wren said. "And a microphone."

"Karaoke doesn't start until six," he reminded them.

"Buddy, I plan to be in my pajamas by then. Can't you make an exception?" She pushed her belly out for emphasis, as if it wasn't already obviously protruding enough.

The bartender smirked and nodded. He was way cooler than the skydiving guy.

"Wren," Charlie said, a reminder that she was still waiting on an answer: *What are we doing here?*

"Because I have not only diagnosed our problem; I have prescribed the solution: We need a little of the good old days," Wren said simply.

"The good old days . . ."

"When things weren't so complicated, and life wasn't always getting in the way."

The bartender returned with drinks and two microphones, flicking a few switches and powering on the karaoke setup at the front of the bar.

"So whadya say?" Wren asked, taking hold of one of the mics and offering it to Charlie.

"All right. We're here," Charlie said, reluctantly snatching the mic with a little less enthusiasm than Wren had hoped for. "What are we singing?"

"Oh, like you don't already know."

They told the bartender to cue up Ford the River's first big single, "17th Summer," and the regular at the end of the bar clapped politely at their enthusiastic off-key performance. The bar was still empty when they were done, so they followed it up with hits from Yellowcard, State Champs, Stand Atlantic, and Baltimore's own All Time Low.

OK, so Wren realized she wasn't exactly taking it easy. But she performed the last handful of songs while sitting on a stool, at least. She'd even switched from seltzer to regular water after the first drink. She was not only sitting, but hydrating. That was progress.

When they were finally breathless and parched, their throats shot and raw, they downed another round of seltzer waters and traded burps in a fit of giggles.

"So?" Wren said expectantly, when the laughter had finally died down.

"What?"

"You know what."

Charlie grabbed a handful of peanuts from a bowl on the bar that hadn't been cleaned since the nineties, a petri dish of disease, and began cracking open one of the nuts.

"If you're asking if I forgive you, the answer is yes."

Wren sighed a loud exhale of relief. "Good. So everything's back to the way it should be."

"Yeah," Charlie said, scratching her head now. "I guess it is. And that's kind of the problem."

"Problem?"

"Never mind." Charlie ate a peanut and set out on shelling the next one.

"Don't do that." Wren gave her a playful little shove. She hadn't come this far to not get everything out on the table.

"Don't you think our friendship has to evolve, Wren?" Charlie said, exasperated, as if she'd been holding this thought in for a long time and simply couldn't manage it anymore. "Nobody loves drunk karaoke, and watching trashy reality shows, and ribbing each other endlessly more than me."

"OK? So what's the problem?"

"I want there to be more to our friendship."

"There is more to our friendship." Wren couldn't believe what she was hearing. They were best friends. They told each other everything. When had that ever been in question? "And we're not even drunk! We're being extremely mature."

She held up her water, her plain water, as if it was proof.

Charlie could only sigh. *You don't get it.*

"And speaking of old times, I decided something," Wren said, improvising and determined to up the ante. "I am coming to the wedding, come hell or high water or newborn baby infant."

"Wren, you can't promise that."

"Yes, I can. I might go into labor at the reception, or if the baby comes sooner than that, I might show up in a wheelchair with my body beaten and battered to hell. But I will throw on a dress and show up for you. No matter what."

To Wren, this was an evolution. She was legendary for flaking on RSVPs, commitments, and pretty much anything planned in advance. A promise to show up was uncharted territory for her, especially with so many unknowns in the equation. It showed depth of character. It showed maturity.

"I don't know . . ." Charlie trailed off.

"Are you saying you won't have me?"

"Of course I'll have you, idiot," Charlie said. "I just need to call the caterer and save you a plate."

"Just one?"

"I'll see what I can do." Wren hugged her friend. Charlie was still a little stiff, but it felt so good to be reunited. "But there is one thing," Charlie said, pulling away suddenly. "There's been a slight change in plans. I literally just found out yesterday but, you know, I wasn't speaking to you."

"What is it?"

"Remember the original venue we wanted but couldn't get

because it was all booked up? Guess who had a last-minute cancellation—the event coordinator wasn't supposed to tell me but she let it slip that the bride and groom found out they were related, sooooo . . ."

"No way, you booked it?!" She didn't remember. Wren was sure they'd talked about it, but she couldn't recall. Pregnancy brain, surely. Or maybe this was exactly the kind of gap in their friendship Charlie was talking about.

"It's been a little insane, OK, completely bananas, trying to switch everything over at the last minute, but YES! It's like I always dreamed of. And I'm so excited you're going to be there to help us celebrate at the aquarium."

"Wow. How about that?" was all she could manage to say.

16

~~WREN~~ ARTHUR: *Survive the World's Scariest Haunted House*

ARTHUR HAD HALF HIS HAND inside the jar marked with a *W.* Wren's jar, full of all her hopes and dreams and greatest adventures yet to come.

It was so strange for her, watching him feel around in there. Those belonged to her! She felt incredibly apprehensive about what he might draw and how it might feel to watch him attempt something she had dreamed of for so many years. It was a little like the time he'd come out of the bathroom after a shower wearing her robe because all the towels were still in the wash. It felt wrong, but for some reason she couldn't peel her eyes away.

"You can't be serious," Arthur said after removing a new slip and reading it to himself. "Survive the World's Scariest Haunted House?"

"I remember that one!" she said. "I'd seen something on YouTube about this haunted house where the actors could grab you, throw you around, tie you up and put you in the trunk of a car, drive you across state lines. Basically do anything they wanted. You had to sign a waiver to get in."

"And this is . . . something you wanted to do?"

"Back then. I'm a horror buff, remember?" Arthur was decidedly not. He'd never been willing to watch the bloody slashers and borderline torture-porn movies she got such a kick out of, outside the one time he thought it might be a good idea to try to impress her early in their relationship. The vision of him peeking out at the "safe" scenes from between his fingers probably had not exactly been a turn-on, and she never forced him to try again. But whatever. He never saw the appeal in an adrenaline rush of fear or visceral disgust. Without anyone to share her dark, twisted side with over the years, it had atrophied into nothing more than a passing interest. Watching trailers for *Saw* movies and reading the occasional Stephen King. "But the place turned out to be just a thinly veiled excuse for the owner to torture people and he went to prison."

"Who could have possibly seen that coming?" Arthur replied. "So I guess this one is out."

"Unless . . ." Wren trailed off.

"No, no *unless*. Can we please not? I'll just pick something else."

"You said you'd do *anything*. You said you'd be me. You promised."

"But the place is closed! It's not my fault I'm getting off on a technicality!"

She didn't want to let him off that easy. And after just a little bit of googling, she was extremely pleased to find out that she wouldn't have to.

❑ ❑ ❑

"I'm starting to think this isn't a legally binding waiver," Arthur said.

They'd driven ninety minutes to the middle of who knows

nowhere Maryland to attend opening night for Vicious Asylum, the only haunted house attraction that would be open this early in the season.

A large man dressed in a slaughtered pig mask had just handed Arthur a sheet of very official-looking paper to sign. Upon closer review, it was all part of the act. "I hereby certify that I am a very brave boy" and that the entertainment company would not be liable for any "willies, heebie-jeebies, or soiled underwear." Arthur begrudgingly signed on the dotted line before the pig man violently ripped the pen out of his hands and roared a psychotic sort of wail directly in his face.

"How great is this?" Wren squealed, squeezing his arm with one hand. The other was cradling a very confused Ferdie, who'd come along for the ride as they waited in line with just a handful of other "victims," as the signage called them.

"I really don't get what you see in any of this," Arthur said. He looked up at the haunted house itself, designed to look like an abandoned hospital or an insane asylum. Strobe lights and smoke machines were doing a lot of the heavy lifting here in creating the supposed atmosphere. A few prop cadavers, gory-looking scarecrows, and spooky skeletons were scattered around as well.

"Too scary for you?"

"No," he said. "Just a little campy. That's what I've been trying to explain to you. It's not that I find horror frightening; I just find it gross and cheesy."

"OK." She laughed. "Keep that energy up. I saw some of the clips from inside and I think you'll be changing your tune shortly."

They reached the front of the line. This would be Wren's last stop. In her condition, going into the attraction would be too dangerous. Tripping hazards, jump scares. They couldn't risk it. Surprisingly, she took the news well.

"Waiva'?" a bloody bride with a cleaver stuck in her head said, speaking in an old cockney accent for some reason. Arthur handed over the paper. "If you find y' pissin' yourself and want out, just say the safe word," she said, fastening a red wristband on his outstretched arm.

"Which is?"

"Tortellini."

He laughed. "OK, now you're just making me hungry."

Wren gave him a kiss on the cheek. "Good luck. I'll see you on the other side . . . hopefully." She threw in a spooky ghost noise for good measure, *OoooOOooo*.

"I think I'll be OK." He smirked.

He walked through a cloud of smoke hanging in the entryway and found himself in a dimly lit hallway, all black lights and bloody streaks on the walls. He now, finally, allowed his bravado to fall away. And he promptly, and quietly, freaked the absolute fuck out.

"*Fuckfuckfuck*," he whispered to no one. He was scared shitless. No, what was worse than that? He was petrified. Could barely move. His legs were frozen in place. This was an actual, literal nightmare. He was a man who feared rejection, failure, and the slightest intuition that someone might be mad at him. Being hunted by a machete-wielding psychopath was more than his heart could possibly handle.

The worst part was, there was something he hadn't told Wren: He had stacked the deck in his favor in order to end up here. He had chosen this. He had cheated.

The thing with Wren was that she wasn't a reasonable person. So when he went through her jar in secret after she'd fallen asleep the other night, he knew he would have no way out if he picked Get My Nose Pierced, Run a Red Light in Broad Daylight, Hold a Live Tarantula, or any of the extremely dangerous and expensive ones: Swim with Sharks, Go Cave Diving, Get My Pilot's License.

There was a way to push himself out of his comfort zone and grow as a person and nurture his sense of adventure and spontaneity without dying, altering his appearance, or giving himself PTSD for life. (The tarantula, in particular, was a hard no.)

So he took a few—just a piddly few—slips out of the jar. He hid them deep inside his GRE study book, a brand-new addition to the house, which he had recently and quite conveniently placed on his nightstand.

Going through a haunted house *at the time* didn't sound so bad, in comparison to some of the others, so he decided that one could stay. He realized only now what a colossal mistake that had been. He hadn't expected it to be quite so haunted.

He tried hyperventilating, drawing quick, shallow breaths and rapidly blowing them out. It didn't help. Then he tried slowing his breathing down, taking in a big, slow lungful of air, holding it, then gently releasing it. OK, better. His legs released, though they were still stiff and wobbly. He took just one step forward. OK. Progress.

That's when a grimy hand shot through rusty bars in the wall—a doorway, as if to a prison cell—with frightening suddenness. Arthur dodged the hand, then peered into the cell and found a cackling, half-strait-jacketed patient grinning at him.

"Hey, pal," Arthur offered. "If you could tell me the fastest way out of here, that'd be super awesome."

He was not going to use the safe word. He'd die of a heart

attack in here before doing that, and there was a good chance he might just do that. He'd never live it down with Wren if he ran out of here like a chicken. He was supposed to be New Arthur. Not afraid of anything at all. Living in the moment. New Arthur should be having a grand old time hanging out in a blood-soaked hallway with scratchy, old-timey music playing over crackly speakers.

The actor in the cell beckoned Arthur to come closer with a curled finger.

"I'm good. I can actually hear you perfectly from here. Any tips or secret shortcuts you can share?"

Maybe there was some way to appeal to the actor's humanity to get him to break character. Any advice on how to avoid the jump scares and take the fastest possible route to the exit would be greatly appreciated.

Another *come hither* from the mental patient. Arthur took a hesitant step toward the bars, and that's when the actor lunged at them, grabbing them with both hands and cackling in Arthur's face. He took a quick step backward and nearly fell over.

"My fault. That's my fault," Arthur said after regaining his breath and soul, both of which had briefly exited his body. "Should have definitely seen that coming."

He continued down the hallway. There were more cells like the first one, hands jabbing out at him, shrieking laughter emanating as he slinked along. For now, he ignored them as best he could. At the end of the hall was a cell slightly different from the others. Darker. The lights barely reaching. And it was fully barred, like a jail, with a figure standing inside.

Arthur was shaking. Scared out of his goddamn mind. Intuitively, he knew he was in no real danger. The actors were all teens and aspiring thespians from the nearest small town, not demented serial killers. But his body was fully immersed in the experience, screaming at him to run. He tried to steady his hands and voice as he approached. What was he even doing here? How did he get from wanting to take more chances in his life to signing his physical rights away to some carnival freaks? He just wanted this to be over, for Christ's sake.

"Hello," a little girl's voice echoed out from the cage.

"Goddamn it," Arthur said.

The figure, the girl, stepped into the light. She was dressed in a sepia-tone dress, with makeup to match, looking like she had just been plucked from Pilgrim times. The woman wore her hair in pigtails and skipped closer to the bars.

"Will you please play with me?"

"Hi, whoever you really are, I want to talk to the human being. Is that OK? Can we have a conversation?"

The woman, playing the role of psychotic little girl, stared at him blankly. Then she began to cry.

"Why won't you play with me?"

"No, shh." Arthur tried soothing her. "Don't cry. Listen, I just . . . I have to get out of here. Do I just keep going this way?" He pointed down the hallway, which curved to the right. "Is there a drooling clown or something waiting to jump out at me over there? Just tell me."

The little girl woman sobbed and sobbed until finally she took a deep breath and opened her mouth to scream: "DADDY!!"

"Daddy?" He didn't know who Daddy was, and he definitely didn't want to find out.

Arthur followed her eyeline. Behind him, where he'd just come from moments ago, was a towering, terrifying figure, illuminated from behind by a flickering strobe. It had to be ten feet tall, whatever it was, and without any warning at all, it was coming toward him, lumbering and skittering across the floor like a giant alien spider, all gangly legs and unnatural, jerky movements.

"Nononononono." He scrambled, losing his footing, hurrying down the hallway, wherever it led, freaky clown be damned. He had to get away from the thing. One look back and all was revealed as the creature stepped into the light: a psycho mime on stilts, holding an ax. Its eyes glowed red, fixated on him and only him.

Arthur ran. Yeah, he saw the signs: NO RUNNING. But, respectfully, fuck that.

He should have held the goddamn tarantula. He should have run the red light. Jail would be better than this.

What was he supposed to do with this mutated giraffe-like apparition bearing down on him, ready to swing his terrible ax? *It's an illusion, it's all an act*, he tried to remind himself. If the horrible mime caught up with him, the actor would let out a terrible scream to maximize the scare and then scurry away into the shadows. He couldn't really hurt him. Could he? Arthur hadn't really read the waiver carefully. What had he unwittingly consented to? No, this wasn't that kind of place. He would be fine.

Except Arthur's poor, trembling body wasn't buying it.

Arthur ran and ran. Soon he entered a new room. Strange shadows danced along the walls, coming from slow swaying objects all over. It was a meat locker, great slabs of meat hanging from gruesome hooks. Plastic? Rubber? Surely, not real. Right? They did seem a little moist, a little too sticky. Arthur didn't stick around to find out what the slabs were made of. He ran through the gauntlet of dead cows like the football players running drills at training camp when Wren forced him to watch *Hard Knocks*. He just had to get through to the other side and he'd be free of the creature, still shrieking out horrifying hisses and squawks in the darkness behind him.

Running full speed now, he collided with a slab of beef and fell to the floor. His hands and knees stung like fire. But something was hot on his tail, so he peeled himself back onto his feet and examined the wounds. A bright white substance, illuminated by the black light, was covering his hands. Blood. Oh God. He was bleeding. He absolutely had to get out of here. Seek medical attention before he fainted in this hideous place.

But first to find an employee. (Not the stilts mime. No, anyone but him.)

Arthur staggered forward and found himself in a new room.

"Oh good," he said, staring into a hall of mirrors. The octagon-shaped room loomed before him, tricking his eyes almost immediately. It was impossible to see the path forward. He would have to use his hands to feel it out.

Suddenly, there was a brutalized ballerina dancing in one of the reflections. She performed perfectly haunting pirouettes, her slashed and bloodied leotard flashing across each of the mirrors.

Arthur really, really did not want to go in there.

But the only way out was through.

He followed the dancing specter. "Ma'am!" he cried. But she spun away, and he smacked his nose on one of the mirrors.

"Miss, I'm hurt," he cried. He couldn't see her anymore. She'd disappeared. He picked a direction and walked. BONK! That was a mirror. He tried another. BONK! His nose stung, eyes watering. In the warped reflection and the flickering lights it was impossible to tell, but he worried it might be broken, his body bleeding in several different locations now.

Grainy music-box music played over the speakers, some haunted circus tune. He tried another path. BONK!

It was then that Arthur sat down on the ground, examined his bleeding hands one more time, stinging like fire, and curled up into the fetal position.

He suddenly found himself envious of Dorothy from *The Wizard of Oz*. *There's no place like home, there's no place like home*, he repeated in his head, even clicking his heels once or twice just for good measure. But nothing happened. The chilling music didn't stop, and he was not lucky enough to open his eyes and find himself in his own bed. He'd have even settled for a random farmhouse in Kansas.

Without warning, the ballerina was standing over him. He looked at her. She stared back, emotionless. Like a dead person. He opened his mouth to speak, ready to forfeit, but . . .

What was the goddamn safe word?

"Fettucine," he said.

She blinked at him.

"Rigatoni?"

Nothing. She opened her mouth and bared her teeth, including razor-sharp fangs. She was a vampire. Of course she was.

"Spaghetti?! I don't know, I can't remember the safe word, I just want to get out of here!!"

She leaned in as if to bite his neck and transfer the eternal curse, when he finally remembered the safe word, coming to him as if delivered directly from the pages of an Olive Garden menu, divined by the Gods of Italian Pasta. They were here to save him. *Tortellini*.

But he wasn't going to say it.

No. He had a choice, and he was going to make the right one for once. It was as if he suddenly remembered that he was not a frightened little boy. He was practically someone's father, for crying out loud. And this pathetic display would just not do.

He had a vision of crossing the road, a tiny person holding his hand and trusting him implicitly to lead the way safely. Trust *him* with their life, the grown adult male child currently crying about a few raspberries on his palm.

What if his son or daughter inherited Wren's unfortunate love of all things gruesome and horrific? What if they were holding his hand right now, clinging to him with their eyes closed with full faith that he would guide them out safely? He could not be curled up in a shivering little ball on the floor. He had to be stronger than that.

Arthur found the strength to climb to his feet. The ballerina hissed in his face, threatening him with her fangs again. But he felt very much like Neo when he was finally able to read the source code of the Matrix. It didn't scare him anymore. He could see the flaking makeup on the edges of the girl's face, the little gap between the prosthetic fangs and her regular teeth. He could hear a hint of that townie twang in her growled threats. The illusion was crumbling before his eyes.

"No," he said simply.

She stopped. Taken aback at his subtle breaking of the fourth wall, his shattering of the illusion. "No?"

"Just no." He dusted himself off and walked calmly past the bewildered ballerina, staggered his way through the rotating vortex tunnel of doom, gently stiff-armed a demented granny holding a butcher knife, and made his way to the door clearly marked EXIT.

But. There was one final trial, and it was a doozy. Someone had strung a gob of spiderwebbing across the hallway leading to the door and dotted it with fake rubber spiders. Arthur examined it and realized there was no way under or around, by design. He'd have to walk through. And if there was anything he hated more than clowns and mimes, it was spiders. Their webs, in particular. The unsettling tickle of feeling it on your body and not being able to see it, the frantic pulling and swiping and swatting of trying to get it off before the spider at the end of it grabbed hold of you and sank its fangs in, or laid its eggs in your ear canal. The humiliation of knowing you looked like an absolute loon to anyone watching you struggle and flail.

It was why he often walked with his arms stretched out in front of him, swirling them in a circle, or batted at the air with a stick when strolling in nature. It was why he only took the well-traveled paths and never strayed where someone hadn't gone before him to clear out all the spiders.

It was all fake, but his heart pounded the same, anticipating the feeling: a caught fly waiting for the slow, painful end to come.

He took a deep breath. Speed would be his best friend. One quick go, no stopping or looking back, and he would be free.

One . . . *Ew, it really was gross, shiny . . . Was the web somehow wet? Never mind.* Two . . . *Was there any chance that it was a real spiderweb, or that real spiders had perhaps found the fake webbing really enticing and taken up residence? Possible, but not likely.* Three . . . *It would be wise to take a few more seconds to analyze the situation, count to five instead.*

But another group was coming, and Arthur couldn't risk the humiliation, so he dropped into a sprinting stance and lunged.

❑ ❑ ❑

When he finally stepped out into the dewy evening air, it felt cool; well, cooler than it had been inside the poorly ventilated attraction. And whether he was cool, hot, sweaty, or covered in strands of stretched cotton didn't really matter. He was alive, in one piece, and he hadn't caved in to his fear. That was what really mattered.

Wren was waiting for him at the exit when he got out.

"So, how was—" He didn't let her finish before pulling her toward him, running the fingers of one hand up the back of her neck and firmly into her hair, and kissing her deeply. It was the adrenaline, he knew. His skin felt tingly and sensitive to every touch, and he felt this overwhelming joy to see Wren again, to be here with her in this moment, and at the fact that she was his. He just had to let her know.

"*Whoa*," was all she could say when he finally let her go.

"Sorry."

"It was a good *whoa*."

"Oh." He smiled. "Cool."

"I heard a little girl screaming in there and worried it might be you," she said. "I know you don't handle it well when teens are mean to you."

He'd be lying if he said he hadn't been worried about that, about being designated one of the "weak ones" and getting extra, unwanted attention from the performers. Or worse, having some brutish farm boy make an example out of him to score points with Wren. He worried about falling and breaking a limb, passing out, and getting maimed by a prop gone wrong and lying there in a pool of his own blood, incoming groups stepping over him thinking he was part of the scenery.

He'd worried about all of that, and he went anyway. And better yet, he had actually made it out.

"It wasn't as scary as I thought," he said. "I did get a little scraped up, though."

He'd forgotten about his hands until now. They still stung and were probably bleeding profusely at this point. He held them up to the beams coming from a nearby floodlight, bracing himself for the worst. But there was no blood. Barely even a scratch. Just dust. Dust from the floor. In the black light, it had looked like a massacre. Turned out it was nothing at all. He couldn't help but laugh.

"What's so funny?" Wren said.

"Me," he said. That was the only way he could explain it.

"OK." She side-eyed him. "Well, meanwhile, I've been holding in the world's largest pee because I didn't want to miss you."

"Go ahead," he said. "I'll wait for you by the gallows."

Wren hurried off toward the port-a-potties and Arthur stood there, still basking. The adrenaline was wearing off, but even with its edge taken off, he felt amazing. Like he could do anything.

For some reason, he thought of the house, the Needle. Maybe it was because Wren had called it a torture dungeon. Or was it a sex dungeon? And he'd just walked out of an *actual* house of terror and found it wasn't nearly as bad as he'd built it up to be in his mind. So what was he really so afraid of? He could do the work and get the house ready for their family, all on a shoestring budget. He wasn't all that handy, and definitely not experienced, but that's what YouTube was for. It's what his dad would have done. It's what his dad *did* do. He renovated their entire house as a wiry little twentysomething, with nothing but a few library books and some hand-me-down tools. If he could do it, Arthur could do it. What's the worst that could happen? He'd been searching for meaning, for purpose, for feeling like he was somebody for a change. Maybe this was what he had been looking for all along.

Wren could be upset; that could happen. But he'd offered her the chance to show him her vision for their life and family, and so far she'd done nothing. Not a speck of research or even sending a single listing his way to look at. Not that he could blame her. She was busy growing a human. He couldn't exactly relate, but it was probably a lot to deal with. Linda Kellerman was right. Wren didn't have the bandwidth to take this on, and it was his job, his responsibility, to make this decision for them. He wasn't afraid of that responsibility anymore.

He checked that the coast was clear, pulled out his phone, and called Linda. She answered quickly.

"Arthur! Are you finally ready to make a deal?"

"Better late than never," he said. "Right?"

17

~~ARTHUR~~ WREN: *Stay in Bed All Day*

WREN WOKE THE NEXT DAY and gently opened her eyes to find Arthur staring at her.

"Hi," she said groggily.

"Hi," he said, smiling. He was lying there in his usual spot with a gentle hand on her belly. He looked like he'd been up for a while.

"Why are you looking at me like that? It's frightening."

"I don't know," he said. "Just pumped to be awake and lying next to you. I take one page out of your book and it's like I have a new lease on life. Is this how you feel all the time?"

She slowly propped herself up. *Do I look like that's how I feel?* she thought. His cheeriness was really grating, especially when she felt like such crap. They'd really been pushing it lately and she was utterly exhausted. Apparently even just watching Arthur do things, and singing while sitting on a stool, was pushing it now. Turns out you can only pretend you're not eight-and-change months pregnant for so long before reality becomes undeniable, like Wile E. Coyote running off a cliff . . . You know the second he looks down, he's going to fall. And she was currently falling. Her feet hurt, her muscles were sore, her back was screaming. And Arthur was all sunshine and rainbows.

"No."

"How did you sleep?" he asked.

"Terrible." She'd been waking up a lot during the night, which was strange. She used to sleep like a log. Her legs always seemed to be restless and it was hard to find a position that was comfortable for more than a few minutes at a time, squishy C-shaped pillow be damned. "You?"

"A little weird. Had some pretty bizarre dreams if I'm being honest. The freaky mime on stilts was there, but, like, he was my mom? I don't know how to explain it."

"You're so chatty," she said. It would be really, really great if she could have a coffee right about now. But truth be told, she was proud of Arthur for facing one of his greatest fears. And since he did so well, that would make it her turn to do the same.

She groaned at the thought of doing anything. Anything at all. But Arthur was grinning at her like an idiot. And that's when she put it together.

"You're holding the jar, aren't you?" she asked.

He smiled even bigger and whipped it out from under the covers, the jar that is, the one with the *A*, and held it out for her.

"You get to be me today," he said. "How fun is that?"

"All right," she said, mentally preparing herself. "Might as well get this over with." She just knew the challenge was going to be Prepare and File My Own Taxes or Learn How to Tie a Bow Tie.

She reached into the jar, which was getting considerably less full these days, and felt around. There were fewer slips than before, but still several left. Still so much to do. They hadn't made that much progress after all, and they were nearly out of time.

Without any drama or showmanship, she pulled one out and read it to herself.

Oh no.

She didn't feel like doing anything, but she also didn't feel like doing nothing, and that's what this was. She'd rather work on their taxes. She'd rather spend the whole day touring cookie-cutter suburban McMansions. She'd rather spend the day studying wealth-building strategies and comparing the long-term performance of different stock portfolios. Literally anything would be better than this.

"Come on, let's see it," Arthur said, craning his neck. She sighed and flipped it around so he could read.

"Yes!" he shouted. "This is going to be amazing."

No, this was going to be a nightmare.

❑ ❑ ❑

Years ago, on lazy mornings in his dorm room, Wren would hear Arthur pacing around the room fully dressed, zipping and unzipping his backpack, aimlessly shuffling the contents inside as he got ready for the day's classes. She wasn't stupid. She knew it was all a performance, meant to make just enough noise to rouse Wren from her slumber. She would be tucked under the covers like a lump of mashed potatoes and he'd be eager to start the day; that was their natural state. But she would play along by poking a single squinting eyeball out of the bedding, as if she hadn't been listening the whole time. And he'd come over and apologize: "Oh gosh, did I wake you? I'm sorry."

She'd grumble and bury her head in the covers. And he'd

say, "Since you're up, we've really got to get to class." She'd pretend to ignore him, or that she'd fallen back asleep. And she'd wait until he got closer to check on her, and when he was close enough she'd reach out and grab for him like a monster, pulling him into the bed, trying to trap him under the covers. And he would try to escape, but not that hard.

She'd nuzzle and kiss him and say, "I wish we could stay in bed together all day."

But that was then. When she was younger and had all the time in the world. Now the clock was ticking on her freedom, her life. And sitting around doing nothing with it was the absolute last thing she wanted to do.

But she had brought this on herself. She had wondered aloud why she couldn't be satisfied just spending time with Arthur and Ferdie, and now that's exactly what she was going to get, in the most highly concentrated version possible. Since it was her own karmic fault, she had to give it an honest effort. Arthur went face-to-face with a vampire ballerina for her. The least she could do was lie here and try to relax.

❑ ❑ ❑

"Uh-oh," Wren said.

"What's wrong?" Arthur said, barely looking up from his book. They'd been lying there for an hour already, he absorbed in a book—*The Happiest Baby on the Block*—and she doom-scrolling. It was like the social media algorithms knew what was happening to her. Through no fault of her own she was being bombarded with content from the crunchy moms, the child psychologists, the pediatricians. It was barely 10:00 a.m. and she'd already been accused of ruining her unborn child's life in numerous ways. The sudden tingle in her bladder was a welcome excuse to get up and move around.

"I think I have to pee."

"OK?"

"How does that work?" she asked.

Arthur blinked. "You usually start by sitting on the toilet."

She slugged him playfully. "How can I pee if we're supposed to stay in bed all day?"

Arthur laughed and doubled over, burying his face in the covers.

"I'm serious!" she said. If she was going to play, she was going to play by the rules.

"We're allowed bathroom breaks, obviously," he said, coming up for air.

"Come on, that's weak. Where's your commitment?"

"My commitment stops well short of a pee-soaked mattress. Just go!"

Wren scanned the room as if hoping an answer would appear.

"What if . . ." she started, a nugget of an idea forming in real time, "we can't touch the floor?"

"Like Floor Is Lava."

"Exactly." She hadn't had much of a childhood to speak of, but even *she* had played Floor Is Lava. She'd played with her brothers, when they all still lived together, and was known for her ability to balance on just about anything, including her now legendary tightrope walk along the length of an extension cord running through the living room. That one had earned her a spontaneous round of applause.

He threw up his hands. "If you want to go for it, I support you."

"Good. Give me your pillow."

"What—" He yelped as Wren yanked his pillow out from under him, causing him to bump his head on the headboard.

"Sorry," she said. "All for the cause."

"What are you doing?"

She dropped Arthur's pillow on the floor, close to the bed. Then she took her own and tossed it a few feet farther. From there, it was a couple more feet to the edge of the bedroom carpet, the threshold where the scuffed hardwood began, and a few more feet from there to the bathroom door.

"Here goes nothing," she said, taking a deep breath, taking the first step onto Arthur's pillow.

"You are so extra."

An extra-long lunge got her to the next pillow, where she stood and steadied herself. She turned around to grab the first pillow again, to build a stepping-stone bridge as she walked across it, but she had misjudged her first stride. It was too far. She wouldn't be able to reach that first pillow again without stepping onto the carpet. Wren squatted down and reached as far as she could and nearly toppled over in the process.

"Having trouble, dear?" Arthur mocked.

"Throw me your other pillow."

She held out a hand, waiting for her supplies to arrive, but instead, a pair of balled-up socks whizzed through the air and clonked her in the head. She nearly lost her balance then and there. It was a direct hit.

"What the hell?" Wren looked up. "Ew, and these are dirty! You're disgusting."

He whizzed another sock ball at her. Wren just barely ducked, nearly losing her balance again.

"I'd hate for you to fall in the lava," he said. "Anything I can do to help?"

And that's when he chucked a pair of boxers at her, which landed on her face.

"Underwear?! Too far, Arthur, too far." She flung them off. "Seriously, I'm about to soak the carpet if you don't toss me something I can use!"

"Good! Maybe it'll kill the roaches."

"Gross." She retched.

Arthur floated a T-shirt into the air, tossing it like a Frisbee, and it landed over her like a blanket. "ARTHUR!"

When she could see again, Arthur had positioned himself in front of her, kneeling on the pillow closest to hers. They looked into each other's eyes, both unsure of the next move, and both burst into laughter.

"Hey," Wren said, "catch me." She sat up on her knees and fell toward him, hands outstretched in front of her. He did the same. They met in the middle, holding each other up like a human tepee. They tried to kiss, but their balance failed, and they toppled over onto the carpet laughing.

"We didn't last five minutes," Arthur said after the laughter had died down, both lying on their backs watching the ceiling fan spin.

"I have an idea," Wren said. "Since we're both here. Let's call it a mulligan. We'll take two minutes. I'll pee, you grab all the supplies you think we'll need, then we meet back in bed. Deal?"

"What kind of supplies—"

"Go!" Wren looked at the alarm clock: 10:04. "Ten-oh-six and not a minute later!"

Wren sought the sweet relief of the bathroom. Arthur slipped and slid his way to the kitchen in his socks, rooting through the pantry like a madman. Mere seconds before the deadline, they both dove back into the bed.

"We did it!" Wren yelled triumphantly.

"We? All you did was go to the bathroom. I was the one collecting rations to get us through the day."

"What did you get?"

Arthur unfolded a ratty kitchen towel and revealed a treasure trove of snacks inside. Peanut butter crackers, a pack of Pop-Tarts, a lone banana, two bottles of water, a wrinkled protein bar, and a tub of room-temperature mayonnaise.

"Mayo?"

"I don't know. I was just grabbing stuff. We can toss this."

"I didn't say toss it."

Arthur began ripping into the pack of Pop-Tarts. "Are you sure we can do this? We still have like twelve hours left until we usually go to bed."

Wren kicked back with the peanut butter crackers and grabbed the TV remote off her bedside table.

"My love," she said, "this is why they invented Netflix."

❑ ❑ ❑

Eight episodes of *Cake Island* later, they were in the exact same place. And all the food was gone. Wren had even dared to eat a fingerful of mayonnaise and then gone back for another.

"Can we take a break?" Arthur said. "My eyes hurt."

Wren flipped back to the Netflix home screen. "I feel so much stupider now. It rules."

Seven straight hours of watching attractive bakers make complicated confections while simultaneously wooing and backstabbing one another had made her feel a few IQ points lighter. And it was glorious.

"Stupid people are way happier, I've always said."

"So what now?" she said, laughing, stroking an extremely content Ferdie, who had curled into a little ball next to her, contouring himself perfectly to the shape of her body.

"I don't know. We just . . . hang out?"

"Hang . . . out?" Wren said, imitating a caveman. "What mean?"

"Make words," he said. "Talk."

They'd been in constant motion these past months, even going back to the night they found out they were pregnant. Wren had scrambled to pick up freelance work, they'd read books and made lists, picked out and assembled furniture. And then there'd been everything that came after the shower. The Ravens game and the house tours, the casino and the haunted house. There'd been almost no time to just sit and reflect. Sit and enjoy each other.

"This is nice," he said, finishing his thought out loud.

"Yeah, it is."

"It seems so silly and so simple, but this might really be the last time we get to do this."

"I thought babies were supposed to sleep all the time."

"They do. But not on your schedule. They're up and down again every couple of hours, all night long, to start."

Wren sat up dramatically, as if he'd just delivered breaking news. "And you didn't think to tell me this before we had sex?"

He playfully shoved her away. "I'm excited, though," Arthur said. "Are you?"

She was getting there.

"I keep thinking about a little human being that we made running in here to wake us up and tell us he had a bad dream and that he needs me to hold him," she said. In truth, she hadn't spent much time picturing what their life would look like. What their child would look like. It had seemed better to avoid it, just in case . . . But imagining it now was filling her with this incredibly glowing warmth.

"Or that he pooped the bed."

"Way to ruin it!" She slugged him playfully. She was usually the one who punctured moments with dark or sarcastic humor. She thought about how they were so different, and yet how alike they'd become. Intertwined, like the gnarled tails of a rat king. No, something cuter than that. Two vines growing so close together you could hardly tell where one ended and the other began. You couldn't pick two people who were more the opposite of each other than them, different worldviews, different personalities, different energy batteries. And yet somehow they were bringing all that together to build one life. It was fascinating.

"How's the book?" she asked, breaking the silence. Her eyes had spotted its worn pages sitting on the nightstand behind him. "Is our baby the happiest yet?"

"Oh yeah. It's kicking the asses of all the other babies on the block." Then: "I know I should be studying, but I needed a little break."

He'd been poring through it lately, making good progress. It felt good to be taking action, but it was keeping him up at night, that book, and he really should be banking sleep before the baby came. How could anyone be expected to do it all at once?

"You're really going to do it now, aren't you? The GREs? Grad school?"

"It's looking like it," he said.

He was stroking her foot with his, rough calluses on his feet and all. It tickled.

"What were your parents like when you were a kid?" Wren asked suddenly.

"What do you mean?"

"Did they have a parenting style, you think? You know, like monkey style or dragon?" She mimed a karate chop and a high kick that wasn't very high, stifled by the covers. "You turned out sort of OK, I guess. I want to know how they did it."

"Wow, thanks." He reached over and gave her a playful tap on the arm. "I guess I would call them *authoritarian* if I'm remembering the term right—I feel like I'm being quizzed on my reading right now, wow. That was probably a cutting-edge word then. They were loving but not particularly affectionate. Very heavy on teaching and setting a good example, very demanding. They had firm boundaries, followed through on consequences, which could be severe at times."

"Authoritarian." Wren frowned. "What's the one where you just let them do whatever they want and you shower them with affection?" she asked.

"I think that's called lazy."

"Whatever. Boundaries and consequences are gross. I just hope they like me," Wren said.

"Me too. But they have to respect you, too. It's a tough balance."

"Eh." She shrugged. "Respect is overrated. If we like each other and we're honest with each other I think everything will work out just fine."

"OK." Arthur paused. "Here's a hypothetical. Baby's old enough to sleep in a crib, in his own room, but he won't stop crying—"

"Irrelevant. He can sleep with us forever," Wren cut in. "I would literally love that."

"Forever?"

"Forever!"

"Doesn't it get weird at a certain age?" Arthur protested. "Also, I like to stretch out."

"Families in other countries share beds all the time! It's only weird because America is filled with uptight prudes."

It occurred to Wren that this would have been a good conversation to have roughly seven years ago, before moving in together. But when were people meant to talk about this stuff, if not too late? Maybe it should be mandatory after the first time you slept with someone, she figured, just in case. *That was fun, and also what are your thoughts on gentle parenting?*

"I like that we're different," Wren said, as if cutting off her own internal argument. "It's what makes us a good team."

"You do?"

"Yeah. Don't you? You can be the cold, distant one who drives them into my warm, unconditionally loving arms. Yin and yang."

"I am not cold and distant."

"I'm just teasing," she said. "You're going to be amazing."

"I hope you're right," he said. "And so are you."

Another lull. They stared googly at each other in the complete dead silence of their bedroom. Somewhere in the background, Netflix wanted to know if they were still watching.

"Hey, so I wanted to talk to you about something," she said suddenly and without warning.

"Me too, actually."

"Really?"

"Yeah. I keep waiting for the right opportunity," Arthur said. "It's about the house."

"Oh, so is mine," she said. "I guess I'll go first."

He nodded, as if offering her the floor.

"I know how excited you were about that house, or the

idea of that house anyway, and how I kind of crapped on it. But I don't think I did a good job explaining why."

"Oh. OK. I'm listening."

"I think I'm . . . afraid of who we'll become if we live in a place like that."

"I know," he said. "You don't want us to become obnoxious HOA people. I get it."

"Not just that. We'll never discover anything new there. We won't find new coffee shops; we'll just go to Starbucks. We'll buy everything we need from Target and Amazon Prime. Go to the same park every weekend. Take trips to the same beach the same week as all our neighbors. I feel like I could map out the next thirty years of our lives and tell you every single thing that will happen."

"I've never thought about it like that," he said.

"Oh," Wren added. "And I'm afraid we'll become Republicans."

"We would never."

"It's happened to better people than us."

Arthur said nothing, his face falling into that blank, slightly serious expression that betrayed nothing except for the fact there was something to betray.

"What is it?" she asked.

"Nothing. It's just . . . you're sure I can't change your mind? What if I promise we can do all our shopping at Trader Joe's? Screw the kids, you never have to join the PTA. We'll drive forty-five minutes so we can buy Fair Trade coffee from local cafés. Whadya say?"

She rolled her eyes at him. "You're making fun of me."

"What I mean is . . . we'll keep it interesting, I promise," he said, squeezing her hand now.

"It's not even really that." She sighed. "It's that I know there will always be a next thing, you know? We'll be house poor, scrimping and saving everything we can to make the mortgage, then for college, and then retirement. I'm afraid it'll never end."

"And we'll forget to actually . . . live."

"Exactly," she said.

Arthur considered this, his face still serious, unreadable.

"I'm with you," he said finally. "But there's just one thing."

Her heart skipped a beat then. The expression on his face was not one that usually came bearing good news.

"In a few years, I do want to start saving . . . for my funeral. I have big plans."

A big grin spread across his face. She gave him a gentle knee to the midsection. The jerk.

"We'll invite all our friends," he said.

"Both of them?"

"Shut up. There'll be an open bar, obviously. And not at the reception, I'm talking in the graveyard. My coffin will be made of glass."

"Can we stop talking about this? You're never dying."

"I'm serious. If you want to be with me, you have to get on board."

"Fine. I assume you want to be buried in the finest suit money can buy?"

"No, nude."

She laughed, hard. The image was so utterly ridiculous it pushed out the horrific thoughts of Arthur being dead, sent them hurtling right out of her brain. When she finally regained her breath, she remembered.

"What were you going to say to me? You said you had something to tell me."

He smiled, leaned in, and kissed her on the nose. "It was nothing important."

Wren had half a mind to press him, but it was exactly at that moment that her stomach growled audibly. Even Ferdie jumped.

"OK, an update on the status of my various biological systems: I'm hungry."

"Really? I still don't think I've digested the Pop-Tarts from earlier. Probably because I haven't moved an inch."

She scooched closer, flashed him a devious grin.

"I can think of one way for you to work up an appetite."

"Oh?"

"But . . . we do have to break the rules a little bit."

❑ ❑ ❑

Wren screamed at him, "Pull! Pull! Harder, damn it!"

She had squeezed herself into the back seat of their car and was pressing the entirety of her weight down onto the Graco Lock-tite 4000 XL. It had taken an embarrassingly long time for the two of them to get it out of the box and attach the headrest and other soft covers, to thread the rage-inducing elastic straps through tiny holes that attached the cloth to the hard plastic.

Now was the final push to tighten the thing in place so they'd never have to do this again.

"It won't give! There's no more slack!"

Arthur was tugging on the strap with everything he had. It wouldn't budge a centimeter.

"If I push down on this seat any harder," Wren said, her voice strained, "this kid, and probably several different bodily fluids, are coming out. PULL."

He propped his feet up on the edge of the car and leaned his body completely backward. This was it. Every bit of weight and might and strength in his body flowed directly into the strap, until finally, he collapsed onto the pavement.

Wren contorted herself out of the car and stood next to him. He managed to climb to his feet, embarrassed by how heavily he was breathing.

"Did you ever figure out who gave us this stupid thing?"

"It's not stupid, it's a marvel of modern engineering. And, no, I asked around but no one seems to want to take credit."

"Well, moment of truth," Wren said. "Wanna give it a wiggle?"

"I'm afraid."

"Me too."

She made a religious crossing gesture as Arthur took a step forward and grabbed hold of the back of the car seat.

He gave it a push. He gave it a pull.

By God, it was secure. It didn't budge more than an inch.

"We did it!" he yelled. "Honestly, I can't believe it."

Wren dusted her hands off. *All in a day's work.* "Should have asked for my help earlier, jerk."

"Believe me, I've learned my lesson. I can't do it all on my own. In fact, I don't think I can do anything at all on my own. Hope you're OK with that."

"I'll allow it if you feed me in the next thirty seconds."

He wrapped his arm around her, pulled her close.

"I don't know. I'm still not that hungry."

"Still?"

"If only there were some other strenuous physical activity we could engage in."

She rolled her eyes. "Strenuous, huh? If either of us breaks a sweat, I owe you five dollars."

"So you're going to pay me to have sex with you? This is the best day ever."

She grabbed his hand and led him across the parking lot, back toward the apartment. He followed eagerly.

"You know, we technically failed," he said. "We got out of bed."

"I think we proved our point."

In the bedroom once again, they lit the dusty old sex candle that had been gathering cobwebs in the corner the last few months and climbed under the covers. They both laughed as they realized that it had been a while. A long while. And that a lot of the angles had changed since the last time. During one kiss, their teeth bumped together, creating a horrendous clicking sound. Wren whipped her bra off in what was supposed to be a sexy move and one of the metal clasps hit Arthur in the eye. Ferdie was staring at them from the corner, ghostlike, asleep with his eyes open, the entire time.

Eventually, they figured it out, and they wondered why they hadn't been doing this the whole time.

❑ ❑ ❑

Arthur was sound asleep at 5:03 p.m. Poor guy. Wren supposed he'd earned it. But, in typical fashion, she couldn't sleep. Far too uncomfortable. And now her thoughts were racing to boot.

Suddenly there seemed so much to do to get ready.

For starters, there was the bassinet she had picked out, still sitting there in the box. She'd heard the old joke about kids liking cardboard boxes more than the toys that came in them, but she figured the baby would probably appreciate it if she actually bothered to put the thing together.

"You want somewhere nice and cozy to sleep, don't you?" she asked her belly.

She smiled, and it occurred to her that she had never done that before, spoken to the baby. Arthur had done it here and there, and had mentioned to her that he'd read in a book that it was supposed to help lay the foundation for a strong bond. She'd read some message boards herself to confirm he wasn't making it up. He wasn't. All the expecting moms did it. There were apps and devices that helped you talk to the baby, recommended books to read them, lists of songs you could sing to them. There were even these ridiculous headphones you could attach to your belly. She had laughed them off at first, then thought that they might be a good way to start the little bugger's pop punk education early, and then looked at the price tag and laughed them off again.

The apartment suddenly felt so quiet. Like something, or someone, was missing.

"It's just you and me now, little nugget. If you want to come out soon, I think I'm ready to meet you." OK, her baby voice was a little bit too similar to her doggie voice, but it was a good start. "What does my womb look like, by the way? I hope it's nice in there. Kick twice if you could use more legroom."

She laughed. She liked this. She couldn't believe she hadn't been doing it the whole time.

It had been a good day. She'd done nothing at all, and it had been good. She didn't previously know that that was possible. Look at her. Sitting here being so responsible, so motherly. Not trying to skirt the rules of pregnancy, not trying to engage in any reckless behavior whatsoever. Just sitting quietly with her own thoughts, and with the baby, snapping the various metal and plastic pieces of the bassinet into its cushiony frame, and most shockingly of all, actually enjoying it. It was satisfying in a strange way, as the metal prongs popped into the holes that would hold them in place, and plastic fasteners clicked into their exact landing spot.

Was this what it would feel like to actually, well, be a grown-up? And if not be one, at least act like that? She was never going to get her childhood back, she realized in this moment. But she could create a good one, a really good one, as the mom she never really had.

Bassinet done. It was a little plain, a little flimsy, but a quick double check of the reviews and safety ratings confirmed it was good enough for now.

The next thing she needed was a go bag. Of course, Arthur had packed his a while ago, and she had put it off. Was there anything more fitting than that?

"Let's go look and see what we've got in the closet," she said to the baby, hoisting herself up off the floor by the edges of a doorframe. She shuffled around inside the master closet quietly until she found her old backpack from college. Ratty, dusty, empty except for a few crumpled papers. It would do.

She began stuffing it like a piñata, haphazardly throwing in a pair of leggings, some underwear, a spare phone charger, a small reading lamp that was out of batteries, a first-aid kit (as if they wouldn't already be at a hospital), a pack of gum.

She had no idea what she was doing. Yes, she could google it, but that was the answer to everything, wasn't it? Fucking google it, watch an influencer reel, read a thousand blog post checklists, skim a YouTube video. She ached in that moment for someone to call who could tell her, show her how this was supposed to be done.

She'd figure it out in the morning. For tonight, Wren was running out of gas. But there on the floor of the closet was . . .

something. A corner of the closet that had been converted into a graveyard of cough drop wrappers, loose change, and if you can believe it, even more outdated charging cables. Buried beyond that was a small bin of her old paints. It had been ages since she'd used them, and they were covered in dust bunnies. More importantly, there was one more thing that caught her eye, buried among the rubble. A small black velvet box that she hadn't seen in years. Wren didn't need to open it; she knew what was in there. But she did want to see it again. She grabbed it, flipped open the lid. The ring was still there, shiny as ever. Hardly ever touched by human hands.

When Arthur had asked her years ago, this tiny thing had filled her with terror. She knew that was not what an engagement was supposed to feel like. It was funny that he'd brought up dying, and his funeral. Because that's exactly what had been so scary. It was never that she wasn't sure he was "the one," whatever that meant, but she had learned early in her life that people sometimes disappeared, whether they wanted to or not. That was not something she ever wanted to go through again.

She was always the Girl Whose Parents Died. It followed her around like a brand for years, people walking on eggshells around her and treating her with kid gloves, for the most part. A few cruel kids used it as bullying fodder, but they were easily dealt with. (Step one: Apply one scoop of dirt taken from a fire ant hill to bully's backpack. Step two: Enjoy the show.) The large majority of everyone else looked at her like she was a fragile antique. Better to keep their distance, just in case. If Arthur got hit by a car or struck by lightning, she didn't think she could live with being the Widow. At least, if they weren't married, she could disappear and start over in the event of the unthinkable, take on an alter ego. Maybe become an international assassin, an exotic escort, or a mysterious railroad tycoon.

Keeping just that little bit of distance felt like a way to keep herself safe. And, until recently, she'd been doing it with the baby, too. Too scared to decorate, to give it a name, to get attached. The baby deserved better. And so did Arthur.

But back then, she'd felt she had no choice but to do the hardest thing she had ever done—she'd said no. She did love him, and she'd told him that, reminded him endlessly, and they'd worked through it. He never asked again.

But he did keep the ring.

Looking at it now, the teeny-tiny diamonds that Arthur had been able to afford at the time somehow still sparkling, Wren felt completely different about it. It was so cute, like a little bike with tassels and training wheels. Adorable. The kind of thing broke young kids who have nothing in their bank accounts but all the love and passion in the world buy. When she looked at it now she saw their family growing, their skin getting wrinkly, dull days full of laughter, hard days full of tears. She didn't want to put it back in its dark place. So she closed the lid, put the box in her go bag instead, and shut off the closet light.

18

"COME ON, LINDA. COME ON, Linda," Arthur grunted in hushed tones, standing out in the hallway of the apartment building so as not to wake Wren, building to a hoarse, frantic whisper-scream now: "Linda!!"

A door across the hall cracked open and an elderly woman looked out through the crack with a single eyeball, the knife she was wielding poking through just under the chain lock.

"For the last time, Mrs. Flynn. I live here. I've lived across from you for years. I help you carry in your groceries every week." No reaction. *Really?* Arthur thought. "I'm not here to rob you!"

The lady paused, then slowly closed the door without removing the suspicion from her face. Mrs. Flynn only ever seemed to recognize him when she needed assistance, and she was big on buying canned goods and jugs of water, as if the zombie apocalypse might occur before she keeled over from natural causes. Those grocery bags were never light. When she wasn't exploiting Arthur for manual labor, he got side-eye and the knife.

The phone kept ringing.

It had only been a few days, but it had all happened so fast with the house, the Needle. Almost immediately after his adrenaline-fueled call to Linda Kellerman, to his complete shock, the sellers had accepted his offer. Shock, because he'd gone in with a total lowball. It was almost insulting, really, how low the offer was. He briefly considered the seller—for some reason he imagined a silhouetted man in a suit like the Banker from *Deal or No Deal*—tracking him down to give him a gloved slap in the face for such a show of disrespect. In reality, the lower offer was a hedge. Though he was feeling confident the moment he made the call to Linda to put in the bid—he was still triumphantly covered in fake cobwebbing, after all—he figured it would probably get rejected and he could be proud of himself for making an attempt without having to suffer any real consequences.

Win-win. Sort of.

After his conversation with Wren the other night, though, the consequences were suddenly looming over him, and they were big and they were scary.

Once the offer was accepted, things moved even faster. Linda scheduled an inspection, which came back completely clean, and Arthur even agreed to a shortened due diligence period. Linda had thought it would make their offer more attractive, and she was right. For his part, Arthur was worried if he had too long to think it over, he'd end up backing out, like always. Ripping it off like a Band-Aid seemed like a good idea at the time.

The only problem was . . . he'd been thinking a lot about what Wren had said the other night. He didn't want to lie to her, hide this from her anymore, and most of all, make this huge life decision behind her back. She'd never forgive him for that. But more than anything, he'd been thinking that maybe she was actually right. In all his excitement to finally go after his dreams, he never stopped to consider that maybe he was going after the wrong one.

Worse still, his window to back out without losing a serious chunk of their, primarily his, savings was closing fast. He only had a few days to make up his mind.

And Linda Kellerman wasn't answering the phone.

He tried one more time, getting her annoyingly chipper voicemail once again. "Linda, it's Arthur. Please call me, OK? Please. ASAP. That's as soon as possible. If it's not too much trouble, of course. No worries if not. But please, soon. K. Bye."

❑ ❑ ❑

Over the last few days, Arthur and Wren had crammed a lot in. Slips of paper were crumpled on both their bedside tables, little balls of them lying around like they'd had an epic Chinese carryout feast and eaten their body weight in fortune cookies.

Arthur had ordered a Cameo video from blink-182's Tom DeLonge, in which Wren's childhood hero had discussed alien life forms and made dick jokes for forty-five seconds straight, all for the low, low price of ninety-five dollars. It was probably the closest they could realistically get to fulfilling her lifelong dream of meeting her idol. And at the behest of the jar, and with Wren creating an excellent "pregnant lady in distress" diversion, he'd snuck onto the set of an unknown movie filming near the Inner Harbor and tried to place himself in the shot, nearly falling into the murky water while staring at someone he swore was Scarlett Johansson. (It wasn't. But maybe it was.)

The jar had other plans for Wren. Indeed, she learned to

tie a bow tie. She'd said it had nothing on wearing heels in the misery department, but it had frustrated her to the point of hurtling the thing on the ground and trying to stomp it to death, like a venomous snake that had somehow fallen from the ceiling. In the end, it looked surprisingly adorable tied around her neck. She could have been the fifth member of Panic! At the Disco. Then she had concocted a frothy mixture in a jar called a "sourdough starter" and been extremely unsettled about the way Arthur talked about it, like a living thing, a pet. But she couldn't deny that the promise of fresh-baked bread literally at their fingertips was extremely enticing.

Arthur did a set of completely improvised stand-up comedy at a local open mic night. It consisted mostly of knock-knock jokes until he tried a little crowd work using burns he'd overheard from his students. The manager proudly told him it was the fastest he'd ever seen anyone get booed offstage.

Wren had read the entirety of *Moby Dick* in a single day—the audiobook, that is, set at 2.5× speed. When Arthur asked her what she thought of it, all she could say was, "The narrator was a little chipmunky for my taste."

All of that and the baby still wasn't here. Wren was beginning to get a little offended, like maybe she was doing something wrong. But Arthur assured her that she'd just made such a nice home for the little bugger that it didn't want to leave.

On the plus side, it meant they could definitely go to Charlie's wedding that weekend. Arthur wasn't necessarily looking forward to another visit to the aquarium, not after everything that had happened. He'd avoided it for years, even citing a made-up puffin allergy to get out of a school trip. But Wren needed to be there for her friend, and he needed to be there for Wren. That was the least he could do now. So that would be a promise kept.

Arthur slipped quietly back into bed, his heart still racing. Predictably, Wren stirred immediately, sensing his presence.

"Hi," she said groggily.

"Hi," he said, smiling.

She looked around with sleepy, squinty eyes and got her bearings.

"Where is it?"

She was looking for the jar.

"You're sure you want to keep going? Being me hasn't been too boring for you?" Arthur said.

"On the contrary," she said, sitting up. "I think me with a little bit of you is a perfect combination. And vice versa."

He had to agree. Being just a little bit more like Wren had done wonders for him so far. He was sleeping better, for a start, not waking up with new worries every couple of hours.

Well, at least it had worked for a while.

"If only there were some way we could take the best parts of both of us and combine them into one person. It'd be the coolest person ever," she joked.

"One of the great unsolved mysteries of science," he said, shaking his head.

She laughed and gave him a playful shove. He leaned down and gave her belly a good morning kiss, then leaned up and gave her mouth an even better one. "Sorry, morning breath," he said, pulling back. She'd always been sensitive to it, even more so during the pregnancy, once likening it to egg salad that had been pulled from the belly of a large tuna.

"Morning breath is a completely natural biological process, whereby saliva breaks down small food particles, which combined with dry mouth creates an unpleasant odor," she said in a nasal voice.

"Is that supposed to be what I would say? I don't sound like that. I'm not a . . . wordy scientist."

"What I'm trying to say," she said in her normal tone, "is give me one more. But no tongue."

He did as he was told.

"Now, are you ready for the jar?" she repeated.

He nodded. "On your nightstand. Behind the world's largest water bottle."

She'd recently bought herself one of those impossibly tall water bottles with lines marking how much she should drink by different points in the day. Drink half by noon, three quarters by dinner . . . He loved to see her well hydrated, but the damn thing never fit into any of their cupholders, and it was so imposing that Ferdie was legitimately frightened of it.

Sure enough, the jar was hiding behind the monstrosity.

"Only one left," Wren said, rattling it around in her hands. "No pressure or anything."

She was right. There was one lone slip of paper, folded awkwardly in not quite half, lying limply on the bottom of the glass jar. How had they gotten through so much of their lists? Where had this pregnancy gone? By in a flash was where.

Arthur reached his hand in, pulled it out, and looked.

"It's . . . blank."

"What? Let me see."

He handed it over. She stared at it in disbelief.

"Must be a leftover clipping from when you cut up the lists," Arthur said.

"But that can't be it," she said. "There was more. I know there was more."

"Like what?"

"I can't remember," she said, rubbing her temples. "My brain is completely giving out on me."

Arthur felt more than a little guilty about taking things out of the jar without telling her, but not just because of the disappointment on her face. He was beginning to feel like he'd robbed himself of a chance to really grow and challenge who he thought he was. But it was too late to go back now, to admit to rigging the game, to fly to Hawaii and book a little swim with hammerheads. It was time for this to be over.

But Wren, for her part, looked like she was about to cry. This was not the triumphant moment he had imagined when they'd started on this journey. No bugles and confetti and drop-down banners. *Anticlimactic* was the word.

"It can't end like that," she said defiantly.

"Why not? Don't you feel ready? I think I feel ready."

"I do. But I wanted to finish something. For once. Any chance you'd reconsider going skydiving? Like right now, today?"

He laughed. "You know I can't do that."

Arthur had come a long way, faced his fears (of both clowns and failure), and grown immensely as a person. But he was still him, and he was not the kind of person who jumped out of perfectly good planes. He would have done almost anything else in the entire world. It didn't seem fair that Wren's biggest dream just so happened to be his biggest fear.

"Not even for me? I think it would be sexy and heroic. Plus, the symbolism would be amazing. Just think, diving headfirst into the great unknown adventure that is the rest of our lives together. Whadya say?" He was unmoved. "Please?"

Her watery eyes looked up at him like some kind of cartoon puppy, impossibly large and quivering. Somehow, Ferdie had gotten the memo that it was time to do the eyes, because he was sitting on the floor staring at Arthur, giving his best attempt behind his furry eyebrows, even placing a pathetic little paw on Arthur's foot for good measure.

"You know what?" Arthur said, eager to get all these doe eyes off of him. "I have a better idea."

❑ ❑ ❑

They walked into the Mad Cow Creamery, and the chilly, vanilla-scented air welcomed them with a blisteringly cold hug.

"Do they have to keep it so goddamn cold in here?" Arthur said, immediately regretting his choice of T-shirt instead of long sleeves.

"It's an ice cream shop."

"Exactly! The ice cream has to stay frozen, not the customers."

"You seem tense. Are you sure you're up for this?"

He was tense because he'd called Linda again and had to leave yet another voicemail. The uncertainty of what was happening, or not happening, was killing him. And he still didn't know quite what to do.

"It's not me who has to be up for it," he said, regaining his composure. "It's you."

"What do you mean?"

He stood tall and signaled to the young clerk working behind the counter, a redhead in a Mad Cow visor. "We'll take one Heifer, please."

Wren audibly gasped. Customers at other tables turned and gawked.

"You have to order, sir. I'll take you over here," the worker said, motioning to a register.

"Right." Arthur went red. He'd gotten a little carried

away, imagined the moment to be much more cinematic. Instead, he dutifully whipped out his credit card, rewards card, and a coupon for two dollars off.

"I thought you said this was a waste of money," Wren whispered excitedly as they approached the counter.

"It is."

"I thought you said the only thing you get is a Polaroid and diarrhea."

"Hey, it's your butthole. Do what you want with it."

"I wish you'd have told me. I could have prepared."

"What would you have done?"

"I don't know, I'm just nervous!"

The employee rang him up but stopped short when Arthur tried to hand over the coupon.

"Oh, we don't accept those anymore."

"Why not? It's still valid; the expiration date's right here."

"I don't know. My manager said there was too much coupon fraud and we had to stop taking them."

Arthur went red again, he, the perpetrator of said coupon fraud. But it was never intentional. It wasn't his fault they kept showing up in the mail! He wanted to explain, but it would only complicate things. And that wasn't why they were here, anyway.

"I get it. Just make sure I get my double Moo Points on this one, OK? I'm almost at a free milkshake."

He handed over his credit and loyalty rewards cards. It hurt a little to watch the card go through the swiper with that outrageous amount on the screen. But it had to be done.

"And you're paying full price," Wren purred in his ear. "Who are you?"

"You can call me Daddy."

"Gross. I will not."

"Sounded cool in my head. Now, are you ready?"

❑ ❑ ❑

"The rules are simple," the redhead recited in a monotone, as if reading from a script with very little zest or enthusiasm. "The Heifer consists of thirteen scoops of vanilla ice cream, chocolate sauce, sprinkles, whipped cream, and one cherry. To win the challenge, you need to finish the entire bowl in under thirty minutes. Good luck, and Godspeed to your digestive system."

The girl hurled a large spoon down on the table, sending it clattering around, and hit the start button on a very loud plastic timer—the kind a kid would use for chores or homework. It sat on the edge of the table and ticked and tocked. Wren stared at the behemoth bowl that had been placed in front of her. The size of a watermelon, at least, overflowing with chocolate and the very beginnings of melted vanilla. It loomed there like a bowling ball, daring her to try. Never before had rainbow sprinkles looked so menacing.

"I don't know if I can do this," Wren said. "It's almost twice as much as a quart from the store. This is insane."

"You talked a big game before."

"That was hypothetical; this is real life! What if I embarrass myself in front of these legends?"

She glanced up at the wall, at the Polaroids of the conquerors who'd come before. They were all the same. Rotund, mustachioed men who were built for this kind of thing. And then there was Wren, whose eyes were almost certainly too big for her stomach.

"Did it say on the menu how many calories are in it?" she asked.

"You really don't want to know."

"Oh boy. Yeah, I don't know about this. I know I said I wanted to do it, but now that we're here, I think I'm changing my mind. This is not going to feel good." She was getting legitimately panicky, sweaty even, though she hadn't had a single bite.

Arthur grabbed her hand. "You can absolutely do this."

"But I'm scared."

"It all starts with just one bite. Anyone can take one bite. Look, I'll be right here the whole way to talk you through it. How's that?"

She took a deep breath and nodded, then picked up the spoon and dug in. Just one bite. But soon a grimace spread over her face.

"Ah, brain freeze."

"It's OK," he said. "That's normal."

"It hurts, Arthur!"

"Shh," he said. "You're doing great."

"I need something for the pain," she cried, massaging her temple with her free hand.

"It's too late for that. Stick with it; the pain will pass. It's almost over."

"OK," she breathed. "I think it's passing."

"Can you try taking one more bite?"

"I think I can try."

She dug the spoon back into the gooey mound, chocolate and sprinkles all running together, nearly spilling over the side of the bowl. She forced a few bites down, making the same faces she used to make when Arthur planned salad for dinner.

She was hitting her stride, though. Had to have eaten four or five scoops by now.

"I'm so proud of you—you're doing it," he said.

"I am doing it," she said, mouth full of at least half a scoop. "I'm the man."

"I love you."

"I love you, too."

A sprinkle flew out and landed on Arthur's cheek. He hoped she wouldn't be disqualified for that. Chocolate coated Wren's face. Drips and drizzles of melted ice cream collected on her shirt. The whole thing was pretty disgusting to watch, but in a way, she'd never looked more beautiful to him.

Wren powered through, one bite, then the next and the next. The clock made its threatening ticks, but Wren was picking up speed.

"Oh my God, you're almost there!" Arthur cried. "I can see it! I can see the head!"

She paused mid-swallow and looked up at him, confusion in her eyes.

"There." He pointed. She looked and, indeed, there was a cartoon cow's head on the very bottom of the bowl, buried under the gooey dessert. And she was excavating it, revealing the full illustration one spoonful at a time.

But suddenly Wren stopped mid-bite. She placed the spoon down.

"I don't think I can," she said, wincing.

"Brain freeze again?"

"Heartburn. Ow, fuck, it stings like fire! And I'm freezing! This is the weirdest pain ever."

She gripped his hand and squeezed with enough force to turn his bones into a fine powder.

"Come on. It's one more scoop and then you can rest. Just one more. You're almost there. Just breathe."

"IT BURNS, ARTHUR! I CAN'T DO ONE MORE!"

The bones in his hand were cracking, but he took the pain and channeled it into his chest.

"Yes . . . you . . . CAN!" he cried.

She let out a primal yell, worthy of Xena: Warrior Princess, and picked the spoon back up.

❑ ❑ ❑

They sat there minutes later, both on the same side of the table now, a sweating, exhausted Wren lying on Arthur's shoulder. They sat there and they stared at it:

The Polaroid. Wren, triumphant, bloated, queasy, victorious.

"You did it," Arthur said.

"We did it."

"You did all the work. I just got to do the fun part," he said, and dipped his finger into the empty bowl, collecting a thin layer of vanilla and chocolate liquid and popping it into his mouth.

Wren looked down at the photo again. Next to them, the defeated timer clock lay on its side. Wren had tipped it on its side like a chess player humbly resigning. "It's beautiful," she said of the picture.

"Yes, she is."

"Arthur?" she said.

"Yeah?"

"I don't think I'm gonna fit in my dress for the wedding. And for the first time in my life, I couldn't give a shit."

They both burst out laughing.

❑ ❑ ❑

Arthur had just closed Wren into the passenger seat, which was no easy feat. He'd parked her on the curb, sitting her gently on a bench outside the shop, and gone to pull the car around. Loading her into her seat was a feat. She was limp and heavy like a firefighter training dummy. But he'd shoved her in there and managed to buckle her in.

As he walked around to the driver's side, his phone buzzed in his pocket. He answered quietly.

"Linda?"

"Arthur, sorry for the delay. I was camping with my daughter, no service. I just got your messages. All eleven of them."

He felt bad about disturbing Linda during her family time, but this was an emergency.

"I've been going back and forth about pulling out," he said. He peeked in through the car window thinking he'd need to come up with some excuse for who he was talking to. But Wren was already completely zonked out in her seat. "And I think, after a lot of thought, the right thing for me to do is to walk away. I'm really sorry about your commission, and for wasting your time. But I think Wren and I need to regroup and rethink our priorities."

A long pause on the other end. The sound of bad news incoming. Linda had given him a second chance after he'd yanked her chain at the McMansion. She was going to rip him a new one for leading her on again.

"Oh, Arthur. It's too late. The inspection period is over and it's . . . There's nothing I can do. I didn't realize you were having second thoughts."

No, that wasn't right. Couldn't be right.

"I thought I had a few more days, right?"

"We agreed to shorten the due diligence, remember? I hadn't heard from you before today so I assumed we were full speed ahead."

The truth is, he didn't remember. He remembered the conversation, and signing some papers, but he'd obviously been distracted. Lost track of time. It was completely unlike him, though, to be fair, he'd been intentionally trying to be as unlike himself as possible lately.

"So what are you saying, that there's no way out of this?"

He stood there under the streetlight, heart pounding, hoping the next words out of Linda's mouth included some kind of loophole, some miracle that he could use.

"There is a way out," she began. He exhaled pure relief. "But you'll lose your earnest money."

And just like that, his heart sank again. When the offer was accepted, he'd written a big check to let the sellers know he was serious. A deposit on the down payment, essentially. It was a significant chunk of his savings, and handing that check over was one of the hardest things he'd ever had to do. It was a dozen summers of mowing lawns, waxing his creepy neighbor's Porsche, and walking dogs while his friends went swimming at the pool. It was every boring chicken and rice dinner at home instead of taking Wren on a date, every hour spent clipping digital grocery coupons and meal planning around the sales, every vacation they never took.

"How much will I lose?" he asked.

"All of it."

19

IT WAS FINALLY THE DAY of the wedding.

Wren sat on the side of the bed, staring into their closet, mindlessly stroking a dozing Ferdie in her lap. A flustered Arthur had run out at the last minute to buy a new shirt. He'd had a bit of a Bridezilla moment before he left.

"I wish we had more time. God, nothing FITS!" he'd said before storming off. Wren found it endlessly entertaining.

And now she was alone, the apartment dead quiet. She stared into the sea of clothes hanging in front of her. Somewhere in there was a floral maternity dress that might just work well enough. But the thought of standing up and wading through everything else to find it was completely overwhelming.

She'd taken the engagement ring out of her bag and sat twirling the box round and round in her fingers, knowing exactly what to do. For her, the deal had been sealed at the Mad Cow Creamery. Arthur had grown, and changed, in amazing ways. But she had changed, too, and that's what mattered most of all. She wasn't scared anymore, of the baby, of commitment, of whatever tomorrow might bring, even if it hurt.

Arthur had shown her that he really knew her, inside and out. He knew what she valued in life and, even though he was fundamentally different from her in so many ways, he respected that. He'd shown that he would always come through, and even push himself beyond his own comfort zone, to help her find happiness and joy. Even in the little things.

For that, she was going to find a way to get Arthur alone in Shark Alley. And she was going to propose to him.

But before then, she had some time to kill. He wouldn't be back for a little while, and the wedding didn't start for several hours.

Her eyes began to drift over the beige, lifeless walls. Over the bassinet and the stacks of books and baby toys. Then to the carpet (also beige) and the blinds (off-white). The two go bags packed and stacked on the floor. Her mind flicked over the checklists and blog posts. Technically, they had everything they needed if the baby were to arrive at this exact instant. But still there was something missing.

She needed her paints. Returning to the closet, she dug them out from behind a power adapter for an HP laptop that she didn't remember ever owning. Most looked dried out and crusted over, but a few colors were still salvageable.

It would be enough.

❑ ❑ ❑

When Arthur returned, Wren was almost finished. He walked into their bedroom and strutted confidently.

"I'm just warning you," he said, "you are definitely going to want to bone me when you see how well this shirt fits."

Arthur stopped in his tracks when he noticed what she had done.

Wren sat on a tarp of kitchen trash bags, surrounded by squirts of paint on paper plates.

"Do you like it?"

He took it all in. She watched as his eyes tracked the streaks of yellow and pink, the swirls of light blue, all of it taking over the main wall of their bedroom.

"It's beautiful," he said. Then, leaning down and whispering: "What is it?"

"It's a sunrise."

"A sunrise, of course."

She was rusty, but still proud of it. If only the baby had needed a snappy, brand-friendly logo whipped up in Photoshop! She would have crushed it. But this was good, too. She was sure of it.

"That's the sun there, and the clouds. It's coming up over rolling hills. It's a little abstract, I know."

"No," he assured her, "it's incredible. I can't remember the last time I saw you paint something. Almost forgot how talented you are. Now I remember. Why a sunrise?"

"Because this room needed something," she said flatly. "And because . . . I wanted to always be reminded that tomorrow is always coming, and it is beautiful."

"And what if we don't stay here? What if they have to come paint over it one day?"

She shrugged. "Nothing lasts forever. But that's OK."

"Hey," he said, offering his hands and helping her off the ground. "I'm really proud of you."

"Can you put the bassinet back? I want to see how it looks."

He walked across the room to where Wren had stashed it

and slid it up against the wall, perfectly centered on the mural. It made a world of difference. Things felt right now. The room was warm, colorful. The type of welcome to the world that a baby deserved.

"Now," she said, "you almost ready to go?"

They brought the go bags just in case.

❑ ❑ ❑

Though the reception would be at the National Aquarium, the ceremony itself was held at a quaint little church in the city without much parking. They were almost late as Arthur tried to negotiate parallel parking between a couple of hulking pickup trucks, trying desperately to not block the fire hydrant that was stationed right there.

"I can get out and help guide you," she'd said.

"I've got it, just relax," he said, putting a hand on the back of her headrest and craning his neck to see backward, even palming the wheel as he spun it round. He was becoming such a dad already.

Once inside, Wren only got a quick, prison-length visitation with Charlie before the ceremony was set to begin.

"You look so beautiful," she told her friend, standing outside the claustrophobic little dressing room the church referred to as a bridal suite. It smelled like hair spray and warm mimosas.

"So do you. I really wish you could be up with the rest of the bridal party, but it would ruin the photos."

"Thanks! Appreciate it."

"You know what I mean."

"I know," Wren said. "Wrong dress and everything."

"And you're the size of a manatee."

"I would slug you right in your perfect face if I wasn't afraid I'd topple over."

Wren kissed her on her cheek and sent Charlie on her way, the comically long white dress dragging behind her. She knew she'd see Charlie again in a few minutes, and then at the reception after. But something would definitely be different between them when she did. Tonight was the end of an unofficial era, an era that started with two single best friends in college having debauched misadventures together. Even when they settled down with Arthur and Tristan, respectively, it still felt like Wren and Charlie's world. The boys were on an extended probationary period to determine if they'd be allowed in. With Charlie tying the knot, and Wren waiting for the right moment to give Arthur his own ring back, the club would be permanently expanding.

❑ ❑ ❑

Wren and Arthur sat and watched the wedding party walk down the aisle to the soundtrack of some pop country song Wren couldn't quite place, wedding-ed up with violins and harps.

The ceremony was held in the church's back garden, lined with rosebushes and beautifully trimmed hedges. The sun was just beginning to dip, giving the light a soft, warm quality that Wren knew would be harnessed into incredible photographs. It was a desktop background come to life.

But . . . it was hot as hell.

Arthur leaned over. "You doing OK?"

"Yeah, why?"

"You just look a little . . . dewy, that's all. If you're not up for this, just say the word and we can leave."

Wren wiped at her forehead. Pretty sweaty. That early fall sun was blasting her directly in the face on its way to making the perfect picturesque sunset.

"Gonna take more than that to take me down. I've gathered here today to witness some holy matrimony and I'm not leaving until I get it."

"Roger that."

The bridal music hit, everyone stood, and here was Charlie, looking flawless and genuinely overjoyed. Her dad, a stoic man who'd never said anything to Wren that wasn't related to the weather, was in pieces as he walked her down the aisle. His lip trembled as he held back sobs and tried to keep his chin up. He was just a fraction of a step behind, giving the illusion that he was pulling her backward. *Don't go.* Charlie dragged him along nonetheless.

When Charlie finally reached the front, she quickly found Wren in the crowd. *Am I good?* her face seemed to ask. Wren gave her a thumbs up. It made her heart flutter, her insides all gooey, that in this, one of the biggest moments of Charlie's life, surrounded by all her best friends and family, she looked first to Wren for support.

They were gonna be OK, the two of them.

"Welcome, y'all. Y'all be seated," the officiant—Tristan and Charlie's friend Malcolm—announced. Malcolm was thin and stylish and had secured his officiant license online a few weeks prior. "Y'all are gathered here today . . ." Tristan cleared his throat. "Sorry, I know I'm saying 'y'all' too much. Guess I'm just nervous."

A small chuckle from the crowd.

"*We* are gathered to celebrate the love of Tristan and Charlie, two of my closest friends, and living proof that a one-night stand can lead to a lifetime of happiness."

A bigger laugh. Charlie's mouth hung open in faux shock.

"I'm serious," Malcom went on. "I know we were all shocked that their second date was something as wholesome as ice cream in the park when their first date had been in the club bathroom. Sorry, Dad." The officiant offered an apologetic look to Charlie's father in the front row, red-faced but smiling. "But, I believe that these two were destined to find each other, somehow, some way, and that their love is one of the purest and most joyful you'll ever see up close.

"But anyway," Malcolm stammered. "I asked Charlie what her thoughts were on the ceremony. And she told me, 'Short and sweet. I want to be married to that man yesterday.' So let's move it along, shall we?"

Some applause. A few people in the back whooped. Malcolm turned to Tristan. "Take it away, hubby."

Tristan took Charlie's hands, looked deep into her eyes.

"Charlie," he started, voice just breaking. "I know you said you'd kill me if I made a long speech and kept everyone baking out here in the sun for too long. But I just want to say, I know that I don't deserve you. You are kind, generous, selfless. I'm in awe of you every day. When people look at me, all they see is good looks, money, endless charisma, a sense of humor, a great physique, and limitless ambition." The crowd laughed. Tristan smiled, too, then got serious. "But you know how much I've struggled with wanting to make a difference in the world. With feeling like I'm not enough. And I just want you to know that I will never, ever give up trying to make you proud. And I'll never give up on us. No matter what. I love you."

Sniffles and a few cheers from the crowd. Malcolm handed the mic to Charlie.

"I have no notes," Charlie announced, staring at him with huge, wet, lovestruck doe eyes. "Just marry us already."

"The last thing I want to say," Malcolm said, to a chorus of groans, "is to tell you to embrace the change. It may seem a simple thing, wearing a ring, signing a certificate. Especially for two people who've already committed to each other, who live together, who have seen each other at their worst.

"After today, your marriage becomes your unquestioned top priority. Yes, more important than the S&P 500, Tristan."

"And more important than your speech, Malcolm!" Charlie said, leaning into the mic. "Wrap it up already!"

Wren beamed. It was amazing to see her friend so happy, so joyously in love. Somehow it was even rubbing off on her, a contact high of sorts. She found herself reaching for Arthur's hand, lovingly stroking his thumb with hers, just the way he always did. PDA had always nauseated her; who the hell was she turning into?

But then Wren started doing some math. If Tristan became Charlie's number one, that would make her Charlie's number two. If Arthur became Wren's number one, and the baby number two (or would it be the other way around?), that would make Charlie number *three*? There was an overall demotion of three life spots happening all at once, which seemed unacceptable. Something would have to be done about this.

But in the meantime, Arthur was looking at her, his own eyes wet, and squeezing her hand, and they were both rubbing their thumbs on the other, and stroking the other's palm, and intertwining fingers that had no business being intertwined, and the whole thing was just so sickeningly lovely.

"Ladies and gentlemen, I now present . . ."

It was time to stand and clap.

❑ ❑ ❑

At the aquarium, Wren found herself nibbling on a cream cheese wonton and peering over a railing and down into the clear depths of the stingray tank. The creatures were so graceful and alien, some strange combination of slimy fish and winged angel. A flaky crumb flew off her appetizer and floated down toward the water, like a bit of fish food. She hoped the rays would like it.

Charlie and Tristan were finishing up a few last-minute photos, just the two of them. The bridal party was done. But she wasn't quite ready to go back to the party. She'd left Arthur to fend for himself for a few minutes, said she needed a minute to think.

And now, as if on cue, here was a person invading her peace. The pained groan of an older man taking a load off pierced the air. It was Charlie's dad, leaning on the very same railing, letting it do the work of holding him up.

"Do you mind?" he said.

"Not at all."

He exhaled a grunt, almost as if he'd just taken the first sip of an ice-cold beer. Wren couldn't help but smile at the similarities between the two. Even their bellies were about the same size.

"What're you doing sitting here alone? They'll be serving dinner soon," he said.

"I'm not finding I have much of an appetite."

"I paid for that fillet. Don't you waste it, now."

Wren chuckled.

"Wren, right?" She nodded. "Yeah, I remember. Something got you down?"

"Just feeling . . . a lot." Sad, happy, excited, nervous. She felt like she was standing on the edge of a cliff. Everything she had ever known in her life was about to change, all of it at once.

Paul exhaled loudly. "Boy, I feel that."

"I like seeing my best friend so excited. And Tristan's a good guy and all. But I'm afraid that I'm going to lose her. Does that make sense?"

"Did you forget who you're talking to?"

"You're just her dad, what do you know? I'm her best friend! You couldn't possibly understand the bond we have," she teased.

"Well, it's good practice, anyway. Feeling this way."

"How do you mean?"

"I hope I'm not going out on a limb by asking if you're pregnant?" he said, as Wren could barely even stand up straight. She also had a permanent grimace on her face from the sheer exhaustion and pain of carrying this kid around.

"Get used to the feeling. You're supposed to celebrate all these milestones that mark the passage of time, but all they mark is your time with them slipping away. Off to school! Sixteenth birthday! Learning to drive! Graduating college! Let's all eat a goddamn cake! And then the day they find someone else to take care of them is supposed to be one of the happiest days of your life?" He blew a raspberry in the air.

"Fuck, man," Wren said. "I haven't even had this baby yet; why are you doing this to me? I came over here to collect myself, not to hurl myself over the ledge."

"You could be eating steak and getting ready to hit the dance floor, but you wanted to sit here and talk to a sad old man who just gave his daughter away. That was your choice."

Wren laughed.

"I guess I should get back. I've never danced at a wedding

before, believe it or not. Won't be too many more of these where I'm going, which is apparently the grave."

Paul nodded. "The next phase of your friendship with Charlie will be new, and it will be different. Will it be better? I don't know. But it will be. So there's that."

"That sucks."

"Tough," he said.

"And what about you and your little girl? What's your next phase look like?" she asked him. She had seen him struggling walking down the aisle. But his tears were gone and now all that was left was this deep, still sadness. Is this what she was going to look like someday, some twenty- or thirty-odd years in the future?

"Oh, I'm screwed," he said. "And they don't even want to have kids, so there's another dagger. Good thing I love my wife, though. I've still got her. That's all I really need."

No matter what else happened, she thought, she would still have Arthur. That's why it had to be this way. Why he had to be her number one, and Tristan had to be Charlie's.

"Now, go on before I drive you even deeper into depression," the old man joked.

"Do you think . . . you could give me a hand off this railing?"

And now it was Charlie's dad laughing.

"I was gonna ask you the same thing."

With that, and a deep, steadying breath, she was ready to do the damn thing.

❑ ❑ ❑

When Wren returned to the bar area, Arthur had managed to snag a private moment with Tristan. She watched the two of them knowing they were only friends by proxy, really, and that Arthur had a vague distaste for Tristan. He wasn't everyone's flavor, after all.

"Just wanted to tell you congrats, man," Arthur said. "If you hate your present, I'm sorry in advance, money's a little tight right now. But if you love it, you're welcome."

"No worries. Your presence is enough of a present," Tristan said.

"Good, I'll return the spoon, then."

Tristan laughed.

"Seriously, you picked a great day to get married. It was beautiful."

"Every day is a great day, Arthur. You know what I always say? It's not just another day . . . it's To-day."

Tristan slugged him in the arm playfully and walked off, ready to continue making the rounds. When Arthur finally turned and saw Wren, he immediately adopted an over-the-top lovestruck look on his face and a cartoonish twinkle in his eye, as if he'd just drunk some witch's bubbly pink love potion in a children's film.

"Why's your face like that?" she asked. "I know it's hard not to get caught up in the romance, but tone it down a little. There are people around."

"Can't help it. It's a beautiful night, I'm happy, I'm in love. Why not smile? Here, got you a mocktail." He handed her a cloudy orange drink in something resembling a wineglass. She took a test sip, face twitching from the soury-sweetness of it, and the heartburn was almost instant.

"Should we get to our seats?" he said. "I think they'll be serving dinner soon."

"I know. My skin tingles when my body knows red meat is nearby."

He laughed.

"But not just yet," she said. "You up for a walk?"

Truth be told, she felt like hell. The indigestion was still climbing up her throat, she felt just a bit clammy and nauseous, and the exhaustion of a long day was beginning to settle in. She didn't know if she was going to make it to dinner. But she was ready. It was time.

"OK," he said, and they strolled. Past the deep-sea freaks like the sea dragons, poky, gangly little things that had clearly been penciled in at the very end when God had run out of ideas. Past the jellyfish and sea nettles, which were far more stunning when safely behind glass. "But if you want to leave, it's OK, I promise."

"No, I'm OK. Let's just walk." She just had to stick it out for Charlie and Tristan's big entrance to the reception, then for the toasts, and then for the first dance and the cake cutting. She could hold it together for a few more hours. And if the baby decided to try any shenanigans, she would have to hold that in, too.

"Hey, you showed up, you saw your best friend get married. That meant the world to Charlie and I know for a fact she would want you to go home now and get some rest."

Damn it, he was right. Wren was notorious for powering through in the name of a good time. Had one too many drinks but not ready to go home yet? Have two too many! Deal with the fallout later. That was always her motto. Being beholden to this child inside her, having a *greater purpose*, was inexplicably causing her to make better decisions. It was starting already.

"OK, fine. I'll go say goodbye, but will you meet me by the sharks? I really want to see them before we go."

Arthur's face went stone white. Wren could almost see the memory replaying behind his eyes. "Oh. I don't know . . ."

"Please?" She touched his hand. "For me?"

"OK," he agreed. "See you there in a minute?"

❑ ❑ ❑

Wren was just able to grab Charlie before she and Tristan were set to make their grand entrance to the reception.

"Little busy, Wren," Charlie said, air-rehearsing some multistep dance routine, hidden away behind a tank of *Finding Nemo* clownfish a few dozen feet away from the reception.

"I know. I just wanted to catch you before we left."

"You're leaving?!" Charlie came to a stop mid-thrust.

"It's for the best. There are so many ways I could ruin the rest of the night for you. I could go into violent, screaming labor; I could puke all over whoever's sitting next to me at dinner."

"I think it's just my least favorite sister. I'd be fine with that."

Wren briefly considered telling her friend about what she was planning to do. She always told Charlie every single thing she was thinking or considering, and even a lot of things she wasn't. That's how deeply psychic their connection was. But she didn't tell her this. Charlie wouldn't have been upset. Wren and Arthur weren't going to make a scene and steal the spotlight. They'd just steal a quiet moment or two in a quiet hallway and that would be that. There were some things, now that she and Arthur were a family, that were going to have to stay between them. That was one way her relationship with Charlie was going to have to change. And that led her to say:

"I think you're right, by the way."

"Right about what?"

"Maybe fighting to keep everything exactly the same between us is a battle we're never going to win, you know?"

Charlie smirked. "Are you saying we have to evolve?"

"To be clear, I don't wanna. But . . . I'm never going to give up on us, and you'll never get rid of me. But you're right that we do have to figure out what it looks like to grow together."

"So instead of drinking and walking around HomeGoods, you think, maybe we could, like, just sit and have a glass of wine one night?"

"And . . . talk?"

"And talk."

"Well, you know me. I'll try anything once."

"God," Charlie said, fanning her eyes. "I really should have married you."

They laughed.

"I think it would be better if I left without making a scene. It was a beautiful wedding, you were a beautiful bride, and I'm so happy I was there to see you get a new number one."

"You're always my number one, you know that."

"You can keep telling Tristan that to keep him in line . . ."

"You know I can hear you," Tristan muttered.

". . . but it's not true. And that's OK," Wren said.

They hugged. Wren felt ten years younger in Charlie's arms. Like a carefree kid. The irony was not lost on her that there was literally a kid between them now, the hug a little more spaced out than before. That was just the way it was going to have to be.

❑ ❑ ❑

Wren was extremely nervous walking down the dimly lit ramps of Shark Alley. Sweating, trembling, fiddling with the ring in her clutch like some big old doof. Was this what guys felt like all the time? It was a miracle anyone ever got engaged and that more people didn't puke from the nerves.

She rehearsed what she was going to say as a sandbar shark swam by her behind the thick glass, almost escorting her. *You good? Need me to eat anyone for you?* its dark eyes seemed to ask. She would tell Arthur that he had always been her future, but she was only just now able to see it without fear. She would not apologize for saying no all those years ago, but she would create a beautiful, full-circle moment that would say it all. He would get it. He would say yes.

Arthur was waiting for her at the bottom, as promised, his silhouette popping against the blue water behind him. A hammerhead shark glided right past him. It was eerie and beautiful, and just a little scary, for many reasons.

"Hi," Arthur said, watching her approach. She could see the apprehension in his eyes. This place held a lot of pain for him, she understood that. But hopefully she could change that.

"Hi," she said.

"You look beautiful."

"So do you."

He laughed.

"No, really, you do," she said. "Blue must be your color."

They stood there together and watched the sharks for a moment. It was hypnotic and peaceful. A few other wedding guests quietly perused around them, everyone in a near silent trance.

"You probably remember the last time we were here," Wren said. Her voice was so shaky, betraying her.

"I do," he said. "It's OK. We don't have to talk about it."

"No, we do. There's something I want to say."

"OK."

She took a deep breath. "You mean more to me than I could possibly say, Arthur. You have always been my future, my everything. I'm sorry it took me so long to say this."

He smiled, but with a confused crinkle in his brow. "So what are you trying to say?" Her heart beat even harder; she was sure he could hear it. This was it, this was the moment.

"Arthur, I—"

"Arthur?!" a voice cried out. They both whirled around. There, in a black dress and gaudy gold necklace, was Linda Kellerman.

"Linda, hi," a flabbergasted Arthur said, accepting a stiff hug from a slightly wobbly Linda, who was holding a glass of white wine. "What are you doing here?"

"I sold Charlie and Tristan their first condo, right before the market went to shit. And I go way back with her parents. What are the odds, right?"

As much as Wren usually loved an awkward, unexpected interaction like this one, she really wished the lady would saunter away, or maybe fall over and roll the rest of the way down the slaloming ramps. She was ruining the moment.

Suddenly, Linda locked onto Wren. "Wren, I'm sorry I haven't had a chance to say it yet, but . . . congratulations."

"Usually you say congratulations *after* someone has the baby. All I've done so far is have unprotected sex. But thank you."

"No, I mean— Oh." Linda went serious, turned to look at Arthur, looked back and forth between the two of them. "You haven't told— Nothing. Nothing at all. You've just got yourself a good man here, that's all. So congrats on that, congrats on the baby, congrats on the sex. All of it. I'll let you two get back to it."

Linda sauntered away, unaware or unbothered that she'd just laid a grenade in the middle of their conversation.

"So you were saying how I'm your future, your one true love, et cetera," Arthur said, trying to play it casual.

"Arthur, why was she congratulating me?"

"Probably because of the baby. You're obviously about to pop any day now. I don't know why she couldn't think to say that in the moment, and not make it weird, but I'm sure that's what she meant."

Wren wasn't buying it. The weird panic in Linda's eyes, the look back and forth between the two of them, the catching of her tongue. Wren was used to belly rubs and *goo-goo-ga-ga*s and people staring at her stomach, and this was not that.

"She said, 'You haven't told—' What haven't you told me?"

Arthur's nervous smile faded. The fight drained out of him. His eyes went soft, pleading.

"Let's not talk about it here. Can we go home?"

Did he do something behind her back with Linda? Did he buy a *fucking house*? It was too insane to even consider. No, he wouldn't do that.

But it was the only thing that made sense.

"Just tell me what you did," she said.

❑ ❑ ❑

After the truth came out, the fight spilled outside, where it was raining. Of course it was raining.

"But that was our money, not just yours!" Wren said. "You don't get to decide that!"

"Wren, I'm sorry I lied to you, I really am. But I've been saving up since I was a kid. I can't remember you ever putting anything into that account."

"Not true!" It was mostly true. She'd contributed a certain amount of her pay over the years to their rent and expenses and usually blown the rest on whatever seemed fun. But she wasn't going to concede the point. "I took under-the-couch coins to Coinstar many a time! And I always put that right into savings."

OK, sometimes she bought herself a handful of Runts first. But still.

"You have to call it off," she said. "You have to get out of it."

The lights of the city and the harbor twinkled on the dark water close by.

"I can't."

"What do you mean, you can't?"

"It's too late. It's basically a done deal."

Wren's stomach dropped. She couldn't believe this was happening. That he could be so reckless, so stupid.

"What were you thinking? That house is a disaster." She was unwittingly pacing back and forth now, mind spinning for a way to make sense of this.

"It's not that bad." His body language was that of a scolded puppy.

"Arthur, it looks like Guantánamo Bay in there."

"You're right, it does," he said, stiffening up just a tad, a little fight coming into his voice. He was getting defensive now. "But it won't be so bad. If you can just get on board, believe in me for once."

"For once? What does that mean?"

"Nothing."

She marched right up to him. He wasn't going to suppress this and bury it down. He was going to say it, or she was going to make him.

"Tell me what you mean."

"Fine," he spat. "All the negging and needling me. 'Oh,

there goes Arthur, scared to go for it, scared to take a chance. Maybe I'll tease him about taking his time and thinking things through! Sure, he's the most boring human being on the planet, but I don't mind much!' It hurts, Wren! I got sick of it, I'm sorry. I guess for a second I just wanted to do something without you doubting I would go through with it. So I did."

She'd never done that, never doubted him. He was just unleashing all of his insecurities on her, and it wasn't fair. She didn't deserve that.

"Even if I did do that, which I didn't, I would have been right," she said. "Because you still can't quit playing it safe."

His jaw hung open. He was incredulous.

"I'm sorry, what part of this is me playing it safe? I'm risking everything, Wren. For us. So we have a real place to live, a real future. It didn't go exactly as I planned it, I admit that. But I am taking a chance, can't you see that?"

"No, you're not. You just don't have the balls to figure out what you want your own life to look like, so you're trying to copy your parents. News flash, Arthur: That life doesn't exist anymore. Not for people like us."

"Yes, it does. You just have to want it. You just have to sacrifice."

"That's not how I want to live my life! Sacrificing everything that actually makes life worth living! Not anymore. If you really knew me, you would know that."

She had him there. For just a moment, he was speechless. They stood there, panting like two fighters between rounds, drizzling rain making them damp.

"Well, at least I'm not afraid to want *something*," he said.

"Excuse me?"

"At least I don't run away from anything that might potentially be good. Your job, our family. Jesus, Wren, do you even want to have this baby with me?"

"I'm going home," she said flatly. She couldn't believe he would ask that, and she wanted to tear him apart for it, but she was tired and out of fight. "I'll get an Uber. I don't want to be in the car with you."

She put in the request on her phone in record time while he pleaded.

"Can you at least request a female driver so I don't worry?"

"Fine." She checked the option on the app.

"I think I might have a discount code you can put in, too, just give me one sec—"

"Oh my GOD, will you just fuck off?! I can't even look at you right now."

That was enough. She stormed off.

"Wren, come on. I know we're heated right now, but it's just a fight. We'll work it out. We have to."

"We have to! Wow, what a fairy tale," she said, voice dripping with sarcasm. "Sad thing is you're probably right. Lucky us."

She huffed down the walkway to a far corner of the brick square outside the aquarium, far away from Arthur, where she could wait for her ride in peace. But first, she shot one last glare over her shoulder in case he dared try to follow her.

He didn't. Only watched from afar until she climbed into the back seat of her ride and floated away.

20

WREN STAGGERED THROUGH THE FRONT door and kicked off her flats, sending them flying down the hallway. She slammed the door behind her. The apartment was dead quiet. It was weird being here without Arthur.

But she didn't want to think about him right now. Or anything at all.

She'd been an idiot. Carrying around a ring, ready to propose to her boyfriend like this was all some modern fairy tale? What was she thinking? Of course it had been too good to be true, too good to last. Nothing good ever does.

It would persist, but she would be trapped. She'd have no choice but to live in the barren house, sleeping on an air mattress while Arthur attempted to fix it up, putting their baby to sleep in a drafty corner somewhere and eventually letting it do its tummy time right there on the concrete flooring. If and when Arthur was ever finished, she'd live out her days as the picture-perfect suburban mom, secretly getting by with various substances that allowed her to feel something, anything.

There she went, thinking again when she'd vowed not to.

She set her sights on the sofa, beckoning to her like a siren, and flopped down into its softness. She turned on the TV. Wren and Arthur had promised they would start *Cake Island 2: The Duel* together, and for a second she felt bad queuing it up without him. But this was, at the moment, the best revenge she could possibly get.

"Ferdie," she called out, "get your ass over here. Mama needs snuggles." She was also going to look into the feasibility of having an entire cake DoorDashed to the apartment so she could do terrible things to it.

Ferdie came limping in from the bedroom, moving glacially but happy to see her, tail wagging almost imperceptibly.

"There's my boy." Wren scooped him up and brought him into her chest, then started the show. "Love you the most, buddy."

The two of them fell asleep like that before the first elimination.

❑ ❑ ❑

In the morning, she opened her eyes with a tragic, naive hope that she'd feel better, that she'd discover a magical spring in her step. But that pit in her stomach was still there, her heart was heavy, and Arthur's side of the bed was empty and cold. She'd never admit it out loud, but there was a part of her that had hoped he'd secretly returned in the night.

No such luck.

He was often up before her, but his spot was always warm, and though it usually annoyed her at the time, she was realizing just how quiet the apartment was without him clanging around, making more coffee, tapping away on his laptop, or "quietly" vacuuming with their little rechargeable hand vac. It made her want to strangle him on many a morning. And now it was gone. Just dead quiet.

All in all, Wren decided that she couldn't bring herself to get out of bed, and neither could Ferdie, from the looks of him. He was curled up in the same exact spot he'd fallen asleep in, contoured perfectly against the bend in her legs.

There were too many feelings weighing her down. What she needed was to disassociate even further; yes, that would be the ticket. But she found herself getting distracted upon resuming the show. Not even suspiciously hot bakers competing in American Gladiator–style games, delivering towering cakes across long balance beams, could wrangle her brain. She needed something even more brain-dead. And that's when she remembered Instagram.

She began scrolling. Here were a few photos of the wedding from friends of friends. People out at breweries. Visiting the zoo with their kids. A "get ready with me" reel. Soon she was absorbing all kinds of kooky misinformation about vaccines and food dye from the momfluencers, but she didn't care. Bring it on. Frosted Flakes leads to kids with low IQ? Sure, why not? Formula linked to colic? If you say so. She wanted more. Maybe she would become one of them and hide her pain behind a baseless campaign against Froot Loops.

The edges of her vision went dark and she lost all track of time and sense of reality, exactly as intended.

Until she saw something that caught her eye. Immediately, she called Charlie, whom she'd been texting on and off with most of the previous night—which just happened to be Charlie's wedding night. She was a real one.

"Hi," she said glumly when her friend answered.

"I was just thinking about you. You doing OK?"

"What, re Arthur? I'm fine. I'm barely thinking about it."

"You should really call him," Charlie said with concern. "He keeps texting me, begging me to let him know if you're OK. I've said you're fine, but—"

"He's just some guy, Charlie. Some guy I've been casually hooking up with. For ten years. Now, believe it or not, I didn't call you to talk about that."

A pause. Wren waited to see if Charlie would let this go or if she would have to be steamrolled, which was never an easy task. They were both stubborn, so stubborn, in fact, that they'd never even once agreed on who was *more* stubborn throughout their entire friendship. An eternal stalemate. Finally, a small sigh came through from the other end of the line. Charlie always sighed like that when she knew Wren was about to pull some bullshit. "OK, what is it, then?"

"I called to tell you that . . . we are so back."

"What? Who's back?"

"FORD THE RIVER. I just saw on Instagram. They kicked off a huge reunion tour a few weeks ago."

"Aren't those guys in their fifties now?" Charlie asked.

"Who cares! They're coming to Baltimore tonight. You believe that? I know you're leaving for your honeymoon in a few days, but we're going," Wren said.

"You want to go to a punk rock show? When you're about to go into labor at any moment? And you just decided to stop speaking to or about the father? You could at least *pretend* to not be suppressing your emotions."

"Maybe I am. Who cares? This is a once-in-a-lifetime opportunity." Wren was getting uncomfortable, her legs pinned in place by a comatose Ferdie and falling asleep rapidly. "These guys hate each other's guts and they're likely to murder each other before they ever tour together again."

"Or die of natural causes, at this point."

"Exactly. I've never seen them live, and this is our last chance. I can be sad later. What do you say?"

"How are you talking me into this right now? It's insane. I'm supposed to be packing for my honeymoon," Charlie scoffed.

"Shut up, I know you did that days ago."

Wren swore she heard Charlie curse under her breath. Busted.

"I will go without you if I have to," Wren threatened. "Then I'll have no one to supervise me."

"Fine, but one rule." Charlie sighed. "I am NOT getting into the mosh pit."

"OK, no problem."

"And neither are you!" added Charlie.

"We can discuss it on the way."

Wren ended the call. She'd always wanted to clip off a phone call mid-conversation, like some Jason Bourne–esque action hero. Plus she knew any further discussion or negotiation would only cause Charlie to rethink their plans.

Now she had to get ready, find something to wear, listen to the official tour playlist, and practice her double devil horns in the mirror to make sure she was still young enough to pull them off. True, most of the people at the show would be her age or older, but she also knew the music was starting to catch on with a younger crowd and she didn't want to be banished to the elderly parents' section of the venue. Oh, and she had to do it all without thinking about Arthur and, ideally, not going into labor before she could figure out what to do about her relationship.

No sweat.

❑ ❑ ❑

A few hours later, she was ready. In another world, Wren would have loved to go all out, outfit-wise, for the show. But she had to settle for stretchy pregnancy pants and a loose-fitting top plastered with the logo for 408, another one of her favorite bands. It had been a while since she'd been to a concert, a long while, but she was pretty sure it was still forbidden to wear a shirt of the band you were going to see. With more time, she might have added a few accoutrements, a spiky wristband, a streak of purple in her hair. But she more than made up for it by layering on an absurd amount of eye shadow, which not only looked punk rock but helped disguise her eyes, which were red and swollen from holding back tears.

In all the excitement, she realized, she'd forgotten to walk Ferdie. He'd surely need a pee before being left alone for the next few hours. Arthur might be back at some point. But then again . . . he might not.

"Come on, bud." She groaned. In her current physical condition, she wasn't going to be any more thrilled about a walk than he was. "Let's get this over with."

He was still sleeping in the same spot on the bed, the same exact spot. It had been hours. The dog could sleep like a vampire, but this was rare, even for him. She sat next to him and tried to gently rouse him. When he didn't twitch immediately, she freaked. Call it instinct. She stood up and screamed.

No, this could not be happening, not to her, not right now. He couldn't be gone.

She left the room and looked up, as if to the heavens. "You've made your fucking point. Go pick on someone else for a while."

The proper thing to do would be to sound the alarm, call Arthur, call the vet. Do something. But what was the point? She'd known all along Ferdie wasn't going to be with them for long, that was part of the deal. And she couldn't be in there with him right now anyway. It activated parts of her brain, parts of her heart, that she'd long since drawn the curtains on. It would hurt too much to try to use that atrophied muscle: hope. Better to just give in to the pain now.

She sat down on the sofa, sinking into it more than ever before, and allowed herself to cry. But it wasn't long before the tears ran dry. She was surprised that this moment wasn't hitting her the way she expected. Not with the force of a freight train or a semitruck. It was more like the disappointment of the inevitable. The last bite of an amazing meal. The closing credits of a movie you don't want to end. You know it's coming, but you're hoping somehow that it won't.

But it did. The whole thing, she realized, was anticlimactic and bleak. She had no amazing parting words for her boy, no great speech or emotional plea. He was there and then one moment he was just gone, and Wren sat on the couch, numb, unsure of what to do next. She knew that's how death was. It wasn't an ending or a new beginning, the way people say. It just left a hole you couldn't fill.

21

ARTHUR WOKE UP TO THE smell of hotel breakfast. Rubbery eggs, watered-down coffee, and more bacon than a person could possibly eat. It was all arranged neatly on a tray, which his mother delivered to him in bed.

"Wakey, wakey . . ." she said.

"Don't say it," he pleaded, rubbing the sleep from his eyes.

"Eggs and bakey!"

He groaned and rolled back over in bed.

"I'll just put this here for when you're ready," she said, placing the tray down on the desk near the foot of the pull-out sofa.

After the wedding fiasco, Arthur didn't know where to go or what to do. So he called his dad, who revealed that they had wrapped up their travels and had been staying in a nearby hotel to get a little extra space while they awaited the arrival of little baby Peterson.

And that's how Arthur ended up sleeping in the "living room" of his parents' extended-stay suite. Which was an ironic place to be, because he barely wanted to be alive.

Arthur could hear his parents hardly bothering to whisper in the next room.

"I don't know what to say to him," his mom said. "He just seems so heartbroken."

"Let me talk to him," said his dad.

A moment later, Arthur felt his father's weight sitting down on the edge of his mattress.

"Hey, bud." It was like he was a kid again, getting ready to be on the receiving end of a tried-and-true "We're not mad, just disappointed" talk after flunking a test in school.

Arthur begrudgingly sat up. "Hey, Dad. Before the heart-to-heart starts, could you hand me the coffee?"

"Sure." He chuckled, then handed over the mug. "You weren't very talkative last night. Want to tell me what happened?"

"Nothing surprising."

"Meaning?"

"I fucked up. I hid some things from Wren that I should have told her about. Or better yet, should never have done."

Neal took a solemn beat. "Fixable?"

"I don't know."

"Ah. Almost anything is fixable with the right attitude."

Arthur took a sip. Scalding hot. Mostly water with floating bits of grounds in it. But there was caffeine in the mug somewhere, and he was going to find it.

"Yes, maybe it's fixable. Probably. But that's not the point. This was always going to happen. Wren was always going to wait for me to screw something up so she could use that as an excuse to bail. I was never going to be enough for her, but I've also never given her a reason to leave. Last night I finally did."

To Arthur's surprise, his dad began laughing.

"Did you just remember a joke or something?" Arthur asked.

"This is absurd, Arthur. You two are having a baby together any minute now! You're not breaking up."

"I didn't say we're breaking up. Eventually she'll answer my calls and she'll forgive me, then we'll be fine for a while. But forever is a long time. Whether it's now or in five years or in ten years . . . I just don't know if it's going to work out. I don't think I'm what she deserves. I don't know if we want the same things."

He didn't know if that was true. He didn't know what he wanted anymore.

"Is it possible," his dad began, taking a sip of his own coffee for dramatic effect, "that this doesn't have anything to do with Wren at all?"

Arthur considered this, despite his first reaction, which was to scoff. It was possible that this wasn't really about Wren, who had never done anything but love him through thick and thin. Maybe the person whose love he was really worried about was his future son or daughter. He had enough data by now to know he wasn't nearly spontaneous or silly enough to be the fun dad. And he wasn't strong and steady enough to be the family's rock. He doubted he was warm and nurturing enough to be an evolved, modern dad, one that maybe stayed at home. He wasn't handy, wasn't successful, wasn't wise or interesting or powerful in any way. What on earth was he bringing to the table, then? Objectively, outside of some kind of biological obligation, what reason would he be able to give his child to love him?

"I don't really want to talk about it anymore," he said finally, exhausted and defeated.

His dad nodded, understanding. Arthur could tell his

father was spinning an epic motivational speech in his head and was about to unfurl some serious wisdom. But instead . . .

"So what do you want to do today, then?"

"I don't know. Sleep, cry, and call Wren over and over until she answers?"

"How about we get out of the room? After breakfast, of course."

"OK," Arthur said. "Where do you want to go?"

❑ ❑ ❑

Arthur and his dad stood in front of the Needle. The FOR SALE sign in the front yard had a magnet plastered to it that read UNDER CONTRACT. Seeing it made his stomach turn.

"She really is a beauty," his dad said looking up at the big windows, the fresh siding, and especially the damp strips of toilet paper that had all but dissolved all over the lawn and the gutters. "I can see why you fell in love with it."

"I may have had a bit of a tantrum," Arthur said, surveying the mess with red-hot embarrassment. Some of it had been picked up by someone, wadded into wet balls and left casually. But most of it was still there. "Mind helping me tidy up?" He held up a couple of trash bags and latex gloves he'd brought along.

"Spoken like a homeowner."

"I don't know if we're keeping it," Arthur said, handing a bag to his dad and rolling a glove into place on his right hand. "I don't know anything anymore. But I shouldn't expect anyone else to clean up my messes."

Arthur started on the front steps and began gathering what was left of the paper. It was like scraping a stubborn sticker off a dish that had already gone through the dishwasher.

"Tell me what's going on. Why wouldn't you hang on to the place?" Neal bent down with some effort, and a loud groan, and joined in.

"It's a pretty facade, that's all. Something I thought I wanted but now that I'm here it's . . . hollow, somehow. Maybe that's because there's literally nothing in there. I'd show you if I could."

Neal chuckled.

"I had a good childhood, you know? I just wanted to recreate that for my kids. But it was never going to happen, not the way I envisioned it."

"I hate to see you give up. If you scraped together some money you could still turn this into something special. Have you tried tightening up the budget, cutting back on things you don't need?" his dad asked. "I know it's tough, but you have to make sacrifices."

"You don't get it, Dad. That's all we *do* is make sacrifices. It doesn't work the way it did when you were starting out." Arthur sighed. On to the front porch, where he reached out to grab any strips hanging down off the gutters. "But in any case, I might be stuck with it, house poor forever, over my head, trapped in an endless loop of renovations and refinancing and still trying to scrape together enough money to retire one day. It's like being on the losing end of a game of Monopoly. You just want it to end, but it won't until you've been slowly bled out for everything you're worth."

But then Arthur had an idea. Just the tiniest flicker of hope. "If I decide to keep it, will you help me fix it up?"

"I don't know if I can."

"I know, I know," Arthur relented, anticipating his father's words. "You put in your days of hard work and now you're enjoying your golden years. And I know you didn't have anyone helping you. I get it."

He knew what his old man was going to say. And he couldn't help but resent it just a little bit, the fact that his dad was so unbothered by the whole world going to shit. Speeding away in their little camper while everything burned in the rearview mirror.

"It's not just that," his dad said, a hint of shakiness in his voice. Vulnerability. "I just don't think I'll have time. What with me . . . going back to work."

"Wait, what?"

"You're not the only one who's stuck, son. Now, I know no one's going to cry me a river, but I've been doing the math and unless I die in the next three years, me and your mom are going to be in serious financial trouble."

"I had no idea."

"My knees are shot, my back hurts, and I don't drive so great at night anymore. Our trip has been fun, but it's also been hell on my body." Where was this coming from? His father had just been all over the country. Arthur had even seen him take a selfie with a mountain goat. But now that he was really paying attention, he could see how much effort it took the old man to get up off one knee. "But the good news is I don't plan on dying anytime soon, and sexually, I'm better than ever."

"I didn't need to know that part."

"I'm just saying, the reality is . . . here we are."

Another reason his dad wouldn't be able to help him with the manual labor. It was easy to forget that he was getting old. Same person, same strong personality, but with a few more miles on him than Arthur often realized. It hit him, for maybe the first time, that his dad would not be around forever.

"Did you already get a job? What is it?"

His father blushed. Honest to God, he turned red from embarrassment. "Driving instructor."

"But you hated teaching me how to drive." He recalled at one point his father took to bringing a thermos of whiskey around on their practice sessions just to manage the stress.

"That should tell you how dire the straits are."

Arthur didn't know what to say, but for some reason, he was having to hold in a laugh. The idea of his father teaching some acne-ridden fifteen-year-old to drive, sitting in the passenger seat with barely concealed rage and frustration, was hilarious to him. If a little sad.

Just then, a group of young boys rode by on bikes laughing.

"Do you wish you hadn't waited so long to do it? To travel, I mean? Do all the parks and everything?"

Arthur thought back. If these weren't his parents' golden years, then when were they? When he'd come home from college to visit, his mom eagerly washing the laundry and dad enlisting him in chores? The years when they'd sit around the house doing puzzles together and working in the yard? He'd always wondered why they didn't do . . . more. He thought they must be bored. Now he was starting to see that having each other, and him, was all they had ever really needed.

"Arthur, I can honestly say I don't regret a single thing," Neal said.

Arthur felt his throat tighten up. "You shouldn't be ashamed of doing what you have to do, of doing work that matters. No matter what it pays."

"Look who's talking," his dad said, almost as if . . . as if he was proud of his son.

In another moment, Arthur would be sobbing and releasing thirty years of pent-up emotion. But he still had something even more pressing weighing on his brain, on his heart.

"What do I do, Dad? If I walk away from this, I lose almost everything we've saved. If I don't, I'll lose Wren."

"I don't know. I'm just an old man with an achy back. But we've always loved her. And you've always loved her. You just gotta decide for yourself if she's worth fighting for."

Arthur didn't have to think about that. He knew without a doubt that she was.

"My offer still stands, you know."

"Offer?"

"A loan. No strings attached. If you still want the house, I'll help with the costs. If you don't want the house, you can use it to get back on your feet."

"I couldn't. You just said you're going broke."

"Not as broke as you."

Arthur couldn't suppress his smile at that one.

But, no. He still wanted to do this on his own. And he knew just how to start. But before he could, another car pulled into the driveway, and he knew by the puffy hair exactly who it was before she even stepped out: Linda Kellerman.

22

Ten years earlier

THEY LAY THERE IN THE hazy afterglow, squished next to each other on the wafer-thin mattress in Wren's dorm. The only light in the room was the glow of her computer screen-saver, strange trippy shapes in vibrant purples and greens dancing across the monitor.

"That was fun," Arthur said.

"Mm-hmm."

"Did you . . . Was it also fun for you?"

"Absolutely mind-blowing. I may never take another lover."

It had been playfully sarcastic at the time but would eventually come true.

"I get it," Arthur said. "Do you want me to go, or . . . ?"

"Just relax, dude," she said.

"Sorry. Just nervous, I guess."

"What are you nervous for? You did the hard part . . . chief."

A moment of silence.

"You forgot my name, didn't you," he said.

"No, no, I know it. It's . . ." It was a grandpa name. Decidedly unsexy. God, why was it so hard to think? "Harold."

Harold didn't sound quite right, but hopefully it was close enough to not offend him.

"Sadly, you're in the ballpark." He sighed. "This is weird, though."

"Why?" She sat up, though it took some effort, and propped herself up on her elbow facing the pale, scrawny boy. He followed suit.

"I've never done something like this before."

"Had sex?"

"Not without getting to know someone first."

She considered this, trying to figure out what to say. It wasn't her first time, but there was probably no good way to say this. She also hadn't really planned on keeping Not Harold around, but there was no great way of saying that either. Still, she didn't want him to walk away feeling icky about the whole thing. Or about her.

"Well, maybe we could get to know each other. Would that make it feel better?"

"I think so."

"OK, then."

He took a deep breath, as if preparing to deliver a monologue. "I'm Arthur. Not Harold, but again, you were close. I'm an English major, and I went to high school at—"

"I don't care about any of that."

"Sorry?"

"I mean, OK, basic trivia is fine, I guess. I'm Wren, I'm an art major and a Capricorn and I have a heart-shaped mole on the bottom of my foot. There, we're caught up. Now tell me something real about yourself."

"Real . . ."

"Like what do you want to do with your life?"

"Be a teacher," he said without hesitation. "I like kids, and I think I'd be good at it."

This guy. There was something so earnest and genuine and naively straightforward about him. He made no attempt to be cool or aloof, had no slick lines up his sleeve. The weed from earlier was wearing off, and yet she found herself feeling even more relaxed the more they talked.

"Shaping young minds, giving back to the community, that's legit," she said. "Me? I want to swim with great whites."

"Sharks?"

"No, just some awesome white people. Abraham Lincoln. Betty White. Mr. Rogers."

She winked and he laughed, laughed so hard he doubled over and nearly fell off the bed.

"So that's your life goal?"

"Well, it's one. Something I want to do before I die. Ideally before I turn thirty."

"Why thirty?" he asked.

"Your life's basically over then, isn't it? The good part, at least. After that it's kids and a mortgage and chronic back pain for the rest of your life."

"See, I want all that. Not the back pain, I guess. But the house and the kids. I want to own a home to raise my family in before I'm thirty."

"We should be writing this down." She slipped out of bed and paused. Were they on close enough terms for her to walk naked to her desk without covering herself up? On the one hand, he'd literally just been inside her. On the other, now that she was facing away from him she wasn't sure she could pick him out of a lineup, if prompted. Before she could decide, a T-shirt appeared in front of her face. It was his.

"Here," he said.

This was not how this usually went. Usually, the more words that came out of a guy's face, the more Wren came to regret what they'd just done, and the faster she wanted them gone. The opposite was currently happening, and she found it absolutely frightening.

She slipped the shirt on, just long enough to cover her up, and ripped out a piece of loose-leaf paper from a notebook on her desk. With a pen, she scribbled her name, and his (which helped solidify it in her memory), and began writing.

"OK," she said. "Another thing you should know about me is that I love football. Have you ever been to a Ravens game?"

They kept at it for over an hour, until the paper was filled with frantic scratches, bouts of wild inspiration, and all their greatest hopes and dreams for the person they would eventually become.

"OK," Arthur said finally. "I think I feel better about this."

Wren feigned a gasp. "That means you just enjoyed hollow, meaningless sex. Could it be so?"

"I guess I did. You convinced me of the merits. Is it always like this?"

"No," she admitted.

"This is the most fun I've had in a while," he said, slipping a hand around hers, his thumb lining her palm. There was something deeply sincere in his voice. An aching loneliness perhaps. A belief that this night was a gift he didn't really deserve. Wren didn't mean to think so highly of herself, but she swore she heard it in him. "Thank you."

She kissed him, for making her feel safe. She'd meant to kick him out hours ago but suddenly found herself unable to let go.

23

A KNOCK AT THE DOOR. Charlie was here. Wren dabbed at her eyes with a tissue one final time and hoisted herself up. She caught a glimpse of herself in the hallway mirror on the way to open the door and was instantly disgusted with how ridiculous she looked. Like a child cosplaying as a sad adult.

"Why are you dressed like Morticia Addams?" Charlie greeted her playfully. Charlie, for her part, wore athletic pants and a baggy sweatshirt with a thick neck, like she was going to Trader Joe's on a random Tuesday. It took her just a second to scan her friend's face and realize that something was deeply wrong.

With some effort, Wren choked out the words: Ferdie was dead.

"Can I see him?" Charlie asked solemnly, right after breaking a powerful, life-affirming hug.

Wren nodded begrudgingly and, for some reason, crossed her hands in front of her waist and bowed her head as she led Charlie through the apartment. Like a morgue director leading mourners to a viewing. In the living room, she'd lit some incense and two battery-operated candles. It was the best way she could come up with to be respectful without going back into the room itself.

But Charlie looped her arm around Wren's and practically dragged her in there. Wren hung close to the doorframe when Charlie finally let go to pay her respects.

"Poor guy," Charlie said, sitting down next to Ferdie on the bed and then immediately standing back up and pinching her nose. "Jesus, he stinks."

"Well, he's dead, Charlie. Have some decorum."

"No, Wren, he literally . . ." She leaned in and dropped her voice to a whisper. "He smells like . . . you know."

"What?"

And then they both heard one. A quiet, wispy puff of wind that could only have come out of a dog's butt.

"It's just the gases leaving his body," Wren said, wafting it casually away from her nose. She didn't know if that was true, but it sounded true. She'd been smelling it for a little while now, but to be fair, Ferdie always smelled like that. His meds had a way of making him extra gassy. "Let's be mature adults about this."

The next one was not quite so ghostly and gentle. Ferdie ripped one. Everyone heard it. It was undeniable. A moment later they were huddled over Charlie's phone googling "do dead things fart." They were halfway through scanning an article titled "10 Things I Wish I Knew as a First-Year Embalmer" when Ferdie's leg started visibly twitching.

"Wait, did you see that?" Wren jumped.

"I think I did."

Another twitch.

"Is he . . . is he alive?" Wren yelped.

"Oh my God, is he possessed?" Charlie asked simultaneously, then: "I like yours better."

Wren scrambled over to Ferdie's side and gave him one more shake, and she didn't know what it was, maybe all the excitement or the new smells from Charlie, but Ferdie's eyes finally flew open at that moment, and a few seconds later he was propped up on his elbows looking around, blinking. The relief that flooded Wren's heart nearly made her collapse. Tears came once again.

Ferdie, meanwhile, looked around with the bleary eyes of someone who'd just awoken from an epic, Rip Van Winkle–level slumber. Wren was certain he had been approximately 87 percent of the way to the afterlife.

"My sleepy boy," Wren said, hugging him and stroking his fur. "You scared me to death."

Charlie suddenly appeared with Ferdie's food and water dishes and set them down gently on the floor.

"So he was just in a fart coma?" Charlie said.

It made sense to Wren. Ferdie had been sleeping longer and longer, getting gassier and gassier. It was only a matter of time before it all crescendoed.

Wren grabbed a piece of the dry kibble in her fingers and offered it to him. He ate it casually, then hopped gingerly off the bed and began lapping water as if he hadn't just returned from the beyond.

Wren could take no more. She collapsed on the bed and stared at the ceiling. Soon she felt Charlie lie next to her, their heads just touching.

"Should we take him to the vet?" Charlie asked.

Wren turned and looked at Ferdie. He was snuggling up to

go back to sleep already, this time on his doggie bed in the corner. Being his exact, usual self. "No, look at him. He's completely fine. He's not the one who's broken, it's me."

"Wren . . ."

"I thought my dog was dead for half a day and he was just sleeping."

"Fart coma," Charlie corrected.

Wren couldn't even laugh. "My maternal instincts are nonexistent."

Charlie grabbed her hand then. "You thought he was dead and somehow he survived," she said, almost matter-of-fact. "Don't get me wrong, your instincts are a total mess. But you obviously gave him something to live for."

"You think?" Wren asked. "Maybe you're right, but I definitely can't be trusted with a human baby. I don't know who ever thought that was a good idea."

Ferdie was one thing. She'd known from the beginning that he had one foot in the grave. It was just a matter of time. Certainly, that played a role in her actions. But she couldn't help but worry about what it would be like when the baby came. Would she be too casual and cavalier about every cough? Too slow to act if, God forbid, there was a middle-of-the-night choking incident? And what if the baby had special needs? Would she be equipped for that? In this test, at least, she had failed miserably.

Charlie was silent for a moment as she considered how best to proceed. "Well, I would say Arthur did. He thinks the world of you, always has . . ." Then: "Do you want to talk about it?"

"What does it matter?" Arthur. The last thing she wanted to worry about right now. "He doesn't want to be with me, or more accurately, with someone *like* me. It's abundantly clear now that he would be better off settling down with someone more serious, who wants the same things as him. We had our fun and maybe we've run our course." Maybe Arthur would be better off with Chipmunk, who was probably gorgeous and outdoorsy and the kind of person who monitored her credit score.

"Yeah, you had so much fun you cooked up a baby. Do you hear yourself?"

Wren grunted. Charlie wasn't going to let up, so she had to give her something.

"I'll call him later, OK? But I'm telling you, we're not built to last." She hated that Charlie was making her talk about this, but she had to admit the deep, black melancholy was starting to wear off now that Ferdie was alive again. "When we get married, and then divorced a few years later, I'm gonna rub it in your face so hard."

"That'll show me," Charlie said. "Now, how about a walk? We can see how Ferdie does."

Wren agreed, and then she peeled herself off the bed and leashed up her boy, almost giddy to be doing something as simple as this, something just minutes ago she had thought she'd never do again.

❑ ❑ ❑

They put on Ford the River and blasted it as they walked. Power chords and distortion and heavy drums backed lyrics about not fitting in, raging against society, and stealing girls from jocks. They moved at a glacial pace with Ferdie, which made for a comical contrast.

"It's probably for the best that we're missing the show. I don't know if I'm prepared to see a bunch of fat, bald, middle-aged men singing this stuff," Charlie said. "I love the songs, don't get me wrong, but I feel like they should have moved on by now."

"Why? They probably realized that they were never happier than when they were ripping onstage with their brothers."

"Isn't that sad?"

Wren didn't think so. Ferdie took this moment to stop and pee on a random mushroom that had sprouted in the grass, signaling his agreement. Wren examined him carefully as he urinated, pooped, and walked. He was perfectly fine; she couldn't believe it. Yes, he was still dying, as all things were. Him a little more so than everyone else. But the little asshole was no worse for the wear after a brush with death, or more accurately, a very intense nap.

"How are you doing with everything?" Charlie asked, not content to make small talk about music.

"Well," Wren said, taking a deep breath. "I'm about to pop out this baby, me and Arthur are in a fight, my entire future is up in the air, and my dog might be a zombie. It's a bit of a roller coaster at the moment."

"Must be hard not to think of your parents at a time like this," Charlie said before taking a few steps ahead. Almost as if she knew she'd just dropped a grenade in the middle of their conversation and was ducking for cover.

"We're doing this again, are we? You're not gonna let it go?" Wren had to work harder than she'd like to admit to catch up.

"You know damn well I'm not. I always win in the long run," Charlie said. "Can you make it up here?" She pointed to a small hill that separated the apartment complex from the highway, I-83, and didn't wait for an answer before she began climbing.

Wren groaned and shared a look with Ferdie, who also looked peeved. See, she got him. But they both began walking up the hill regardless. Pumping her legs and glutes for all they were worth, it *was* hard for Wren not to think of her own parents' funeral, which she missed. Wren's uncle thought it might be too hard on her to attend, so instead of closure, instead of their lives having an end point, the tragedy of their deaths just dragged out forever and ever. The pain subsided a little bit every year. But she realized that without that ending, the next phase of her life never really began.

At the top, Charlie sat comfortably on the ground and watched cars whizz by through the thin tree cover. Wren sat and joined her. There went an ambulance without its siren, and there a minivan, and there a long Buick probably driven by a grandma who could barely see over the steering wheel. She watched them all go by and she thought about how she desperately wished her mom and dad could be there when she brought the baby home. She allowed her eyes to go soft, the steady stream of cars blurring together like a river, coming to terms with the fact that that could never be.

"They would be proud of you, you know," Charlie said, as if she were sitting front row in Wren's brain watching all the thoughts go by, munching on a big bucket of popcorn.

Wren knew this was a test of their so-called evolving friendship. And this time, she was determined to pass.

"I think about them a lot, and I always wonder. Usually, I try not to think too hard because I don't suppose I'd like the answer, the honest answer," she said. "But thank you for saying that."

Charlie's mouth hung open. "What, no sarcastic line? No inappropriate joke?"

"It's only because of hormones," Wren said. "Don't think

you have some magic power to make me be honest and vulnerable. It's this stupid baby. Been happening more and more lately." She reached over and grabbed Charlie's hand. "But I really appreciate you."

Charlie wrapped her in a hug and held her tight.

"I have one more thing for you," Charlie said, pulling out her phone.

"What now? A video montage of starving animals? I can't cry anymore."

"I've been texting with your brother." Wren went silent. "You should really reach out to him."

"I don't know . . ."

"You don't have to decide now. But I did get him to send me this."

Charlie showed Wren her screen as a video played. Grainy, jumpy footage from an old camcorder. A dated kitchen, all brown with wooden trim. A four- or five-year-old girl sitting at the table, drawing with oversize crayons on a coloring sheet. Two slightly older boys doing zoomies around the house, creating the equivalent of a human cyclone.

"Is that . . . me?" Wren said. Charlie nodded.

Then the camera panned over to the kitchen counter, where a dark-haired woman was dumping handfuls of chopped apples onto plates.

"My mom." Charlie nodded again. "Is she smoking?" She was, the lit cigarette dangling out of her mouth like a farmer chewing on a bit of straw. "Man, it sucks that cigarettes kill you, because it looks so cool."

Her mom *did* look cool, wearing a tank top, some kind of tattoo on her back visible. Even Wren could tell, they were the spitting image of each other.

"What's Mom serving up today? Let's see," a man's voice

said, narrating over the footage. Her dad. The camera zoomed in on the plates as Wren's mom sat them on the table. Apples and peanut butter and jelly on white bread, crust lovingly removed.

"Mommy's PBJ!" little Wren said.

"Don't say I never gave you anything," her mom quipped. "Love you, you little twerps." She went around and kissed them all on the cheek. Little Wren barely noticed while the boys ducked and dodged the best they could. Wren thought that was tragic. She wondered how many more times her mom had made them lunch and given them a kiss after this footage was taken.

"I make the kids PBJ every week," her dad said. "And does anyone ever thank me? *Nooooo.* But we throw a parade when Mom makes it three times a year."

"It's better when Mom makes it," little Wren said.

Wren's mom approached the camera and gave it playful double middle fingers. "In your face."

Then there was laughing, and sounds of a tussle, a tickle fight maybe, the camera spinning around and pointing at the ceiling at one point. And finally, black. That's where the video ended.

"Wait, that's it?"

"That's it."

"That forty-five-second clip . . . is all that's left of them?" It didn't seem fair. There had to be more.

"What else do you need to see?"

Charlie had a point. There would never be enough. Never enough photos or videos, never enough time. But she could see in that brief clip that her mom was a lot like her, a spicy little firecracker, and that she loved her kids. That was all that mattered.

"Nothing," Wren said.

"How do you feel?"

"At peace. At least, I think? Does peace feel like a horrible cramp in your lower abdomen?" She winced in pain, put her hand to her stomach as if that might stop it, and in a few more seconds, it was gone.

"Wren," Charlie said, eyes wide and alarmed. "I think you need to call Arthur."

24

THE VELOCITY SKYDIVING INSTRUCTOR WAS not thrilled to see Arthur walking through the front door of his office. It was Arthur's last gambit, one last thing to try after the man had told him over the phone that all his slots were booked up and there was no way he'd be able to accommodate him for a jump. At first, Arthur was relieved, but no. He had to find a way to do this. Right now. It was the only way to end this day, this particular day, and he wouldn't take no for an answer.

"She's not here. It's just me," Arthur said.

The guy looked skeptical, stood on his tiptoes and peered over Arthur and out the front door to make sure the bad lady wasn't lurking somewhere.

"Well, anyway, I don't see what that has to do with anything," he said as he began sorting through a pile of release forms. Standoffish words aside, Arthur could tell the man was instantly more at ease.

"It's been my girlfriend's lifelong dream to, in her words, 'fly like a bird.'"

The Aussie laughed. "Bit corny."

"I agree. But I thought maybe if I went in her place, she could . . . not live vicariously, but . . . maybe she'd get that feeling again, that anything is possible. Because I would never, ever, ever do this in a million zillion years. But for her, I would. I would do anything."

"Well, now you're making me feel bad."

The instructor rapped his fingers on the countertop, thinking it over. Good Lord, he really was handsome, Arthur thought.

"All right. Fine. I've got a group coming through soon, and I guess we could jam you in. It'll probably be fine as long as we distribute the weight evenly on the plane."

"I understand," Arthur said with a sigh. "I appreciate you hearing me out."

"Mate, I said *yes*."

"Wait, really?" He'd been expecting a no, definitely hoping for a no. His brain couldn't even compute what was about to happen. And had the man said it would *probably* be OK to fit one more person on the plane?

"Really. Now, sign this waiver before I change my mind."

The instructor slid a piece of paper across the counter for Arthur to review. There was no time to be an Arthur about this. No time to overthink. Arthur scanned the legalese—*release the company of all liability, understand the risks, bodily harm and even death, yadda yadda*—and, regretfully, signed at the bottom.

"Say, just curious," he said as he scribbled his name. "Do people ever die doing this?"

"Sometimes. About one in half a million."

The logical part of Arthur's brain was reassured by the "half a million." He knew intellectually that he was more likely to die driving home, or during the next lightning storm. The rest of him was focused in on the "one."

"Hardly ever happens here, though," the instructor added kindly.

"I'm sorry, *hardly* ever?"

❑ ❑ ❑

Arthur could hear very little over the roar of the plane as it readied for takeoff.

But he could still feel his cell phone buzzing up against his body, buried deep in several layers of clothing. He managed to finagle it out and answer with his nose, since his fingers were gloved.

It was Wren calling. He wasn't supposed to answer his phone on the plane, but he had to know if everything was OK.

"Hello?"

"Arthur!"

"Hello?" He could barely make out her words.

"Where the hell are you? Why is it so loud there?"

"Uh—it was going to be a surprise! Are you OK?"

He couldn't hear her response. The plane's engine was too loud, and it sounded like the call was breaking up. A hand signal from one of the other instructors on board advised him to hang it up. Wren said something else that he couldn't make out.

"Wren, I can't really hear you!" he shouted. "So I'm just going to talk! Um, I think there's a non-zero chance that I'm about to die. I probably won't, don't worry! But it's kind of clarifying. I had an epiphany just now. I had it all wrong, Wren. I thought you always wanted me to be someone else. In reality, you just refused to let me settle for anything but the best that I was capable of. And I love you for that. It's not always comfortable with you, and I wouldn't have it any other way. We do want the same things, Wren. We want each other. We want a life together. That's all that matters. The details come later. Figuring it all out, *that* is the adventure. I'm sorry for lying to you, for ruining so many things. But I'm jumping out of a plane any second now, to show you that I am capable of surprising you, to show you that—"

"ARTHUR!" her voice finally broke through the noise in a scream. "GET YOUR ASS TO THE HOSPITAL!"

"I— Wait, it's happening? It's time?"

"THE BABY IS COMING. NOW. LIKE, NOW NOW."

"Mate," the Australian instructor said to Arthur. "Put it away."

"Just hold on," Arthur told him. "Wren, I'm coming. I promise, I'm coming!"

Arthur hung up, tucked his phone away, and grabbed his instructor by the jumpsuit.

"I'm sorry, I gotta get off," he said. "You gotta turn it around, land it somehow!"

"Sorry," the guy said. "Only one way off now!"

❑ ❑ ❑

Minutes later, Arthur's instructor was painstakingly securing their harnesses. They were strapped together, and he was checking each and every buckle, every clip.

"I don't want to sound like a dick," Arthur said, "but is there any way we can hurry this along?"

The guy just looked at him, like, *You're kidding me, right?*

"Got somewhere to be, do you?"

"Sort of, yeah!" Arthur yelled over the noise, which was

deafening now, the jump door open and wind whipping inside the cabin. "My girlfriend is having our baby!"

"Now?"

"Yeah, now!"

The instructor took this in, looked around, and passed a hand signal back to another instructor, who was waiting with her own passenger.

"Best I can do is cut you in line and have you go first! You ready, mate?"

"Thank you— Wait, what?"

Did he just say *first*?

The pair waddled over to the open door and Arthur stared out. There was nothing. Just open blue sky and a haze of clouds all around. He couldn't see the ground. Shouldn't there be a cornfield down there somewhere? A Little League baseball diamond? Something, anything to remind him that he was still on earth? Vertigo kicked in; his head began spinning. His stomach lurched and he thought he might throw up. All the bravery and urgency he'd been feeling moments ago had apparently been sucked right out the open door.

"Hold on, wait."

"We've got the green light, we gotta go!"

"One sec, one sec!! I don't think I can. I don't think I can do this."

"You have to!"

"But what if we die?! I can't die the same day my child is born. Wren will be traumatized forever. And I don't even have a will yet! I can't. I can't."

"Take it from me, as a dad and a skydiver with over a thousand jumps under my belt," the instructor said, leaning in even further, "you're never gonna feel fully ready! But you are!"

"You think?"

"Hey. It's gonna be a helluva story to tell your kid one day, yeah?"

"Yeah. Yeah, you're right."

"On the count of ten."

"OK."

They counted together.

"One. Two—"

"TEN!" the instructor yelled, and with one final push, Arthur was airborne.

❑ ❑ ❑

Arthur burst into the hospital room, hair still matted from his helmet, fresh rings around his eyes from the goggles. All of it made even more ridiculous by the surgical mask the nurses made him throw on, which only accentuated his dishevelment.

He was expecting chaos, a war zone. Screaming and blood and a dozen medical professionals tripping over one another as they hurried to deliver the baby.

Instead, the room was dark. Quiet. His own panting aside, the room was completely peaceful.

Wren was lying in the bed, torso propped up slightly, a woozy, relaxed look in her eyes. Arthur ran to her, grabbed her hand.

"Did I miss it? Oh God, I'm sorry. I don't know what I was thinking."

"Shh," she said. "You're harshing the vibe."

Arthur didn't understand.

"Where's the baby?"

"Still here." She pointed to her belly. "It doesn't happen that fast, dummy. Charlie got me here in plenty of time."

"She couldn't stay?"

"I'd already kept her long enough. She had a honeymoon to get to, and I knew you'd make it."

A sigh of relief that he had, in fact, made it. More than relief. Arthur felt as if someone had just suddenly decided that the apocalypse was called off. If he'd missed the birth of his first child, he'd have never forgiven himself. That was the kind of moment you could never get back.

"I know that," he said. Some semblance of logic and reason began returning to his brain as the adrenaline wore off. Flashes of passages from books and blogs appeared to him. Things like length of contractions and average duration of labor and how dilated Wren would need to be before she could start pushing. "I was just so desperate to get here, I had no sense of time. It felt like it took forever."

The jump had been exhilarating, but after the initial rush had subsided—and after allowing just a moment to imagine himself as Superman, flying through the air to save Metropolis—all Arthur had wanted to do was land. Eventually, they did. In a big empty field, where they had to wait an eternity for the shuttle to come pick them up and take them back to the start.

It all took way too long.

"You seem surprisingly calm," he said, as if just noticing.

"It's the drugs," she said with a big lazy grin. "I want them all the time."

"I should never have left you alone. I'm an idiot."

"I told you to."

"I shouldn't have listened." Then: "I take it you couldn't hear me, when we were on the phone."

"I heard enough." She squeezed his hand, glad he was

here, but somehow still distant. "But words can't change everything. They don't erase you lying to me. They don't prove that you're actually capable of change."

"I jumped out of a plane."

"Admittedly, a pretty good start," Wren said. "But just a start."

He paused, resisting the urge to be defensive, to deny, to turn things around and hurl criticism at her. That, he knew, would probably be a pretty bad move, given the circumstances. Men had been thrown out of the delivery room for much less. Instead he let it all wash over him. It hurt to hear, but it was well deserved. Luckily, he'd had a feeling she might say something like that.

"I did lie about one more thing," he said, pulling away just slightly. "I wasn't really giving it my all this entire time, the bucket list. And . . . I made a few extra stops today before I got on that plane."

"What do you mean?"

"Here. I wanted to be able to show you."

He pulled his cell phone carefully out of his pocket and angled it so she could see. She cocked her head, confused, as if he was about to pull up YouTube and start showing her old *SNL* sketches, which he was wont to do on occasion. But no. On the screen was his own face, sitting in the car, holding the camera in selfie mode. The version of himself from earlier that same day began to talk.

"OK, Wren, I knew you'd never believe me, so I wanted indisputable evidence." The camera swooped in uncomfortably close to Arthur's face as he searched for a button on the screen, the inside of his nostrils unfortunately all too visible as the lens autoshifted to macro mode, and then he flipped the camera around to show an empty intersection. Somewhere rural, lots of green space and horse fencing in the background. "I drove out to the middle of nowhere looking for the perfect place, and I think I found it. Now, you can say what you want, but I think we can both agree that, in front of me, right now, is a red light, right? An honest-to-God red light. And I'm going to run it."

Present Wren had her jaw open as if watching a contortionist twist his body into a pretzel. She was rapt. But she said nothing, not yet.

Back on video, Arthur continued narrating. "Now, I've looped around three times checking for cops and red-light cameras, and I haven't seen a single other car come through, so I think we're good." A quick flip back to his face. "I'm gonna do it but I'm still gonna do it my way, see. Now, here we go." Back to the road.

"I hadn't been that scared behind the wheel since I took my driver's exam." Real Arthur chuckled. "I kept imagining some tractor trailer flying in out of nowhere and leveling me, and never making it here." He watched her face. She was still glued, but silent.

"Three . . . two . . . one . . ." his voice narrated.

The camera shook as Arthur hit the gas, the light still clearly red, and Phone Arthur let out a little squeal of glee as the landscape blurred around him. Almost as if on cue, red and blue lights began to flicker on the edges of the screen, and a police *whoop* followed. "Oh God . . ." A panicked Arthur fumbled for the camera, knocking it over, where it landed at his feet and angled up at him, giving him far too many chins as he dutifully pulled over.

He pressed stop on the video.

"For the sake of time, we'll skip the part where you see me grovel like a frightened child to get out of a ticket. Besides, I have something better to show you," he said, quickly adding, "Totally worked, though."

He was getting nervous that she still hadn't reacted. Not so much as a grin or a pity laugh. He naively hoped that the epidural had inadvertently subdued her sense of humor, but it was also extremely possible that he was striking out. Back to the screen, Arthur swiped and hit play on a new video.

Black. There was only black. A male voice that was not Arthur's spoke.

"Whenever you're ready. Don't be nervous, but do be gentle. I'm right here."

"Well, this has certainly taken a turn," Wren quipped, sitting up a smidge. Finally, something.

"I think your thumb is in front of the camera," Arthur's voice narrated, and suddenly the image became clear after a haze of beige slid away from the lens. Arthur's whole body was in the frame now. In some kind of store, Wren could tell by the fluorescent overhead lights. And there were glass containers around him. Tanks. A pet store.

Someone other than Arthur was filming. The man. Arthur was visibly shaking.

"Just reach your hand in and lay it flat, palm up. Let her come to you."

"Is that?" Wren asked, squinting to see. "Oh my God."

The random pet store employee, as if watching her reaction in real time, came closer and zoomed in on a chunky, prickly tarantula inside one of the tanks. And in an instant, Arthur's shivering fingertips entered the frame right next to it. "Her."

Wren grabbed Arthur's arm and buried her face in his sleeve. "I can't watch this . . ." But she was still peeking through her fingers with one eye as the tarantula's spindly legs began moving and positioning the spider directly on Arthur's palm, which was glistening with sweat. The camera zoomed out and Arthur, looking up and away and thinking about a happier place, held the spider out in his hand, as if offering someone a mint. She seemed content there in his palm, still and docile. A petrified smile spread onto Phone Arthur's face.

"You did it, man," the store employee offered. "Told you she wouldn't bite you."

"Wait, what's she doing?" The spider was on the move.

"She's just exploring."

"Tell her to explore somewhere else. Stop her!"

"OK, stay calm . . ."

"HELP!!"

The video cut out abruptly.

"Wow. That was . . . a lot. Are you OK?"

He couldn't tell if she was being genuine or patronizing, but knowing her, probably both.

"It wasn't actually so bad, until she started sort of . . . skittering up my arm." He reenacted with his fingers on Wren, and she giggled.

"I'm impressed. That took bravery. Not for most grown men, but for you."

"Thanks. Downside is, they wouldn't just let me walk in off the street and hold a tarantula, so . . . I had to buy it. We have a pet tarantula now—sorry—and I really, really don't want to talk about it."

Wren considered this for a moment before nodding her approval. "Fuckin' metal. I like it."

Arthur clapped his hands together casually as if concluding a sales pitch. "So . . . what do you think?"

She raised an eyebrow, deep in thought. He could feel her

eyes scanning him, evaluating his efforts and weighing whether or not they were enough to atone.

"What else you got?" she asked.

He had her. She was in. She was hooked. He just had to close the deal, and luckily he had one more card to play.

"Well," Arthur began. "I did take a video of this, but it's mostly just me crying, so I thought I'd just show you the result."

He brought his hands up and slowly—ever so slowly, for maximum dramatic effect—removed his surgical mask. Removed it so that she could see his fresh, shimmering nose ring. Solid gold—well, gold-plated stainless steel, anyway—straight through one nostril. Not quite like an angry bull, but close enough.

"You did not!" Wren couldn't help but to reach up and poke it, make sure it was real.

"Ow. Careful, it's still pretty tender."

"I honestly love it. It suits you, and I think your students will love it."

"Really? I feel like an idiot. No one gets these anymore except thirty-year-old women who go to punk rock shows."

She gave him a playful tap on the arm.

"You never know, it might grow on you."

Arthur doubted it.

"Well, that's it, that's the end of my presentation. I wanted to do more, but I ran out of time. I had to get to you."

"It's OK."

"But I brought you these," he said, reaching into his pocket and pulling out a handful of slips of paper. "We can put them back in the jar, tackle each of them together. I don't know if I'll keep the nose ring, or ever sleep again knowing there's a tarantula in our apartment, but I will jump into a volcano for you, I will go cave diving, whatever that means, I will go snorkeling with sharks and go plucking catfish out of muddy holes in Mississippi. I will do those things for you and I will do them *with* you. I will be your one hundred percent partner in everything you want to do. I promise."

"I don't care about any of that anymore," she said, pushing his hand away.

"You don't?"

"It doesn't matter who I wanted to be back then, what I wanted my life to be like." She took a breath and he felt as though he were in free fall again. Was he about to lose her for good? "What matters is that you and I make it together from here on out. Now, can you hand me my bag?"

She pointed. In the corner was her duffel bag, her go bag. The swell of relief had turned his legs to jelly and he could barely manage his way over there, but he did so dutifully.

"I need something out of it," she said.

He did as he was told, retrieved the bag, and Wren reached inside one of the pockets and pulled out the small black box. She opened it and held the ring up, the fluorescent hospital lighting bouncing off it. His stomach did a backflip when he saw it.

"Are you . . . Are you stealing this from me?" he said with a shocked smile. "This was supposed to be my moment."

"You already got to do it once. Sorry I screwed it up."

He nodded: *Go ahead.*

"Arthur Peterson, would you do me the great honor of not having this baby out of wedlock?"

He could barely contain himself. Being here, with Wren, their baby coming into the world any moment now, finally committing to each other for a lifetime and beyond. His body shook as he tried to hold it all in.

"I want to spend all my tomorrows with you," she said.

He didn't hesitate. "Yes! Of course, Wren. Absolutely, one hundred percent *yes*."

He held his hand out, as if she might slide the ring on his finger. "Oh my God, what am I doing?" He laughed. "Here." He took the ring. "This is yours. It's always been yours."

He put the ring on her finger. Her finger, which was a little puffier these days. No matter. He got it on there. It had just enough friction to stay.

This was everything he'd ever wanted. Her beaming smile said the same. He kissed her now, as passionately as he could, as if it were the first time, or the last time, and he wanted every time he kissed her for the rest of their lives to feel exactly like this.

Suddenly, a buzz in his pocket interrupted the moment. Arthur looked down at his phone to see who it was. It was a message from the skydiving instructor:

> *It's Thomas from Velocity. The full gallery and the video will take a few days, but wanted to get you a few shots to show off. Congrats, papa.*

"Is it your parents?" Wren asked.

"No. I guess I did have one more thing to share."

Arthur turned his phone to face her. On the screen, a photo, at the very first moment of weightlessness, right after the initial jump, Arthur's face contorted in sheer terror, Thomas smiling behind him and giving the "rock on" sign.

"Oh my God, I'm so glad there's photographic evidence of this. I almost didn't believe it," she said. "Any more?"

There was. In the next photo, he was mid-dive, his face even more screwed up. Then one more on the ground, Arthur and Thomas posing triumphantly after a successful jump.

"Some hurry you were in to get here!" Wren teased. "Couldn't miss that photo op for the birth of your child."

"I figured you would have wanted me to enjoy the moment at least a little bit."

Wren smiled. "You really jumped out of a plane. Wow." She was still laughing, but it was winding down, and she began repeating herself. "You jumped out of a plane. You *jumped* out of a *plane*."

"Sure did."

Then:

"Why the hell would you jump out of a plane?!" She smacked him on the arm for emphasis.

"Ow!"

"You could have died. At the very least been horribly disfigured. What if you'd broken your legs on the landing? Leave me to take care of a newborn and your paralyzed ass at the same time? No, absolutely not. You are never going to do anything like that ever again."

"You don't have to tell me twice."

"But all that being said," she said, taking a deep breath and calming herself, "consider me surprised. In the best way." She was getting sleepy, settling back into the bed and letting her eyelids fall just a little. It had been a long day for her already, with more to come. She'd need her strength.

"So what now?"

"Now . . . we wait."

Arthur dragged a chair over, held Wren's hand tight.

"I'm not going to leave your side. Never, ever, ever again."

She patted his hand with hers.

"Good," she said.

Five seconds later.

"Arthur."

"Yeah?"

"Before you never leave my side ever again, could you go find me a snack? I think I'm still allowed to eat. Maybe a Jell-O or something."

There she was.

"Of course. Anything for you."

25

THEIR SON WAS BORN ON September 14 at 9:32 a.m.

Hair, none to speak of. Eye color, unknown. They were still shut, his face all red and puffy like he'd been out drinking the night before. He was covered in goo and blood. Honestly, an ugly little thing. Wren stuck by that opinion. Nothing like the freshly manicured grown-ass babies they trotted out as newborns in the movies.

But he was her ugly little thing.

When she first laid eyes on him, well, it was the closest she'd ever come to having a spiritual experience. It was almost like she could feel the cosmic scales tipping just a tad, the universe thrown off-balance for just a moment.

There was a brand-new person in the world.

A person with a name, with a personality yet to be discovered—or determined? A person who would laugh and cry and love and win and lose. A person with a future.

The magnitude of it all overwhelmed Wren for just a couple of seconds. It wasn't exactly the rush of maternal love she had been expecting—it was grander than even that. An infinite appreciation for all life, all of the world and universe, everything.

Yeah, it sounded ridiculous even in her own head. But there it was.

There was no switch-flip moment where she suddenly felt like a mother. But whatever it was that she had felt was pretty cool. And that would do for now.

The nurses took their little boy away quickly and all the woo-woo spiritual stuff passed Wren right by as she succumbed to physical exhaustion and a little blood loss. The medical team cleaned him up and performed their checks and tests. Eventually, one of the nurses came over and told her that he weighed in at six pounds, two ounces.

"Is that good? Did we win?" she asked, a little woozy still.

"It's great," the nurse said.

Dr. Abadi even made an appearance to help stitch her up after some minor tearing.

"Eh, what's up, Doc?" Wren said, barely awake.

"Wren, I'm focusing," Dr. Abadi said. "So please be vewwy, vewwy quiet."

"Did you just make a joke?"

"What, I'm not allowed?"

Wren felt as though she had accomplished something of great significance, getting this no-nonsense professional to loosen up, even just a little. When the doctor was finished, she patted Wren on the shoulder firmly. "Excellent job." That felt even better.

Soon, Arthur came to check on her.

"You did it." He kissed her forehead, wiping away the sweat. "You really did it. He's perfect."

"He needs a name."

"There's plenty of time for that. Just rest."

"You need to give him a normal name. If I pick, he'll get beat up at school."

"Are you sure?"

She nodded. She didn't have the energy to do this part.

"Whatever you want. Just choose quickly or I'm going to start calling him Xavier."

"OK, OK. Will you choose the middle name, at least?"

"Yeah?"

"Oh yeah, go crazy," Arthur said. "Go nuts in there. He'll only hear it when he's in trouble, and the wackier it is, the more humiliated he'll be when we reprimand him."

"Now, that I like."

She'd need to give it a little thought, but she was pretty certain she could work with this plan.

"One more thing, speaking of names," she said. "I don't want to change mine, when we get married. It's nothing against Peterson, it just doesn't feel right."

"OK."

"But I also have no real connection to Morris. It's fine, I guess. It barely feels like mine, but I also don't want to completely let it go."

"I'm confused. What are you saying?"

"Some people combine their last names, make a new one together."

Arthur thought about this. "The Metersons."

"No."

"The Porisses."

"No." She laughed. "It was just an idea."

"We'll figure it out. Just rest. They're already looking like they want to kick us out of here soon."

The idea of going home filled her with dread, but she was too tired to give it oxygen. She let her eyes fall all the way closed knowing it might be her last chance for a while.

❑ ❑ ❑

Soon they were moved to another room, a recovery room, and their son was delivered to them on what looked like a little rolling drink cart, tucked up in a blankie, sleeping peacefully. Their little baby burrito.

The nurses kept telling Wren to "get some rest," and then kept coming in to check her vitals every seventeen minutes, flicking on all the lights, waking everyone back up. No rest was gotten.

Before long, Arthur's parents arrived, bearing balloons and flowers, puncturing the peace and quiet in the room in a way only grandparents can.

"We came as soon as we could," Laura said. "How are you guys holding up?"

Neal went right for the baby. "Can I pick him up?" Arthur nodded.

Laura walked straight past them and told Wren to scooch over in the bed. She did. Arthur's mom wedged in beside her and put her arm around Wren, stroked her hair. Wren leaned her head on Laura's shoulder. It occurred to her that she would be allowed to call Laura *Mom* soon. Weirdly, it didn't seem weird at all.

"What can we do to help?" Arthur's dad asked. "Don't be shy. Anything at all."

Wren and Arthur looked at each other; she gave him a nod of approval.

"Well, Wren and I were talking," Arthur said. "There is one thing that we might need."

"Name it," Arthur's mom said.

Wren wondered if Arthur was going to chicken out. She knew how much he hated asking for help, and when he was forced to, how embarrassed he'd always feel. She watched his face for the telltale red cheeks and averted gaze. This time, she couldn't find them.

"How would you guys feel about taking our car and driving it back to your place?" he said.

His dad looked puzzled. "OK . . . And what about the Airstream?"

Wren stepped in. "Is it as comfy as it looks?"

❑ ❑ ❑

Roughly twenty-four hours later, they were discharged. Sent out into the world with this fragile, squishy little thing swaddled up in a blanket and told, more or less, *Good luck!*

"That's it?" Wren had said in the parking lot as a hospital orderly practically yanked her wheelchair out from under her. "This feels illegal."

One time she'd gone to urgent care for a cut and left with seven pages of painstaking instructions on wound care. But apparently having a baby required no such documentation.

"We'll see the pediatrician tomorrow," Arthur said. "We can ask her our questions. We just need to survive tonight."

They arrived home and Arthur opened the door.

"You ready?" he asked.

"Why do I feel like I'm carrying a bride over the threshold? Wow, this feels like a big deal."

She took a step into their apartment's foyer and immediately felt like sobbing, in the happiest way she could ever recall. She could barely choke out the words:

"Welcome home, buddy."

They'd barely made it through the doorway when a small figure came running—Ferdie. Running. Geriatrically, yes, but running just the same. Wren could barely believe her eyes. The little guy ran right up to Arthur and just about jumped into his arms. Arthur scooped him up and squeezed him tight, receiving a lick directly to the face for his efforts.

"Ferdie, what the shit is this?" Wren said. "Betrayal. And you." She was looking at Arthur now, smiling like an idiot as Ferdie cleaned every bit of hospital off his cheek and ears.

"What can I say? I guess the little guy did grow on me after all."

"Arthur, don't lie," she said. "You loved him from the very beginning. Now, come on. We're home."

She grabbed his hand and the four of them walked into the living room together, their very first moments as a family together, where they were met with—

"WELCOME HOME!"

The noise startled them. Wren felt Arthur's arm shoot out in front of her, push her back as he leapt in front, ready to kick an intruder in the crotch. All instinct.

It was Charlie and Tristan. They were there in their living room, jumping up and down like maniacs.

"Jesus. You scared us," Arthur said.

"Give me that nugget, right now," Charlie said. "Oh, and also how are you feeling and whatever?"

Wren smiled and handed the bundle over. "Meet, drumroll please, Liam Ace Morrisen."

"Ace?" Charlie asked, rocking and swaying with baby

Liam, completely lost in his eyes. "As in number one? First? First of many? And who the hell is Morrisen?"

"Just something we're trying on," Wren said. She took a look around. Home looked . . . different. There were distinct vacuum lines in the carpet. "Is it cleaner in here?"

"We tidied up a bit," Tristan said. "Sorry we didn't have time to do more. There's a few meals in the fridge, and you should have a DoorDash gift card in your email."

"And wine," Charlie added. "I brought lots of wine. It's in the kitchen."

"In the kitchen, you say?" Wren said, already halfway there. When she got there, a glorious selection of reds and whites was spread out on the counter. She didn't even know where to start. She wondered if she could drink them all at once.

Meanwhile, Charlie was completely transfixed by Liam, lost in his eyes.

"You OK?" Arthur asked her.

"Yeah." Charlie sniffled. "Yeah, I'm OK." She handed Liam gently back to Arthur and said, "But do you think I could talk to Wren alone for a second?"

26

ARTHUR AND TRISTAN WAITED UNCOMFORTABLY in the building's lobby to give the girls some space. Arthur bounced Liam mindlessly. He was calm and sleepy.

"So what's that all about?" Arthur asked.

"Well, there's no easy way to say it, I guess. But we're moving."

Arthur's heart dropped. "Oh," was all he could say.

"We love it here and everything. But I finally convinced Charlie that there's more to see out there."

"You know Wren's gonna kill you, right?"

Tristan laughed. "To be honest, I could use a little bit of a fresh start. Figure out what I want to do next. I hope she understands that."

Liam let out the most adorable little yawn, his tiny arms trying their best to stretch.

"Can I?" Tristan asked.

Arthur nodded and handed him over. Tristan held Liam like a plate that had just come out of the microwave. Arthur laughed and helped him adjust.

"You can put one arm under here, and a hand behind his head. Always support the head."

"You're so good at this."

"I'm just well-read. In reality I have no idea what I'm doing."

"Could have fooled me."

A long silence while Tristan, getting the hang of it, rocked Liam back and forth, mesmerized by him.

"I don't know how to thank you guys, for everything you've done," Arthur said out of the blue.

"No need," Tristan said. "Happy to help a friend."

"You pushed your honeymoon back to help us out. That's above and beyond."

Tristan smiled and shrugged.

"I once read about an experiment where students watched a thousand balloons fall from the ceiling. Each balloon had one of their names written on it. They were each tasked with finding the balloon with their own name. Do you know how many were successful?"

Arthur shook his head.

"Zero," Tristan said. "Then they did it again. And this time the students were instructed to pick up a balloon and give it to the student whose name was written on it. In minutes, everyone had their balloon. Pretty amazing, right? I think about it often, and what it says about happiness."

Arthur sighed. "You saw that on LinkedIn didn't you?"

"Yes. But it's still powerful."

Arthur laughed. "You're one of the best people I know, Tristan. You treat people with kindness, you treat everyone like a friend. If that doesn't make a difference in the world, then I don't know what does."

“Thanks for saying that.”

“But if you ever decide you want to be poor and have less flexibility, come and talk to me about teaching. I think you’d be great at it. Your catchphrases would kill.”

Tristan laughed. “Maybe.” Then, as if struck by inspiration: “Maybe I could run an online course, teaching people how to become their own boss; there could be different modules, and there—”

“Never mind, you’re hopeless. I take it all back.”

The door opened behind them and Charlie emerged, immediately wagging a threatening finger at Arthur. She had makeup running down her face and was visibly heaving.

“I. Am. Not. OK,” she said dramatically. Then she walked up to Arthur and hugged him as hard as he could ever remember being hugged in his life. “But I will be. You take care of her, you hear? If you don’t, I’ll find you, make a suit out of your skin, and do it myself. Got it?”

Arthur got goose bumps. All he could say was, “Yes, ma’am.”

He took Liam back and said goodbye to his friends, then took one deep breath before heading back in. Their first night alone with Liam. He’d read all the books, been on a crazy journey of self-discovery these past few months, and still he had absolutely no idea what to do when he walked through that door.

The pediatrician would help. All they had to do was get through one night. How hard could that be?

❑ ❑ ❑

Liam wouldn’t stop screaming.

By midnight, they’d tried everything. Run through the

checklist of reasons babies cry. He'd eaten enough and wouldn't take any more. He had a fresh diaper. Wren had tried rocking him. Arthur had tried bouncing him. He spat the pacifier out over and over. Nothing worked. Cries and screams and screams and cries.

What had happened to their little cooing angel?!

Arthur covered his ears and winced. Liam had cried at the hospital, but my God, it was so much more piercing here. The hospital had a steady hum of activity, machines whirring, people walking and talking outside. Their apartment was dead quiet except for the guttural wails of their newborn. Arthur felt as if his head might explode.

"Check the thermostat, maybe it's too cold in here?" Wren pleaded while cradling Liam.

"It's on sixty-eight; I don't think it's that. I really wish you'd let me re-swaddle him; it's coming loose."

"My swaddle is not the problem."

"Should we try feeding him again?"

"We just tried that! He's full."

"Maybe he's got gas pains. Try burping him."

"He ripped a huge one after he last ate; it's not gas."

"THEN HOW THE HELL DO WE MAKE HIM STOP?!"

"I DON'T KNOW, DO YOU WANNA TRY ASKING HIM NICELY?!"

The yelling continued. Things were said that would be regretted later. But also, this was wartime. There were no rules. There was only survival.

Eventually, suddenly, and finally, the cries stopped, winding down into adorable little coos. Arthur walked over quietly to take a look at the little bundle in Wren's arms. He'd fallen asleep, just like that. Thank fuck.

Arthur and Wren looked at each other, locked eyes, and started laughing.

"I think we handled that well," Wren said in a low voice.

"Totally. We didn't buckle under the pressure at all. Go us."

Wren held out a fist and Arthur bumped it with his.

Together, they walked into the bedroom and laid Liam down in his bassinet, carefully, slowly, as if defusing a bomb. Once he was down, they both backed away with their hands up, careful not to disturb the air and somehow wake him again.

"Ready to do this again in a few hours?" Arthur whispered.

"Do we have to?"

"We don't have to; we get to," Arthur said.

"That's it, you're not allowed to hang out with Tristan for a while."

Arthur laughed. "I can finally admit. He's not so bad."

Silence. Only little heart-shattering noises coming from their son, sound asleep in the bassinet a few feet away. Arthur opened his phone, swiped his way through TikTok until he found a video with bold, aggressive text overlaid: **Newborn won't stop crying? 3 HUGE things you're doing wrong!**

"Anything helpful?" Wren said. Arthur paused, then closed the app.

"Nope," he said, holding his thumb on the icon and deleting it from his life forever.

They lay down on the bed. It was too early for them to go to sleep, but they also felt like they couldn't make even the smallest peep of noise. They were trapped. But there were worse things.

"We never got to talk about the house," he said out of nowhere. It had been looming over them since the hospital.

There never seemed to be a good time to discuss it. “It’s over; I got us out of it.”

Wren shot up.

“You didn’t have to do that. How much money did we lose? Arthur, I was being selfish; we could have made it work.”

“No, you weren’t, and we couldn’t. I can admit that now.”

“So . . .” she said. “How much money?”

“Believe it or not, none.”

“I’m sorry? I’m no real estate attorney, but even I’m pretty sure it doesn’t work like that.”

“Let’s just say Linda Kellerman took pity on us.” After he’d run into her while cleaning up the mess—the mess he himself had created—he apparently looked like such hell, so down and broken, that she just couldn’t bring herself to rake him over the coals. The home, it turns out, was owned by a big property development company Linda did a lot of work with. She had sway, she said, and could probably get them to rip the deal up. It didn’t hurt that she felt a little bad about breaking the news to Wren prematurely after a bit of wine at the wedding.

“So we got off scot-free?”

“Not quite. She made me promise to volunteer at her Spring Cleaning Dumpster Day, and she’s going to drop off about twenty boxes of hideous baby clothes we have to pretend to love.”

“So she’s made herself an honorary grandma,” Wren said. “Small price to pay.”

Silence. Only little coos and baby snorts.

“So what do we do now?” Wren asked.

“I think we still need to move.”

“Because you hate this place.”

“Are you kidding?” he asked. “This is where we stopped being a couple—just a pair of lovebirds running on hormones and Lean Cuisines—and became a family. Even before Liam came along, we were learning how to be a family. We took our lumps and came out the other side better for it. We did it all here. How could I ever hate this place?”

Wren searched for Arthur’s hand, found it, and gave it a squeeze.

“I think you’re right,” Wren said. “It’s time for the next phase.”

Arthur squeezed back.

“But we’re gonna be so broke if we move into a bigger place. Are we gonna be OK?”

“We are. That part’s going to suck. But I say, *If it’s not good, it’s not over.*”

“Another Tristan-ism?” she asked.

“Nah. That’s all me.”

❑ ❑ ❑

In the morning, a knock at the door woke Arthur far too early, right in the middle of a good stretch of sleep from Liam. Wren slept through it, somehow, but Arthur shot up instantly. Without so much as half a second of transition from deep in the dreamworld to full-strength reality, he was disoriented, bleary-eyed, and highly annoyed. Arthur stormed quietly through the apartment, determined that if this was Mrs. Flynn asking him to help her carry a hundred pounds of dog or cat food or drums of oil or whatever heavy-ass thing she was bringing into her apartment today, he was going to lose it. He and Wren had worked tirelessly over the last eight hours to have some semblance of a normal circadian rhythm. Liam had other plans. He was up and angry, then hungry, and then alert, and just when he had finally broken them, he decided it would be hilarious to lull his parents into a false sense of security, allow them to doze off, and then start screaming to start the whole process over again.

But now, he was finally down, temporarily at least. And whoever had knocked had somehow managed to wake only Arthur. Arthur was determined to keep it that way.

He flung the front door open without so much as a look through the peephole. Greeting him with smiling, nervous faces was a gaggle of children—his former students. There was Martin, in the front, and behind him floppy-haired Grant and extremely tall Mackenzie and a few others he'd taught over the last two years. Martin held a bouquet of flowers and a card.

What were they doing here? It had to be some kind of mistake. Maybe they'd announced the news at school, but instead of telling everyone that Wren had delivered the baby, they accidentally told everyone Arthur had slipped into a coma. The kids were here to celebrate and draw crude things on him while he lay there helpless, he knew it.

"Congratulations on the baby, AP," Martin said instead, handing over the flowers and light pink envelope. "From all of us."

"What are you— You guys didn't have to come here." He'd hoped to be more elegant as he realized that they were indeed here for him, because they cared, but found his throat closing up rapidly. Surprised and overwhelmed couldn't possibly do it justice. It was like being back in the dreamworld all over again. He was half expecting one of the kids to morph into his father. "This is too much, really."

"Well, we all chipped in and got you a present, but *someone* forgot to attach the card," Grant said, as Martin's face grew red. "So we decided to bring it by. Sorry it's a little late."

"And sorry it's pink," Martin added. "We were all sure it was going to be a girl."

"That reminds me, you owe me five dollars," Grant chimed in, nudging Martin.

Arthur laughed. "I don't care about the color, it's perfect. But I didn't get a present from—" He stopped mid-sentence, realizing. "The car seat. That was all of you?"

"Well, and our parents," Mackenzie added with a hunch of her shoulders. "My mom headed up the collection."

The parents were involved, too? They actually . . . liked him? This really was too much. With the exhaustion coming into play, he was dangerously close to breaking out into a hefty, on-his-knees sob right here in the hallway. The kids were being nice to him now, but there was no way they'd ever let him live that one down.

"I gotta be honest, I didn't think you guys liked me all that much," Arthur admitted. "Martin, I let you down. And the rest of you . . . I don't know if I was always giving you my best."

"You didn't let me down, AP. My grandma wouldn't let me buy the trumpet, but chasing you with that bat was the first time she'd been up off the couch in weeks." The kids laughed. "I'm serious, once she knew she could do it, everything changed. She's been walking, cooking. She even changed a lightbulb the other day—I'm not kidding!"

"And I definitely would have failed seventh-grade English without your video about how the object of a sentence would drink a soda versus the subject," Mackenzie said.

"Oh yeah, that was fire!" a few of the others chimed in.

"Oh," was all Arthur could think of to say. It was a lot of

information to take in, knowing that yes, they had trolled him and teased him and made his life pretty difficult at times, but maybe that's just what kids were supposed to do. That's what his kid would probably do one day. In the end, he had gotten through to them, some of them. In the end, he had made a difference after all.

"I guess, you're welcome, then." He nodded his thanks again, turned to head back inside, and then paused. "And hey—I'll see you all around the halls."

27

Two weeks later

TRISTAN AND CHARLIE WERE WAITING for them outside in the parking lot, as promised.

"Thanks for coming to see us off," Arthur said. "We would have come to you, but . . . I wouldn't have a clue where to park this thing in the city."

"This is how it's gonna be now, huh?" Tristan teased. "We come to you, wherever you are, on your terms. What do we get in return for being the fun uncle and aunt that always show up?"

"An extra person that loves you?"

"Yeah, damn it, that's pretty cool."

They both turned in unison and began ogling the Airstream. For Wren's part, as soon as she locked eyes with Charlie, it was all over. The sobs came, and they came hard, for both of them.

Wren practically lateraled Liam to Arthur and ran to her friend, devouring her in a hug.

"Fuck you for crying," Charlie said.

"Fuck you for leaving," Wren said. "You give me two

weeks' notice before you leave me forever, like we're working at IHOP or something?"

A small laugh.

"Couldn't you at least stay until we get back?"

"I wish I could," Charlie said.

"Is Tristan making you do this?" Wren whispered. "Just give me a signal and I'll get rid of him."

"He's not making me do anything, I promise."

"It's just that we made a deal," Wren said. "First one to leave Baltimore . . ."

". . . gets a tattoo of the other's face."

"Don't tell me you're backing out," Wren said.

"I wouldn't dream of it."

The two finally pulled away and locked eyes again. Charlie took a deep breath, as if preparing to make a confession of undying love.

"Wren, you've always been—"

"Buh-buh-buh. Do not. Don't even think about it. There will be no eulogies today, OK? You're moving, not dying."

"Are you sure? It's a killer speech." Charlie wagged a little piece of paper in the air—the speech, evidently. It was a meaty piece of paper, folded over many times. Wren was tempted. Enticed, for sure. But no. Not today.

"Tell me at Christmas. You're still visiting, right?"

Charlie nodded.

"And you should start looking at flights for my birthday, and Valentine's Day, obviously."

"And President's Day," Charlie said.

"Oh, yeah, we can't spend President's Day apart."

"And National Ice Cream Day. And it's probably best if we spend all of Women's History Month together, just to be safe."

"I think that covers all of our bases."

"For Q1."

Wren smiled. "Right."

It was time to go, so she walked to the truck, where Arthur and Tristan were just finishing up the most ridiculously stiff man-hug she'd ever seen in her life, saying things like *See ya, bud* and *Later, man*. Would it kill men to show a little real emotion?

Arthur opened her door and Wren slid inside, but as he began to close it, Wren stuck her foot out to block it open.

"Charlie, you're the best friend I've ever had and the most wonderful human I've ever met and I hope you and Tristan have the most adventurous fantastic thrilling first year of marriage of all time OK BYEEEEE!"

"No fair!" Charlie squealed as Wren closed the door, then held up her speech again and mimed tearing it up.

Arthur climbed in and closed his door, started the engine, and shifted the truck into drive.

"Are you OK?" he asked Wren.

"How can I not be?" she said, but her shaky voice betrayed her. "Now, hurry up, I want to see the Pacific Ocean before it boils over."

They'd mapped most of it out in excruciating detail. Arthur figured they could get there and back in just about two weeks if they minimized their stops, which he knew full well they had no intention of doing. He had created an intricate itinerary that would keep them on schedule, for the sake of baby Liam's routine, and Wren was going to inevitably wreck it with unplanned detours to see wacky roadside novelties. And they wouldn't have it any other way.

It would be the adventure of a lifetime, or the start of it, anyway.

"Any final thoughts before we go?" Arthur said.

Before Wren could answer, Liam chimed in from the back seat with a wet, shockingly loud fart. Ferdie, curled up on a blanket next to the car seat, lifted his head a smidge and sniffed the air in approval.

"What he said," Wren said.

EPILOGUE

"EVERYBODY HURRY UP AND GET in here!" Arthur shouted from the living room, a happy Liam on his lap babbling and chewing on a plastic set of multicolored car keys.

Wren and his parents rushed in, holding glasses of champagne.

"Jeez, what's the rush?" Wren said, settling in next to her boys on the couch.

"I don't want to miss it, that's all," Arthur said, then, looking around: "I said everybody!"

And now here came Tristan and Charlie from the other room, in hideous holiday sweaters, red-faced and puffy from wine and too much of Arthur's mom's homemade charcuterie board.

"By the way, I have a few notes on the tattoo sketch," Wren said to Charlie as they found their seats. "Since it's my likeness, I feel like I should get a say."

"We can workshop it," Charlie said.

"OK, do we all have a drink?" Arthur said.

Everyone held up their glass.

"Do we all have someone to kiss?"

Each couple squeezed together.

"Does anyone have a poopy diapy?" Arthur asked, holding Liam up and giving him a quick sniff.

His dad raised a teasing hand, and his mom immediately pushed it down, taking the opportunity to lock their fingers together.

"Here we go, then," Arthur said, pointing the remote at the TV and hitting a button.

On the screen, a cartoon New Year's countdown began, with a band of jungle animals wearing party hats and dancing around with kazoos as a little jingle played.

I can't believe
It's New Year's Eve
So much to do
So much to see
A brand New Year
Ready to begin
Let's all stand up
And count from ten

The countdown began and the crew all shouted along, and when it hit zero, the living room erupted in cheers. Arthur wiggled Liam in the air, held his fist and pumped it like the little dude was at a rock concert. Then he handed him over to Wren, who laid a big fat kiss on him. Liam's face remained blank, his eyes wide and confused—*Someone save me from these people.*

It was 7:00 p.m.

Arthur and Wren excused themselves from the party to go into the next room, one of two—TWO!—bedrooms, and put Liam down in his crib.

They hadn't moved far from their old place, after all. The new apartment was still pretty shitty. It had a few poorly patched holes in the wall, outdated appliances, grout in the shower that had seen better decades. But it was slightly bigger and it had a pool and a playground, or as Wren was keen to call it whenever she wanted to feel fancy, a *swim tennis*. It also had a real, live maintenancc department that attempted to fix things and kept up with the regular bug treatment. They were still throwing their money down the proverbial drain in rent every month, with very little hope of ever saving enough money for . . . well, anything. But, for now, it was perfect. And now, really, was all anyone ever had.

❑ ❑ ❑

Liam was exhausted and went right to sleep, Arthur and Wren both giving him gentle kisses on the forehead—until they went to leave the room, sneaking out as quietly as possible. That's when the cries started up.

"You go," Wren said, "I'll get him down."

"You sure?" Arthur whispered back.

"Absolutely, I got this."

Arthur wanted to protest, but Wren needed the win. She took pride in being the only one who could get Liam to sleep, with a patented combination of humming punk songs and rubbing his belly. Whenever Arthur tried, Liam cried and cried for Mommy, which sucked, but he didn't take it personally. She was soothing and sweet and beautiful. He didn't blame Liam one bit.

He sat back down on the couch next to his parents, both nibbling on cheese and cured meats, and both thinking they were the only ones slipping bites to Ferdie, who was snuggled between them both. It was going to be a gassy night, but Arthur figured their old boy deserved to live it up as long as he could.

"Doesn't get any better than this," his dad said.

"Can't argue," Arthur agreed. "How's work?"

"You know, not bad. It's amazing working with young people today, really feeling like I'm making a difference."

"Dad. Tell the truth."

"Oh, they're all crazy. Completely incompetent. We're all doomed." He smiled. "But I'm doing my best."

"We're really glad we came, Arthur. It's not every day that we get this kind of time with our only grandson," Laura chimed in.

"I heard the way you said *only*." Arthur groaned.

His mom reached around and squeezed his shoulder. Just then, Wren reappeared and flopped down on the couch next to Arthur, squeezing her way in.

"I give up. You're in."

"That was fast."

He could hear Liam wailing in the background.

"None of my techniques were working. I even hummed 'Adam's Song' and he only cried more! I think we're in a sleep regression or something."

"Regression? He *just* started sleeping. How can he be regressing already?"

"There's a new regression basically every couple of months. This is our life now."

"Someone's been reading up."

"Quit stalling. You're up, Papa."

Arthur hoisted himself off the couch, not feeling overly optimistic. He slipped into the dark room, the cries almost deafening, and hurried over to Liam's side.

"Shh. Hey, buddy. I'm here. Daddy's here."

He placed a hand on Liam's chest and kept it there, felt his little body breathing. The cries stopped. Liam grabbed at Arthur's fingers, eventually settling in with a firm grip around his dad's pinky. Liam was fresh out of swaddling, sleeping with free arms for the first time in his life, and this was the first time that he had grabbed Arthur's finger like this. It was amazing.

After what could have been five or fifty minutes hunched over the bassinet, Arthur was pretty sure Liam was asleep. But when he went to tug his hand away, he felt his son's grip tighten, and he decided to lie down on the floor—surely, a more comfortable position—until he was fully asleep, hand stuck through the side of the bassinet.

And that's when everything went black.

❑ ❑ ❑

Wren startled awake on the couch. The living room was dark, quiet. Someone had thrown a blanket over her, but it was clear that everyone else had long since headed back to their respective hotel rooms. The new apartment was bigger, but not big enough to accommodate a baby and multiple guests.

Wren came to and realized Arthur was sitting next to her; that's what woke her up.

"What time is it?" she asked, rubbing at her eyes.

"Two a.m." Arthur said. "I fell asleep in there. Clearly."

"I fell asleep out here. I don't remember the party ending."

Arthur laughed.

"We're pathetic."

"I know."

"We missed New Year's."

"Well," she said, sitting up now, pushing through a yawn. "We're awake now, aren't we?"

"Wanna light off some fireworks? Take a few shots?"

"I want to go back to bed. Or a cup of coffee. I honestly can't tell which."

Arthur laughed and collapsed, laying his head in her lap. For his part, he fumbled around for the glass of water he'd left sitting out earlier and chugged it greedily before setting it back down.

Wren reached under the coffee table and produced a book, *The Princeton Review GRE Premium Prep* course. "Want this?"

"Ah, thanks," he said, feeling guilty. He took the book and immediately placed it under his still-sweating glass.

In *this* apartment, they had decided, they would be coaster people.

"You always used to say the New Year was a blank canvas," she said. "What do you see us painting on ours this year?"

"Honestly?"

"Yeah. Dream as big as you dare."

"I have absolutely no clue," Arthur said.

"Really?"

"Really. Do you?"

Wren thought about it. Nothing came to mind. "I don't." Then: "Are you sure about grad school? I really thought this year was gonna be the year."

"I'm sure. I just want to enjoy life this year. Enjoy the kids in my classes. I have plenty of ideas for that, that don't require me to work and study twenty-four-seven. I realized I don't need to always be advancing. I can just *be*."

"Well, if you're happy, I'm happy. But if I'm being honest, as the financially responsible breadwinner of the family, grad school would have put a lot of pressure on me."

"You haven't even started yet."

"And I'm already sick of it."

Wren had been feeling herself since acing a Zoom interview for an assistant creative director role at a local agency. All while, in her words, being "more incontinent than Liam." Arthur didn't mind her gloating. She deserved it.

"We'll just . . . try to survive," Arthur said. "We'll take it one day at a time and try not to die. And after that . . ."

He trailed off, but she knew exactly how to finish the sentence for him.

". . . Anything's possible."

Acknowledgments

It takes more people than I ever thought to write a book. If we're being anatomical about it, it was my fingers that pressed the keys that ultimately created this story, my brain that dreamed up the characters and the jokes and the set pieces. I'd love to blame someone else—but that was pretty much all me.

However, *A Last Time for Everything* would not exist without many other people, including:

My wife, Sarah. Every evening spent holed away in my office, banging my head on the keyboard while she refereed the kids' latest street fight; every weekend at a cabin in the mountains, searching for inspiration in the woods in the days before a looming deadline while she gave our aging dogs their forty pills per day. Those pockets of focused work would never have happened without her in my corner. If I know anything at all about romance (which is debatable), it's only because I learned by loving her.

My daughters, Natalie and Hannah. They are my biggest fans and also my toughest crowd. Depending on the moment, I can make them pee themselves laughing or groan in disgust with my attempts to amuse them. They help make my skin thick and my life filled with laughter and joy.

My mom and brothers, whose never-ending support and excitement never fail to make me feel like a real somebody.

My agent, Andrea Blatt, who helped shape this initial kernel of an idea into something that we thought might actually be really special. And the whole incredible team at WME Books—Lucy Balfour, Nicole Weinroth, Sanjana Seelam, Celia Rogers, Caroline Cox—who have pulled off impossible feats for my books and my career that I never could have dreamed of.

My editor, Cassidy Sachs, who took a chance on another book from me and patiently guided me through the Book 2 Blues. And the whole hardworking team at Dutton—John Parsley, Nicole Jarvis, Jamie Knapp, LeeAnn Pemberton, Ella Kurki, Dora Mak, Kathleen Soriano-Taylor—who have believed in and championed my writing.

Finally, a younger me and Sarah, pre-kids, pre-dogs, pre-everything. We were broke, dumb, and in way over our heads. I wouldn't change a thing.

About the Author

EVAN S. PORTER is a novelist and writer who has contributed to *Parents* magazine, the *Onion News Network*, AskMen, the Good Men Project, Upworthy, and more. He lives in Atlanta with his wife, their two daughters, two dogs, and not much in the way of elbow room. His debut novel, *Dad Camp*, was published in 2024. *A Last Time for Everything* is his second novel.